BEIN
COLOUR

by **Richard Alderson**

First published in Great Britain as a softback original in 2018

Typeset in Dante MT Std

Editing, design, typesetting and publishing by UK Book Publishing

www.ukbookpublishing.com

ISBN: 978-1-912183-70-8

ACKNOWLEDGEMENTS

As this is my first novel, I have a lot of people to thank for their support and much needed guidance.

First and foremost, I must thank my family. My wife Alison, daughters Sarah and Rebecca, son-in-law Jordan and the new addition to the family, my grandson Zac. With a special mention to my mother and father-in-law, Anne and Norman. If wasn't for these people telling me to go away and stop boring them and to stop talking rubbish, I would never have had the drive to prove to them that I could write an entire book!

For the professional advice and guidance, I extend my many thanks to ***UK Book Publishing***, in Whitley Bay. Ruth, Jay and the rest of the staff did a great job in keeping me on track and assisting me with my, apparently, deeply flawed efforts. I thought I was pretty good, but you know, you've got to humour these people! (They were pretty good, honestly!)

Then there's the front cover. Jay, the amazing artist, at UK Book Publishing, respect, 'nuff said'. Then there's Martin Shaw @ ***Martinshawphotography.com***. Wow! Cool, professional and very polished. You will see what I mean if you have a look at his website.

The model, well, the guy on the front anyway. If you don't recognise him already, that's the living legend, ***Dave Benson Phillips.*** Giving more creditability to an already awesome book. If the fact that this guy is on the front doesn't tell you how exciting the book's going to be, then nothing will!

It took many years to come up with an idea that would eventually become a story. I wanted to write something that people would enjoy reading, just for the hell of it. There will be critics, of course, but if it puts a smile on one person's face, then I have succeeded.

Don't take my word for it, keep reading.

Enjoy!

Richard Alderson

CHAPTER 1

The computer screen stared at him. He returned the stare. The spread-sheet wavered, a little flicker of the screen broke the reverie. He blinked, refocussed his eyes and leaned slightly forward. Glancing down to the right at a pile of papers, he located the digits and figures he needed and added them to the data on the screen.

In the background, Valerie took a phone call from a client. Brendan had always found Valerie attractive. Her manner of dress reflected her organisational skills. The phone call ended and she got up, pushed her chair away with the back of her legs and walked towards the manager's office. When doing so she had to squeeze past Brendan's desk. He could smell her perfume. He looked up at her and she looked down at him. He thought there was a connection, but her body language gave nothing away. Having now gotten past the furniture obstacle course, she made her way across the small space to the manager's door. Knocking politely, she entered without waiting for an acknowledgement. Once over the threshold she turned and gently closed the door behind her. She didn't sit. Brendan could see that she did not like being in the manager's presence. Unable to help himself, Brendan continued to watch the scene.

The manager leaned back into his chair, angling himself so that he could see Brendan. Occasionally, during the conversation the manager nodded. By this time, Brendan's stomach was beginning to ice up. He had the old familiar feeling of impending doom. The talking eventually came to an end. Valerie turned and opened the door. The door was purposely left ajar. Looking furtively at Brendan, Valerie made her way back through the office obstacle course and sat in her chair. Curling her ankle around the chair leg, she pulled herself under the desk and continued with her work.

The feeling in his stomach still hadn't receded. Valerie, not giving anything away, had only made matters worse. She faced her screen and tapped on the keyboard without looking his way. Brendan noticed that the manager was on the phone. At first the conversation seemed quite sociable, but as the conversation went on, he could see that Blackmore was uncomfortable. Eventually the call came to an end. Brendan's anxiety had increased. He became visibly agitated. He wondered if perhaps at some point he might end up with ulcers in his stomach.

After what felt like an eternity, as expected, Brendan was gestured for. He rose, looking to Valerie for support – none was forthcoming and so, feeling alone, he reluctantly made his way through the same obstacle course to the office. Taking a deep breath, he walked through the open door.

The fat bloke sat behind the desk in his too tight suit. Brendan could see in his eyes that he was just as anxious. Blackmore had spent too many years sat on his backside in front of the TV and drinking too much at the Freemasons' Lodge. He had built his accountancy firm through his masonic connections, not because of any skill. This meant, like everyone else in this area, he felt trapped. So, when an opportunity arose that meant he could take his frustrations out on someone, he made the most of it. He was aware that Brendan felt anxious as he stood in front of him.

"It seems you've cocked up the Forbuoys Account."

Brendan looked at him, taking a moment to realise what he meant – he was referring to the local newsagents.

"It seems that you've missed the VAT calculations from May to August. Which will mean, not only more work, but causing this company acute embarrassment."

It took a good deal of effort for Brendan not to laugh at the blubber of lard in front of him. 'The Company' consisted of three people: a fat lazy blob of a man, an ice bitch behind him and, by his own admission, a highly anxious, overweight, black guy who couldn't get a 'proper' job.

Brendan realised that it was pointless arguing with him and conceded to the error, saying that he would collect the books and would have it sorted by tomorrow. This would of course, be done in his own time.

Smiling that he had 'one over' Brendan, Blackmore dismissed his underling and let him return to work. Feeling the butterflies leave his stomach, Brendan made his way back to his desk and slumped back into his chair. Valerie didn't even look.

At home, Brendan had finished updating the books. His eyes ached with the effort and he could feel the faint beginnings of a headache. Rubbing his forehead, he rose from the desk and made his way to the back kitchen. He rummaged through the cupboards and found a bag of crisps, eating them as he did some more hunting in the cupboards for something a little more substantial. He muttered to himself about having non-convenient convenience food.

Whilst waiting for the grill to warm up he leaned back against the counter, deep in thought. He was reminiscing about his past life and what a failure it had been. Constantly being told what to do, when to do it and how. Ignored at home, bullied at school, and now demeaned at work, which had all accumulated into the anxious, nervous wreck that he was. Feeling depressed, he harboured a deep need to change his life. How he would do this, he wasn't sure.

Looking across the room, his eyes fixed on the books and notes that he had just completed. The pile of paperwork reinforced his thoughts on the need for a change. He stacked the work and put it into the awaiting storage box, along with his briefcase. Having now cleared the table he suddenly felt a little philosophical. He thought, is that it – if I clear away my work and clutter, what exactly am I left with? The answer seems to be, not a lot! He moved to his armchair in front of the TV. Reaching over for the remote on the nest of tables, he paused, putting his arms on the sides of the armchair and stared into space. The need for a call to action kept prodding him. He felt restless, but was not exactly sure why. In the background, he could hear the grill fan whirring away and he noticed the slight movement of the streetlight outside of his terraced house.

His reverie was interrupted by the grill's alarm. He rose from the armchair and went into the kitchen to turn off the appliance. Even the food was superficial. Everything's been designed for convenience. He thought, 'Hell, I even work for another's convenience.'

Frowning, he looked around the room. He suddenly realised that none of it mattered. He had been through school, tried hard to get his qualifications, gone to college and then university and did the same. Got this job, which he hated, then set about acquiring material items that he and others expected. Again, he felt conflicted. He, rightly so, felt proud of his accomplishments and yet no longer felt an attachment to any of them. This, he decided, was a big problem. How was he going to fill a void that he hadn't even known was there? Given that he now felt no need for material items, this made the situation worse. If he were to pursue the purely material, he would eventually obtain it, but what then?

Suddenly jumping up from his seat, frustrated, he picked up the used plate and carried it into the kitchen and put it next to the dishwasher. Sighing he turned back to the living room. As he did so he noticed the corner of a magazine protruding from the coffee table. He didn't know why he noticed it this time because it had been there for months. Striding over to the table, he bent down and grabbed the side of the magazine. In pulling it out a couple more fell onto the floor, ignoring them, he looked at the front of the publication.

It was a copy of 'Back Street Heroes'. He'd bought it on the spur of the moment a few months back, after he'd been on a bike trip, with the idea of upgrading his bike from his present six-fifty. On the front cover stood a large tattooed man with his custom bike. He wore a leather waistcoat over his naked upper body. The man wasn't exactly in peak physical shape but he exuded confidence and seemed somehow to be the master of his own destiny. Staring at the picture, Brendan considered his thoughts. Somehow, he knew what he was going to do. He knew the direction his life was going to take, but the question was, how was he going to start? At present, he was a junior accountant in a backwater of a town. Still, he felt the need to move forward with the idea.

It was three-thirty on Friday afternoon, a cool, bright day. Brendan stepped out of the office and made his way home. He carried a small briefcase and held his head upright. His usual slouch had gone. With his new sense of purpose, he felt buoyed and invigorated. Briskly making his way home, he eventually arrived at an early twentieth century Edwardian terrace.

Fishing in his trouser pocket he extracted his key and unlocked the front door. When he entered, he noticed it seemed colder in the house than outside. In the corner of the room stood his computer. He stooped and turned it on, along with the screen and printer. He prepared a cup of tea and finally sat at the computer. The computer desktop showed a picture of a motorcycle in the desert, intimidating yet inviting. He paused for moment and took a sip of his tea. He then placed the cup down and settled himself so that he could get into the right frame of mind for the task at hand. For a moment, just a fleeting moment, he hesitated about what he was going to do. That moment quickly passed and he placed his hand on the mouse and clicked open his publisher program.

The digital clock at the bottom of the computer screen showed a time of 23:47. For some unknown reason, he doubted it and looked at his wristwatch. He thought, 'Christ's sake, where did the time go? Just as well it's Friday.' Feeling a little stiff from sitting so long he got up from the chair and walked in a small circle to loosen himself up. Once his muscles had eased he picked up his handy work from the printer and put it onto the table next to his comfy chair.

The next morning Brendan awoke refreshed. His sense of purpose quickly returned and so he got himself ready with a sense of urgency. As he sat eating his breakfast he looked at his previous night's handy work. He had made a handful of A4 posters advertising for people to join a new motorcycle club. There wasn't a name for the proposed club; it was simply a picture of a motorcycle and a meeting place, which was to be the Angel pub at the marketplace in Loftus. Smiling to himself, he finished his food and made his way to the back of the house.

In the backyard stood an outbuilding, which had four doors in a row. A no-longer-used toilet, an old coal scullery and two further storage sheds. These had been used for wood and to contain his wheelie bin. The doors on the building were painted green, to match the exterior of the house. The floor of the yard was concrete and covered in a thin layer of green moss. Making his way across the small yard, he opened the furthest door to the right and his motorcycle presented itself. A Yamaha Drag Star 650. A near bottom of the range custom cruiser. The bike had a significant amount of chrome to appeal to the middle-aged mass market, who fancied themselves as a weekend easy rider, such as himself. He pushed the machine out of the shed, being careful not to knock it against the brickwork. He managed to get it into the middle of the yard. Putting the bike on its stand, he put the key into the ignition and turned it on. The engine was loud, reverberating within the four walls of the yard. Having revved the throttle two or three times, he let the engine settle into a steady burble. Satisfied that the bike was running OK, he turned it off and went back inside the house to retrieve his helmet and gloves. He pushed the bike onto the back street, closed the gate and mounted his steed. He patted his chest to make sure the posters were OK and then, a little unsteadily at first, set off on his advertising campaign.

CHAPTER 2

Mike generally worked on his own. The only time he worked with anyone else was when there was a particularly big job, such as an engine removal. For that he would call his uncle, John, who was, at the age of fifty-nine, semi-retired. Mike had been on his own since his father's death fifteen years before. He had never felt the need for anyone else. The majority of the work could be done single-handed. Occasionally, he reflected on how his father had worked and realised that he had done the same. Mike had been so happy with his dad that he never thought it strange to be done in any other way. Mike was very fastidious in work and extremely tidy, which helped him to avoid unnecessary accidents. Because he was so meticulous, he had a good steady flow of business, which kept him busy. This had helped him to overcome the loss of his father. Since his dad had died, he was sure he could still feel his presence, reminding him of the times that they had spent together. When he was fourteen, Mike had been told by his father that he had autism. This meant that Mike was perfectly normal, except when he had to deal with intense emotions – then he might have a 'meltdown'. This explained his actions as a child. He still had 'meltdowns' as an adult, but experience had taught him how to control the outward appearance of its effects. This made him 'appear' normal to others in most cases, but perhaps reserved and introverted, maybe even a little gruff. His work let him focus and gave him an excuse to minimise the contact he had with others. He had a reputation for very good work.

The car on the lift was not going to fix itself. Shaking his head, he looked up and put the spanner onto the slightly rusted nut and twisted. Surprisingly, it came loose almost straight away. "Dad, it's OK, we just need a new exhaust and rubber." He had worded what he was thinking, without realising. He stopped, put the spanner onto the lift platform. He slowly took off his gloves and began to cry. He couldn't help it. At the back of his mind he understood that he was having a meltdown, but he made no effort to control himself. No one was there to watch him. Feeling the wave of grief finally dissipate, he went to the bathroom, ran some cold water and splashed his face. At this he felt instantly refreshed and better already.

Coming out of the bathroom he looked across at the car on the stand. Striding over purposefully, he got back under the lift and continued with his work. This was the last job of the day and time was knocking on. Just as the lift hit the floor, the customer walked in. Giving a practised smile, he said that the customer's timing couldn't have been any better. Looking relieved that he didn't have to wait, the customer returned the smile. He paid for the work and drove the car from the garage as Mike closed the door behind him. He took out the final bags of rubbish to the skips at the back of the premises, then turned out the lights and made his way to the door at the side of the garage, which led to his flat upstairs.

He worked his way upstairs. He didn't bother to turn on the lights to the corridor. He had been up and down so many times, he could have been blindfolded. The door slammed behind him, the latch caught and the door locked itself. The only noise now was the clicking of his boots as he walked along the short corridor. The tone of the footsteps changed as they went from a tiled floor to the thinly carpeted wooden stairs. He ascended to his fortress of solitude.

Minutes later, he was in shorts, T-Shirt and barefoot. Picking up his dirty coveralls he went back to the kitchen and set about doing his daily laundry. With the washing machine starting its cycle, Mike began preparations for his evening meal.

Pots done, everything shipshape, he then went into the living room. There was a three-piece suite, and next to one of the single seaters stood a coffee table. On the table, lying page down, was a novel that he had begun to read, 'A Brave New World', Aldous Huxley. Perhaps it wasn't the best book to have chosen; it fed his contempt for the modern world. He couldn't help but feel a certain affinity with 'John the Savage'. Like John, every now and again – and this was one of those moments – he gave credence to the idea that perhaps he wasn't 'normal'. But, as his father had said 'What is normal?'. After an hour or so he was finding it difficult to read, the daylight was fading and he didn't want to switch on the electric light. He put the almost-read book as he had found it and stared into the dark room. He did this every so often. He let the emptiness fill him. The blankness was a sort of reset for his head. He was aware that it was happening, in fact he consciously let it. It was a type of meditation that he did when he felt alone. Strangely, when the emptiness enveloped him he no longer felt alone, it was a comforting solitude. When he brought himself back to reality, returning to the dark room, he felt internally refreshed.

Waking the next morning, he felt a strange pang of loneliness; he wanted contact with others. The feeling soon passed as he went straight into his usual routine. The routine of his daily life helped to supress his emotions. Emotions were something that he found superfluous and so if they were carefully tucked away, he would have no reason to deal with them. Once again, he descended the stairs, footsteps echoing as he went. A last-minute check that he had his keys to get him back in and to open the garage. He then locked the flat door. The day was cool and bright and had a fresh breeze that invigorated him.

He walked around from the side to the front of the garage and opened the large heavy shutter that enclosed the workplace. The time was eight AM. He would open until one PM as it was Saturday. Having secured the door into position, he then switched on the lights and made sure the lift operated correctly. Having done this, he meandered his way back to the office, switched on the light and flicked the kettle on. Through the week, he wouldn't have the kettle on until ten, but a Saturday allowed him the time to indulge. He had three bookings and there was always the chance of 'pop in customers', so although it was more relaxed, he never shut early. Besides, his routine wouldn't allow him to.

Mike was on his second job, a half service and a quick oil change. He noticed the 'put-put' of a motorcycle engine outside. A couple of minutes later a man's shadow broke the straight lines of the sunlight at the garage entrance. He heard a shout of 'Hello!'; another Hello followed a few seconds later. Then, he heard footsteps approaching the lift. The steps came to a halt to his right. For a third time, another 'Hello' broke the silence.

"Just give us a minute," replied Mike gruffly. He hated being stopped mid-way through a job. He was hunched over a red Vauxhall Corsa, checking for a potential head gasket leakage. After a couple of minutes of wiping metalwork, he stepped back and exclaimed "Bugger" to himself. It looked as though his worst fears were going to be realised. Wiping his hands with a cloth, he turned and looked at the person stood next to him. Black, bald, approximately five-foot eight, overweight, medium build. Although he was dressed in Cordura bike gear, Mike could tell he was the type who spent most of their time in a suit. The man was a casual biker, the type who generally killed themselves on the North Yorkshire Moors. He guessed the man had a six-hundred cc custom cruiser of some kind, most likely black, chrome and very clean.

The man spoke. "Sorry to bother yer, mate."

Yes, not from this area, thought Mike, the clue being the accent.

"Yer couldn't do me a favour and put this poster on your board?" The man thrust a coloured piece of A4 paper his way. Turning the paper so he could see the information, he saw a picture of a motorcyclist straddling an aggressive looking motorbike. Big black words arched across the picture stating 'Bikers Wanted for New Club'. Under the picture, more writing gave details of when and where the recruitment day was going to be. Looking up from his studying of the literature, he looked at the man in front of him. He was trying to equate the advert in his hand with the man who had given it to him. He didn't exactly fit the bill of a biker.

"So, what's this about? I know it's a bike club, but why start a new one? Why not go to Redcar and join the Raiders or whatever?"

Looking a little embarrassed, the man stared down at the floor. "Well, it would be our own local one, fresh, without influence from other people, who don't know this place and how we think." Realising he hadn't introduced himself, he stuck his hand out and said apologetically, "Sorry, my name's Brendan Sykes. I live on Westfield Terrace and I work up at Blackmore's Accountants up the road."

Having given his credentials, he kept his hand raised expectantly. Reluctantly, Mike took the hand and shook it in the practised manner he had become accustomed. Looking eagerly at Mike, Brendan said, "Well, would you put it up for me, will it cost?"

Looking at the poster, Mike replied, "No."

Brendan couldn't hide the look of dismay that flashed across his face. Brendan said, "What do you mean, no, as in, won't or it won't cost?" Brendan looked at Mike expectantly.

"No, it won't cost. I'll put it up." Mike said it, but had no idea why he had done so. Normally, such a request would have been dismissed out of hand. Mike walked toward the bench that was under the noticeboard which contained all the relevant work and safety notices and put a small spanner on top, so it wouldn't flutter away. He turned back to Brendan, and as he did so, Brendan smiled and said, "Thanks, mate, why don't you come up yourself, you might like it?"

Acknowledging the request, Mike said he'd think about it. Thanking him again, Brendan turned and walked into the sunlight, blinking as his eyes adjusted, moving out of view as he put on his helmet. Mike heard an engine start up. Smiling to himself, he guessed '650 Drag Star'. The engine rose in pitch and then Brendan rode past the garage door.

'Knew it!' Smiling, Mike went back to the car. He cursed to himself, remembering that he had to face a head gasket change, which involved taking half the engine off.

Mike thought to himself, what exactly would he be doing, if he wasn't doing this? He resigned himself to the task, but he was going to have some food and a cup of tea first. As he ate his sandwich, he leant against the bench and stared at the car. The processes of what he was going to do were going through his head. He came to the end of the sandwich and twisted round to pick up his cup of tea. As he did so, he noticed the poster that Brendan had delivered earlier. Thinking it might be best to put it up now whilst he had a moment, or he would no doubt forget, he pulled out a couple of pins from the corner of the noticeboard and lined the piece of paper up with the rest of the literature. As he hung it up, he read it properly for the first time. At the thought of motorcycles, he looked across at the bundle of sheets in the corner of the garage, under which his father's bike stood. He thought to himself, why not? For the first time in his life he was making plans to purposely socialise with others. Of course, he would have to get the Beemer out, the Bellisima wasn't powerful enough and besides, it was his dad's. Smiling to himself for making the decision, he walked toward the car. It was going to be a long night, so he'd better hurry; he had an appointment to keep.

CHAPTER 3

He sat for a moment. Sighing, he looked at the dashboard clock. It said 14:30. He had just completed his last delivery. He was in Guisborough, outside Mr Bakeall's, the baker's. He looked down at the passenger's seat. There was a box; in that white cardboard box were four cakes. His mother always gave him a few extra for the deliveries, just in case any got damaged. He hadn't damaged any cakes, so this meant he could eat them – after all, what use were they now?

First, he picked up a peach melba. Giving it a quick glance, he then popped it into his mouth, in its entirety. After about four or five chomps, he swallowed and then looked in the box again. 'Hmm'; the sound was involuntary. Having made his second choice, he deftly made another pastry disappear.

Adjusting himself, which was a little difficult at six feet four and with a body weighing more than four hundred pounds, once settled he looked forward, put on his seat belt and started up the engine. The diesel engine chugged into life, the van moved slowly forward toward the main road. Turning left, he followed the road that led to Loftus. Having arrived at the factory, he made his way to the units where the vans were kept. His mother had made the business grow from a kitchen table into a factory that now dominated the small business park. What other small units were on the site, were also rented by the same business for other uses, such as vehicle maintenance. Darren had, of course, helped her to build the business, but had always stayed in the background – she was the main driving force. Darren dealt with the practical aspects of machinery installation, vehicle maintenance and deliveries.

He parked up and squeezed out of the mini-van. Walking toward the back door of the vehicle, he took off his white coat, presenting a large pot-belly, covered by a tatty looking T-shirt. He opened the doors to reveal racks of trays on rollers. They were all empty except for a few crumbs and greaseproof paper. What cakes hadn't been delivered were either on the front passenger seat or in his stomach. Darren carried the trays over to the unit. The sliding front door was already open. He walked in from the sunlight and into darkness. It wasn't dark, but the contrast between the inside and outside was quite stark. He waited for his eyes to adjust and then continued over to the wash area. A worker stood in front of a large sink and Darren placed the trays on his left. Turning to face him, the man looked at Darren and nodded his thanks. Darren smiled his acknowledgement, and because of the loud background noise showed eight fingers, to indicate how many more were to come. Giving a thumb's up, the man carried on with his work. Darren completed the unloading and then set about cleaning down the van. Once finished, he parked the van up and put the keys on the board. He noticed three more sets of keys already there, which meant there were another twelve, still on their runs.

He needed a coffee. He'd been up since four-thirty, for the early start of deliveries. Making his way toward the factory, he waved to another van that had just finished and shouted hello to various people. The factory was a medium-sized affair, but it was the biggest building in Loftus. Entering a side door, he made his way down a dark corridor, occasionally passing a window that gave a view of the workings of the complex. Large stainless-steel boxes and ovens filled the interior. The warmth from the shop floor was such that the rest of the building didn't require any heating. Generally, it was keeping cool that was the issue. Having now reached the cafeteria, he opened the double swing doors and lumbered to the counter. Irene smiled as he approached. She was a little plump, typical of a well-fed, almost pensionable-aged woman from the area.

"What can I get yer, darlin?" Irene asked cheerfully.

"Just a coffee."

He fetched some change from his pocket and put it into her proffered hand. She put the money into the till and then set about making his usual cappuccino. Wiping down the machine when it was complete, she turned back to him and handed him the coffee. Thanking her, he carried it to his favourite table at the far side of the canteen, near the window, so he could watch the comings and goings. Staring into the middle distance, he sat and didn't really think of anything at all.

After a few minutes, his reverie was broken by an intruder. Planting himself in front of Darren sat Jason. Jason was a childhood friend. They had stayed as acquaintances, but the formative bond that they had had as children hadn't stood the test of time. Jason, like many others in the area, worked at the factory; it was, after all, one of the biggest employers in the area.

"So, how yer doin?"

"OK, sp'ose." Darren didn't really want to talk.

"So, what yer thinkin about?" Jason persisted. "You look miles away."

Darren paused for a minute, and focused on Jason and said, more to himself, "You know what, I don't know, I don't actually know what I want or why."

Darren was a big lad, not because he was muscular, but because he overate. He knew it, his mother knew it and the people he met every day knew it. Because of this he had low self-esteem. He still enjoyed his video games. He also had an avid interest in motorcycles. He owned a Triumph Triple III. It was the only bike he could find, big enough to accommodate him comfortably, without having to go to the expense of buying a Harley Davidson. He always thought that Harleys were a bit overpriced and for the time he rode, he couldn't justify the cost. The video games he played until late each night and he ate while he did. On a Sunday, he went on his bike, on his own. He found that people invariably let him down, so he tried his best not to associate and create any form of lasting bond. Of course, he was polite and held conversations with people. He was, when communicating, erudite and engaging, but generally he kept himself to himself. Darren, unsurprisingly, still lived with his mother. She was the only woman in his life. Unusually for such a set-up, his mother wasn't domineering, even though she spent most of her time telling other people what to do. She tried not to bring her troubles home, but like most mothers, she did spoil him. He had a good wage and she bought him whatever he wanted. She wanted him to learn about the business and take it off her hands, but she could see he wasn't particularly motivated that way. He had no sense of purpose. Being his mother, she knew that he always felt let down by others. The first being his father and then she, of course, knew about his friends, when he was younger. She was hurt for him. Contrary to his appearance, Darren was a tidy and fastidious individual. His car and his bike were always clean and his living habits were disciplined and thorough. Everything was always kept in its place.

Arriving home before his mother, he set about making tea. He rummaged around the kitchen for ingredients and when he managed to collect them together on the counter top, running through the recipe in his head, he started to make chilli con carne. Nothing too taxing, but filling just the same. The kitchen was markedly different from the one he had sat in as a child. They now lived in a four-bedroomed detached house, as opposed to a two-bedroomed terrace. His mother would be home in the next half an hour and they would eat together. She would talk about the business in her usual excited manner and would tell him how they were going to expand. Although he felt genuine delight for her success, he himself could not share the enthusiasm. She had started the business to bring in an income after Darren's father had left them and to focus on something else other than the failed relationship. Since then, the business had acquired a life of its own. In a way, with hindsight, although it had hurt him to think of what his father had done, he was pleased as it had brought them closer together than they would otherwise have been. It had also given his mother the opportunity to show her potential.

Darren sat at the kitchen table, playing with his mobile phone, while he waited for the food to cook and for his mother to arrive. Suddenly, he slammed the mobile phone down in frustration and said to himself loudly "God damn it, I'm bored". It was then that he recognised the feeling that he had had, when he had been talking to Jason earlier. He felt a deep need to change his life, perhaps not throw it away, but to make changes so that he felt it was worth getting up in the morning. Flicking back his long hair, which had come out of his man bun, he got up and checked the food. As he gave it a stir to stop it sticking to the pan, the front door opened and his mam came in.

Maureen was a woman of sixty-six years, but very fit and active for her age. Her hair was just beginning to turn grey but the veins on her hands gave away her true age. She wore a neat suit and carried a small briefcase. She put the case on top of another counter top and then walked over and gave her boy a hug. He returned the embrace and smiled.

"Did you have a good day?" he asked.

Without looking up she said, "Not bad, gave a couple of discipline warnings out, two new starters horse-playing, but other than that, quite good."

She sounded like a woman who had found her calling, and was enjoying every minute of it. She sat at her usual place and Darren turned to complete the meal. Within a few minutes, he returned to the table with two hot plates, one piled significantly higher than the other. He put the bigger one in front of his mother. She looked up at him, smiled and said, "Funny!"

Grinning, he swapped them back round and then sat down opposite her. He concentrated on eating, she concentrated on talking. To acknowledge that he was listening, he asked the odd pertinent question.

This went on until the meal was finished. His had disappeared a long time before hers. After he had cleared away the dishes he sat back down at the table. She looked at him silently. He didn't like it when she did this, because he knew she was going to have a bright idea of some kind, usually involving him.

"You can come with me tomorrow." It was a demand, not a request.

"Where?" he said with resignation.

"I'm doing a tour of the customers in the local area, to make sure they're happy."

Rolling his eyes and shrugging his shoulders like a petulant teenager he said, "OK." Yes, he felt frustrated; something really was going to have to change.

The nice blue Volvo waited on the drive. His mother had been out fifteen minutes earlier to get it out of the garage. The air was a little brisk and dew still sat atop the blades of grass on the lawn. Turning to lock the front door, Darren gave the handle a last wiggle to make sure it was secure and then walked to the car. Smoke from the exhaust surrounded the car as there was no wind to dissipate it. Opening the passenger door, bending over to slide the seat right back, he then got in next to his mother. Maureen, as always, was dressed in an immaculate suit. She looked at him and smiled.

"Very nice, maybe you'll get yourself a girl before long, if you stay dressed like that."

Maureen's comment made him feel uncomfortable. Not only did he not like being in a suit, but the subject of women embarrassed him. He sat awkwardly in the car, the suit felt stiff and his hair felt tight. His hair was pulled into a pony tail and his beard was shiny, having been conditioned. The suit fitted, just. It had been especially made to fit his height and girth, but that was two years ago.

"Are we going to be long?" he asked with a sigh.

"About half an hour at each place; we're going to five places."

She could tell he was reluctant to come with her and she also knew that he realised it was pointless to argue. They fell into silence.

They arrived at the first bakery. It was in a terrace shop in Brotton. After finding a parking space on the street, they both got out of the car. It was early Saturday morning, which meant there wasn't too much traffic on the road and only a handful of pedestrians, mainly people who had gone to the newsagent's next door to the bakery. As always, he received a few glances because of his size, otherwise they were ignored. In front of 'Carr's Bakery', always the gentleman, Darren opened the door to let his mother through first. The shop was cool, to keep the produce fresh. Behind the counter stood an assistant. Seeing the couple walk through the door, the assistant said, "Hello Mrs Barnes, I'll just give him a shout."

Turning around from behind the counter, the assistant walked through a strip blind that hung on the doorway. The mother and son heard shouting. "John, they're here." A slightly muffled response came back: "OK, Just a minute, I'm on my way". About a minute later they heard thumping as John came down some stairs at the back of the building. Finally, the strips parted on the door and a clean-shaven man in jeans and T-Shirt appeared. Walking around the counter he shook Maureen's hand, then Darren's.

"Well hello you two, come on out back and we'll have a cuppa."

Following him to the door he had come out of, they entered the blackness of the store room.

"It's OK with the drinks, John. We had one just before we came out and you're the first visit," said Maureen.

Nodding that he understood, he continued to lead them upstairs. John was quite fit and almost skipped up the stairs. Maureen followed him and held the bannister rail for support. She was slightly out of breath at the top, but otherwise OK. Darren on the other hand was struggling, not only because he was so unfit, but because he found it so hard in the narrow stairwell. He was conscious that his suit was rubbing against the wall and it might be getting dirty. When he finally reached the top of the stairs he arched his back, tried to calm his breathing and patted his shoulders, to see if any paint or dust came off. His mother gave him a stern look and tightly shook her head. Seeing her gesture, he lowered his arms and followed her into the office. Bowing his head, he entered the office and then sat with the other two. Of course, Maureen did the talking, mainly asking John how his business was going and how the lines she was sending, were selling. The discussions went on about improvements to the products and service.

Darren was bored. The voices soon turned into a drone in the background. Maureen had specifically told him that he couldn't use his phone or any other device and that he should take notice of what was happening when he visited customers. Every now and again he would proffer a nod and smile when he thought appropriate, but otherwise he feigned interest. It was during his surveillance of the room that he spotted the edge of a piece of paper on a noticeboard. The office was a loose term for the room where they sat. All three of them were seated at a canteen table in the corner of a large room. The actual 'office' was in the furthest corner away from where they were sitting. From the position of the noticeboard, he deduced that the paperwork that had caught his eye would most likely be social. Now, Darren had a problem. He had to sit and endure all this business stuff, while his curiosity made him feel frustrated. After what seemed like an eternity, the conversation finally ended. Everyone stood and did the usual routine of courteous hand shaking and smiles.

"Well, thanks again, Maureen, a pleasure as always," said a genuine sounding John.

"No, the pleasure's mine and I hope the bairn gets better soon." Maureen was by now, holding the 'office' door, waiting to leave. She looked over at Darren expectantly. Surprisingly, he didn't look like he was ready to go straight away. Frowning, she looked at Darren and said, "What is it?"

Returning the look of the other two, Darren said, "John, I know it's rude, but I was looking at your noticeboard here." He gestured to the board. Continuing, he asked, "I noticed a picture with a bike on it, would you mind if I had a look?"

Smiling, John walked over to the noticeboard and searched through the paperwork, until he found the requested sheet. Tearing it, he handed it to Darren. "No one here's interested in bikes, so just take it."

Smiling in return, Darren thanked the man and then followed his mother back to the car. He read the poster properly and then thought to himself, 'I have something to do this weekend, I'm going to a bike meet.'

CHAPTER 4

Malika Acharya worked at his father's restaurant. The reality is that it belonged to him, as his father had been dead for the last six years. He had loved his father, but like most Asian parents, he had been strict. Looking across the empty restaurant, he sighed. His father had done well after arriving in the UK. He had started out as a bus driver and then in 1978 he had opened a small restaurant. Then in 1988 he moved the business to bigger premises, which is where it was now. They had made the move from Middlesbrough, where they had a steady clientele, and had taken a huge chance in a backwater town, called Loftus. Much to everyone's surprise, it took off and soon gained a reputation for quality. Of course, quality only comes from a strict and exacting attention to detail, which was instilled into Malika.

More for something to do, Malika walked around the fifteen tables in the large room. Looking at the detail of each setting, he made sure that the table cloths were flat, cutlery clean, glasses sparkling and the napkins were sharp edged. After about ten minutes of this he gave himself a little nod and decided that he was satisfied. He then walked back to his station next to the till. After a few minutes, which took it to 18:50, the first of the waiters turned up and then in quick succession the other two entered the restaurant. As the last came in, Malika looked at his watch. He did this as a statement to say that he was in charge. He never had to berate them for tardiness. At 18:58 the three waiters stood in a loose group in the corner of the room, chatting amongst themselves. Malika walked over to them. They raised their chins as Malika straightened ties and collars. Once done, he went to the door and unlocked it. No one rushed in; it was Thursday. Thursdays were always quiet. The only time things got busy mid-week, was when a celebration party came, and as it was mid-September, there was little chance of that. It was going to be a long, quiet night. The demeanour of the staff showed that they knew it too.

All night, the clientele consisted of three couples and one group of four men, who had obviously been drinking. Despite this, there wasn't any bother and the evening went over quietly. At nine PM, Malika had sent two of the waiters home. Bringing them in had been a mistake, but as they say, it's better to be over-prepared, rather than not prepared. Eleven o'clock finally arrived. There were no customers to hurry out. The last had left an hour earlier. He had let the last waiter go at ten past ten. The tables had been tidied after each customer left and there were a minimum number of dishes to wash. Malika walked into the kitchen. The chef wasn't there. Looking from side to side for the missing worker, Malika then opened the back door to the rear yard. Stood outside, the chef had a mobile phone in one hand and a cigarette in the other. He looked at Malika sheepishly.

"Sorry, it was quiet and I knew there wasn't anyone else," he said apologetically.

Malika looked at him with a tinge of disappointment. "You know my opinion. Get yourself away, everyone else has gone."

Repeating a mumbled apology, he slunk past and went into the kitchen. Whilst holding the door, Malika stepped in behind him. The chef disappeared into the far cloakroom. Malika could hear him retrieving his belongings. A few seconds later, the chef shouted his goodbyes and the front door closed behind him.

Malika was still stood at the back door holding it open. He wasn't quite sure why he stood there. Originally, he had wanted some fresh air, but the fumes from the cigarette had put him off. Realising the pointlessness of the exercise, he stepped in and locked the door behind him. Walking to the front door he did the same. Once everything was secured, he set about stacking the dishwasher and cleaning up. At last, Malika had finished and once again found himself standing alone in the vast expanse of the restaurant. After a moment or two he went back to the cloakroom and switched off the light. Doing the same in each room, working his way back to the restaurant. Just as he was going to switch off the last light, he stopped himself. Of course, he had forgotten to set the alarm. He walked back behind the drinks counter and located the alarm box. He set the alarm and picked up his coat, which was draped over the seat nearest the door. One more glance about, then he stepped out of the door backwards and locked it. He then decided that he wouldn't put his coat on and so left it over his arm. He made his way to the car and unlocked it. Getting behind the steering wheel, he slammed the door shut. The clock said 00:32. The silence in the car was like a blanket. He felt comforted by it. He was in solitude, but didn't feel lonely. This was supposed to be nirvana. The essence of being self-sufficient. And yet he felt that there was something missing. He had felt it as a teenager. The feeling that he had to do something, but at the age of sixty-four, had he not done everything? Shaking himself, he leant forward slightly and turned the key. The engine growled into life. Looking backwards, he reversed out of the parking bay and then straightened up. Changing gear, he then set off on his journey home to Saltburn. The roads were quiet as would be expected now at this time of night, especially mid-week. He finally arrived home. He pulled up outside the Victorian terrace and then made his way up to the house. He decided to get a cool shower before going to bed. Yet again, another rollercoaster of a day in the life of Malika Acharya had ended. Getting into bed, he knew he would be waking to face the same day tomorrow.

He awoke with a start. He didn't know why. He hadn't had a bad dream. The world outside was quiet. Blinking himself properly awake, Malika looked to his left. That's where Saavi used to sleep. He felt a sudden pang of loss. He missed her. In his younger days, he had been a rebel, or at least that was as far as his father was concerned. There had been a lot of arguments in the house about whom he should marry. At that moment in time, he hadn't wanted to marry at all. He smiled to himself. Those days were so long ago and yet they seemed just like yesterday. He looked at the curtains at the bedroom window, swaying in the gentle breeze. He noted that it was a bit cooler than yesterday. A few minutes wouldn't hurt, he thought. He lay his head back on the pillow and continued to reminisce. His father had been a good man, but he was living in a foreign land and so held onto his customs and culture. This gave him a sense of security, but it meant that the rest of the family were in the same cultural prison as him. As a teenager and into his mid-twenties, Malika wanted to break out. Partly because of the raging pheromones of his youth, but also because he lived in a different world to that of his father. Malika understood society in a more accepting way and wanted to make choices of his own.

Because of the racism that Malika suffered at the hands of British society, he had eventually, if not subconsciously, given in to his father's demands. A young woman was sent from India. The girl was seventeen. He himself was twenty-five at the time. They were told that they were to get to know each other and they would be married when Saavi turned eighteen. That way, the British authorities couldn't question their activities. So, the wedding was set for September – it was now February 1978. Malika quickly got the impression that Saavi was as happy about the situation as he was. However, with parental persuasion, of which there was lots, Saavi and he went on various dates. After a while, about a month or so, Malika realised that he thought of Saavi a lot. He even started to think of how he would make her smile. He knew that he had hoops to jump through to satisfy the religious and cultural niceties, but none of that mattered, if Saavi smiled. Eventually, September arrived. It was the day before the wedding.

"Father, I would like to discuss the wedding. Saavi and I have come to an agreement and have decided that we will not marry unless you concede to our demands."

Malika's father looked at him incredulously. "Demands?" his father repeated under his breath.

"Yes, if we are adults, then we have choices. If we are to do as we are told, then we are prisoners. In which case, as prisoners, we have nothing to lose."

Amused and yet taken aback, his father raised his finger up as a gesture to wait. In a tactic to embarrass his son, Malika's father called both Saavi's and his own family into the room. Moments later, the front room was full of people. The women sat on the furniture, the children on the floor and the men stood. Everyone was silent. Suddenly thinking that this might not have been such a good idea, Malika looked at the floor. In that moment, he realised that this was his father's plan. He wanted Malika to be humiliated and give in to familial pressure.

Raising his head, he looked directly at his father. Their eyes locked across the room. The elder's eyes showed a mix of anger and pleading, the younger's a look of defiance and humility. Both men tried to calculate the other's next move. Breaking the stare and the silence, Malika took a deep breath.

"Saavi and I have decided the following. This should be a time of celebration. How can we celebrate, if half the family must pay money to the other? We do not want the dowry."

After a moment's silence, all hell was let loose. Things calmed down after about twenty minutes. The first to speak was Saavi's father. "Is what we offer not good enough? Do you feel insulted?" The tone was a mixture of relief and being aggrieved.

"No, it is not," came the reply.

Eyes wide in disbelief, Saavi's father paced up and down. "I have given everything that I have, what else can I do?"

Malika's father said nothing and continued to stare at his son.

Putting his hand up, Malika gestured for peace so that he could explain himself. "I, no, we do not want anything from you, but your blessing, that is the most precious thing you can do. No man could, nor should, give more. A dowry is used to induce a man's family into accepting a person, who is perceived as a worthless burden, an expense to be disposed of. By bringing Saavi to me, I have become the richest man in the world."

At this there was a hush in the room. They all looked at Malika's father, who remained impassive. The women then looked at each other, the other men looked astounded. It was then that hell really did break loose. Saavi squeezed his hand, Malika's mother rushed over to him, weeping and hugged him. Then it was the turn of each of the women in Saavi's family. Again, Malika and his father's eyes locked. Malika had turned the entire situation round. The family would be closer, but his father would have less money. He wasn't completely sure, but he thought he saw the corner of his father's mouth twitch into a smile. It was fleeting, but he was sure it was there.

His father, a couple of weeks after the wedding, had asked him why he had given away the dowry.

He explained: "Dad, you're trapped by your culture and so is Mam; to a degree so am I. Saavi must be free to make her own choices."

His father then asked, "But why do that, what's the point, she is still in the family?"

Sounding far wiser than his years, Malika said, "True freedom comes from giving, not taking. I want to give her my love, not take her family's possessions. This marriage is a mutual giving of love, which frees us both."

Looking him in the eye, his father understood. With tears in their eyes they hugged.

It was 2013 when she died. Cancer got the better of her. He had watched her deteriorate rapidly. She had been told in October 2012 that it was incurable and she gave up the fight the following March. He sorely missed her and even now, as he lay in his bed, when he thought the grief had finally passed, he felt a tightness in his throat; a tear welled up and ran down his cheek. Malika finally resigned himself to the fact that he had to get up. He did the usual routine, took a shower, brushed his teeth and hair and groomed his beard. Got dressed, breakfast and then set about the day's business. Orders for the restaurant could be done from home. He worked in his little office, alone. He had finished up in a little over an hour and then decided he had some shopping to do. He got into his car and arrived at the supermarket fifteen minutes later. He parked up and fetched about in his pocket for a pound coin. He then walked over to the trolley cage in the middle of the car park. Putting the pound in the security lock, he pulled a trolley free and as luck would have it, it had a wonky wheel. Which meant that every now and again, without warning, it would spin, sending the trolley in random directions. Cursing his luck, he made his way into the supermarket.

The down draft of the ventilation hit him as he passed through the door and then he was assaulted by out of date pop music, which was being pumped into the air over the tannoy system. Trundling along with his erratic trolley, Malika walked up and down the aisles collecting his necessaries. The supermarket reminded him of Saavi. He used to walk with the trolley behind her as she nattered on about the family goings on. He was always oblivious to what she said, but the fact that he was with her was enough. He would notice the way her dress flowed and how the light reflected off her earrings. But most of all he noticed the depth of her eyes whenever she looked at him. Those eyes, black, deep and full of intelligence and life. Even when the cancer was at its worst and she was obviously suffering, he loved the depth of those eyes. Pulling back from his reverie, he returned to the supermarket. The music seemed somehow louder and the light a bit brighter. In thinking of Saavi, he felt more connected to everything, in a spiritual kind of way. Pausing to think on it, while pretending to look at some washing powder, he concluded that he needed to do something different. Perhaps the universe was telling him to expand, somehow. Smiling to himself he thought, what can a man, particularly an old Indian man in the UK do? He needed to look about himself. The universe, he felt, was telling him to look for clues. He continued his shop with a strange feeling of anticipation.

Finally arriving at the till, he was greeted by a young man sat on the chair behind the electronic register. "Good afternoon, sir, would you like any help with your packing?" It was a practised question, asked without any sincerity, by a boy who had no intention of helping. Malika had the urge to say 'yes', to see what the reaction would be. But, right now he had other things on his mind; the feeling of anticipation wasn't receding. He thought that he was simply getting himself uptight because he felt lonely. His mother and father had passed away and of course, he was without Saavi. He asked for a few carriers and began packing his groceries. He tried to sort the goods into the appropriate bags, but the boy was going too fast, scanning them through and a queue was beginning to form at his till. So, he ended up bunging the goods into the nearest bag, much to his irritation. He paid and put the four full bags into the trolley and made his way to the exit. As he did so, he came to the customer notices. There were the usual cards with furniture for sale, a car and a bicycle. What caught his eye was the A4 picture of a motorcycle. Intrigued, he read further. The poster wasn't particularly professional, obviously done on someone's home computer. There was a picture of a large motorcycle with an intimidating looking man in a helmet. The emboldened letters proclaimed that a new motorcycle club was going to be formed and anyone was invited. The meeting place was going to be a pub along the road from his restaurant, the Angel. The meeting time was to be two PM tomorrow.

Malika thought he would give it a miss. There were probably going to be white right wing fascists. Men who wore Nazi Swastikas, took drugs and went around the streets like insecure fifteen year olds telling everyone how 'bad' they were. It had been a long time since Malika had ridden his bike; in fact it had been twenty-five years since he had sat astride his little two-fifty. Bikes had become a lot more powerful since then. But, for some reason, the poster seemed to attract him. Perhaps the universe was giving him a clue after all. As he decided to away from the board, dismissing the idea, a gruff voice got his attention. "Saw you looking, Paki." A tattoo-covered, overweight man whom Malika assumed to be in his early fifties nodded toward the poster. "You haven't got the balls, Pakis like you don't, that's why you lot come here, you're too weak to look after yourselves, so we have to." The male's voice conveyed undisguised disgust when he spoke and looked at Malika.

"I'm British Indian, not Pakistani," Malika replied politely.

"All the bloody same to me, I wish you'd all just bugger off back home."

Taken aback by the uncalled-for comments, Malika looked back at the poster. His mind had just been made up for him; the universe had spoken.

CHAPTER 5

Looking at his mobile phone, he smiled at a comment that had been posted on Facebook. As he continued to read, he let out a snort of laughter. Turning her head, his mother glared at him.

"I wish you would put that damn thing away," she said in Urdu.

Returning the look with contempt, he begrudgingly switched off the app and put the phone in his pocket. With his hands empty, he sighed and put them on the counter top and drummed his fingers. Again, his mother turned and gave him that look, but said nothing. Taking a deeper sigh, he withdrew his hands and stood silently. He then started to rock backwards and forwards from his heels and onto the balls of his feet.

"Get out of the damned shop, go in the back and do some stock-taking or something," his mother said, with a touch of venom.

He was irritating the hell out of her. Tutting his defiance, he glanced in her direction and stalked out of the shop. He entered the gloom of the stockroom. There wasn't really that much stock and what there was, he had already sorted. He had updated everything on the computer years ago, bringing the shop out of the Stone Age. Despite the efficient innovation of computerised stock control, it hadn't improved the business.

For something to do, he clicked the kettle on, got out two mugs and made his mother and himself a mug of tea. He took a steaming mug to the front of the shop. The busy woman straightened from her stoop. The shelf behind her was still damp from her cleaning and the products were on the floor. Accepting the mug with a weak smile, she cupped her hands around the container and took obvious pleasure from its warmth. She looked reflectively at her son. After a moment, she said in a calm voice, "I know you're bored, but if you're going to run this place, then you're going to have to put some effort into learning how things work and be a bit more professional."

He gave her an apologetic look. "Mam, I don't know if this is what I want. The problem is that I don't know what I am supposed to do."

They both stood looking at each other, trying to assess the possible response. As this contemplation went on, the door to the shop chimed. Breaking away from the conversation, Muhammad went behind the counter as his mother put her mug down and went back to cleaning.

The man who entered was one of the regulars. Tall, with a balding head. He walked with a slight stoop around the shoulders. He made a bee-line to the milk fridge and then had a slow browse at the papers and magazines, before picking up the same paper that he always bought. When he arrived at the counter he asked for some cigarettes. As this went on, he talked about the weather, as he always did. Again, as usual, as he did every Friday, he pretended that he had almost forgotten to buy some lottery tickets, like it was a guilty secret. Muhammad returned the false smile as he handed Mr Stoop his change. Mr Stoop was Muhammad's name for him. He had names for most of the regulars, for his own amusement. Mr Stoop made his way out of the shop and then the door clicked shut on the catch. Muhammad turned to go to the stockroom when the front door double dinged again. Sighing, he returned to his station. The couple who had entered, split up. It seemed that they weren't a couple, just two individuals who had arrived at the same time.

In the background, he could hear his mother stacking the shelves that she had been cleaning. He heard the woman say, 'excuse me' as she made her around his mother. It seemed she was going down the booze aisle, whereas the man was at the magazine rack. After an indeterminate amount of time, seemingly coincidentally, they both arrived at the counter at the same time. Smiling at each other, they both looked somewhat sheepish; they both said at the same time "After you". It was painful to watch the interplay and coy smiles, but the deadlock was broken when the male said, "No, ladies first." With a wide smile, the woman stepped forward to get served. She paid for her goods and grinned at the man, then she moved aside so that he could be served next.

As the man turned to leave, he noticed that the woman hadn't gone. She was waiting for him. She flicked her long auburn hair and smiled at him. She then said, "Don't I know you, I'm sure I've seen you before?"

Smiling, he replied, "No, I don't think so, but I would know, I wouldn't have forgotten you."

It was cringe-worthy, but worked nonetheless. Her demeanour didn't change – if anything, she was more interested, now that a conversation had started. Talking as they made their way to the door, the man held the door open and she ducked under his arm. Before the door shut with a double ding, Muhammad heard the woman laughing. He waited a minute or two in case of any more customers and then went to the stockroom for his mug of tea. Picking it up, he took a sip and quickly realised it was on the cold side of tepid. Wrinkling his face, he walked over to the sink and poured the contents down the sink. Sighing again, he flicked the kettle back on and made another tea. Why couldn't things like that happen to me? He thought of the couple who had just left. They were going on an adventure with each other – whether it lasted for one day or forty years. They would each have someone to go into the unknown with.

For some reason, unbeknownst to him, the room he stood in, seemed oppressive and even darker. He felt as though he needed to do something and expand his world view. He had a degree and could seek opportunities elsewhere, but then he would miss his family and home. He felt conflicted: he loved his parents and was aware of the expectations they had for him. He didn't want to let them down. He was, as far as he could see, going to be stuck here for the rest of his life. His thoughts were interrupted, when at the same time, the kettle clicked off and his mother put her head around the door and said "Busy?" He turned to his mother, smiled and said "Always".

His parents, they had had a hard life. After moving from Pakistan to the UK, they had lived in Bradford, where they were subject to systematic racism. They sought shelter in the Pakistani community, but were given short shrift, because of their more lax and liberal attitude toward religion. They were good people who wanted to 'fit in'. However, because they tried to simply be themselves, they were rejected by both communities. Muhammad too, had been subject to abuse by both communities, but not in such a sustained manner. He, perhaps because of his parents' influence, did not seek to align himself with any group of people. When he asked his father about their predicament, his father's response was to say 'God has sent us to learn something for ourselves, we all ultimately walk alone and so must seek our own answers. No methodology, religion or group can decide our destiny, we must do that ourselves'.

Muhammad didn't have many friends. Those with whom he had associated tended to be for business orientated purposes. Because of this, he would feel bouts of loneliness. He had a yearning to connect with others, in the same way that the random couple had earlier. When he was a little younger, he had tried hard to connect with other Pakistani teenagers in Middlesbrough. His father had bought him a car. A Subaru Impreza. This car was high powered and very quick, enough to impress any teenager. He had had many arguments with his father, as the insurance was so high, let alone the price of the car. His father eventually gave in to him as he realised that Muhammad was trying to fit in with others, as he had done in his own youth. After many concerted efforts of trying to make friends, Muhammad began to understand that he was being used. No one ever called him unless he was to take someone somewhere or they would want something from him, such as money etc. As time went on, his 'friends' would talk to him about going to mosques or religious meetings. What then became apparent to him, is how all the people he had gone out of his way to associate with, all thought in the same way and when there was any attempt to deviate from the accepted norm, there began a backlash of emotional blackmail or straightforward intimidation. Fortunately for Muhammad, he lived a good few miles away. This gave him the space and time to consider the circumstances. Eventually, with the combination of being used by others for their convenience and demonstrative lack of intolerance, Muhammad decided to withdraw from the people whom he sought out.

His parents, throughout his ordeal, had tried their best not to interfere with his decisions and actions. Ironically, their faith gave them the belief that their son would make the right choices for himself. They would have been disappointed if he had gone down the route of intense religion, because it would have narrowed his world view. After his decision to withdraw from the activities in Middlesbrough, Muhammad had sold his Subaru and let it be known to those in the bigger town that he had done so. He bought a motorcycle instead. The phone calls from his friends ceased. When he rang them, as he then expected, he was rebuffed with excuses so that they could terminate the call. Although he was disappointed with the loss of the connection with others, he knew it was for the best. So, Muhammad ended up where he had started, a sad lonely individual, in a dark corner shop, in a back-wood town.

His mother looked around the doorway at the back of the shop. Muhammad put his mug down and followed her out. She beckoned him over to a set of shelves and asked him to help move them so she could clean underneath. Having moved the shop furniture to his mother's satisfaction, he queried her. "How do you manage? It's just that you and Dad don't go away or anything?"

Looking at him in a sympathetic way, she raised her right hand and cupped his face. "Muhammad, you are lonely, because you feel a lack of connection with the world. If you look, everything you need is within you. When you need something, it will appear. Your father and I share a little of each other's universe, which means we fulfil each other's needs. But remember, ultimately, we are all on our own and our choices are also our own." She brought her hands down and gave him a look of understanding. "While you're thinking of universal truths and enlightenment, go get me a bucket of hot water and put some bleach in it."

Smiling at her, he nodded and turned. Going back into the dark of the backroom, he found a bucket, bleach and the mop. He filled the bucket and took it to his mother. Looking with thanks, she said, quite profoundly, "Allah will let you know what you are to do, don't worry."

He hoped so.

Early next morning, his dad walked into the shop and stood behind the counter. He opened the paper that Muhammad had put there for him. He read, whilst waiting for the customers who would pop in before work. The first customer came with coveralls on, probably a factory worker from the steel plant at Skinningrove, on the other side of the valley. The next was an older man, who had tied a dog up on the railings outside the shop. Thereafter, there was a steady stream of customers, each making their early morning starts, each with a disdain for having to get up so early. Muhammad studied the people as they came and went, looking for some clue as to what kept them happy and allowed them to function day to day. He did not see anything that he could recognise. Daylight eventually broke, not that it made much difference to the quality of light in the shop. However, the rain had stopped properly and outside the sunlight reflected off the water and dry patches were beginning to appear on the ground.

The radio had just announced that it was eight-thirty-five when the black guy in the motorbike gear appeared. The man smiled and picked up a couple of small items and as he was paying for them he asked Muhammad's father how much it would be to put a poster in the front window. After discussing the price, the man agreed and paid the fee;

he then left and walked into the sunshine. Having slouched about for a while, Muhammad walked over and picked up the A4 piece of paper that had been left.

"I'll put it in the window," he volunteered.

His father nodded and he then bowed his head to continue reading his paper, which took a while, because English was his second language. Muhammad walked to the front of the shop and moved the panel that was in front of the window, so that he could place the new advertisement. He looked around the board and unpicked a few out of date adverts and shuffled a few more about. Finally, he unfolded the paper to orientate it for display. Looking at it, he saw a picture of a motorcycle, with a man upon it. Of course, having an interest in motorcycles, he read further. The advert was to join a motorcycle club. For some unknown reason, he seemed to suddenly have an undue interest in going to this meeting. He had no idea why. It occurred to him, despite his age, that he had better talk to his parents about it. The meeting was to be tomorrow afternoon. He normally didn't work on a Sunday, so there might be a good chance he could go. He hadn't been on his bike for a while; it might be good for a change. He finished putting the poster into the newly organised space and then, with a little effort, he put the panel back into its place.

Muhammad talked to both of his parents about the poster and what it meant. His mother, as expected, told him to go for it. His father, however, had his reservations.

"Of course, I can't stop you from going, nor would I want to give the impression that I am trying to, but you must remember that this sort of thing is the domain of working class right wing males with a chip on their shoulder."

Muhammad countered the argument by pointing out that it was a black man who had brought the poster in. Shrugging and seeing the determination in his son's face, Muhammad's father no longer laboured the point. Feeling that he had got his parents on side, he went to the shed at the back of the shop yard and unlocked the door. Inside was a cover. Stooping down, Muhammad grabbed the bottom and pulled it over to reveal a slightly dusty, but otherwise, pristine Suzuki Hayabusa. As he had with the car, he had bought the most fashionable bike on the market, at the time. It wasn't exactly a bike club type of bike, but until he understood 'the lay of the land', he wasn't going to spend more money. His father walked up behind him and put his hand on Muhammad's shoulder.

"Listen, son, I know you want to do something different, but this might not be a good idea." The concern in his voice was very real.

To answer him and allay his fears, Muhammad put his hand on top of his father's. "Dad, not only do I need to get out and mix a bit, so does the bike. You bought this for me and it cost a bloody fortune; I should get some money's worth out of it!"

Removing his hand, his dad said, "The money doesn't matter, it never has. I only want you and your mam to be happy. Besides, you should be concentrating on girls and marriage now."

Smiling at him, Muhammad said, "I thought we had talked about this; besides, you never know where this might lead."

Tutting, his father, with a hint of amusement in his voice, said, "I could only imagine what sort of girl you would meet, doing this sort of thing."

As he finished his sentence, Muhammad's mother clipped his father on the side of the head. "Don't you get any ideas either."

The two men smiled at each other and then his father turned and put his arm around his wife. As they walked away, he heard his father's voice. "You didn't say anything like that when I had my bike ... Ouch!"

CHAPTER 6

She was twelve years old when she got her first prosthetic leg, then had had it replaced every couple of years as she grew. Her leg gave her confidence. But, as she predicted so many years ago, she had been and always would be, as far as she could see, patronized. Whether she liked it or not. Wherever she went, people always gave her sideways glances or in some cases outright stares. She had gotten beyond the point of being bothered what people had thought of her; this made her overly defensive. At times, when she thought relationships with others might have worked, sexual or otherwise, she drove them away. This also made it difficult securing a job. She had gone to school, college and had begun university, but dropped out after eighteen months. Because the social aspect of her course became too much for her. She had considered correspondence courses, but the expense was proportionately greater than normal university. So, she ended up drifting through life. Eventually, she landed a job as a barmaid at her local 'The Angel'. It wasn't too bad – like most pubs, there were rowdy nights, but generally, it was a quiet place. It was a reflection of the town. Tonight was one of those quiet nights. A couple of men sat in the far corner, away from the window, playing dominoes and a couple, she supposed were in their forties, sat at the other extreme of the room. The couple were close to each other and talked in hushed tones. Occasionally, a little giggle or laugh came from their direction. They were obviously dating.

Sighing to herself, she bent over and picked up the small crate of empty bottles. Clinking along, which was exaggerated by her limp, she took it to the backroom for collection. The smell of beer, ironically, was lessened when there was more of it. A faint smell of cigarette smoke caught her attention. Looking up she saw a slight wisp of what she could smell. The back door was slightly ajar and she knew that the landlord was having a sly draw. She put the bottles onto the appropriate shelf and walked over to the open door and stepped through. Sure enough, Paul Mason, the pub landlord, stood with a slightly hunched back, leaning against the wall. He looked over at Sophie as she came out of the door. Squinting, to reduce the smoke getting into his eyes, he nodded in her direction.

"Hi boss, thought it was you."

"Yeah, well, just escaping for ten minutes."

He sounded a bit down. The man had taken on the place with business in mind, not to be part of the community. The place wasn't making the kind of return that he wanted, so he often felt frustrated. His wife had left him six months earlier, which only served to make him feel even more depressed.

"You OK?" Sophie asked with genuine concern.

He was a decent bloke, a little intense maybe, but at the end of the day, he had given her a job when many others hadn't. He had never made a pass at her and appeared to really respect her.

"Yeah, thanks for asking." As he said it, he flicked the tab end on the floor, he then searched for it and stood on it to ensure that it was properly extinguished. He walked towards her and then stood about four feet from where she was. "If I could get a buyer for this place, I'd piss off and start again. God, I need a holiday and a fresh start."

She felt sorry for him. She had had dreams that were dashed and so she sympathised. He gave her a quick glance and then walked inside. She stood on her own. The smell of the smoke had begun to clear and so she drew into her lungs some fresh air. She felt a little better.

After a few moments' solitude, she went back into the gloom of the back-store room. She picked up a board and set about recording the present stock. She had to move a few boxes here and there, and every now and again asked Paul about the situation of an order. She eventually finished the stock take and went back behind the bar. Paul had just finished serving one of the domino guys. He turned to her.

"Finished?"

"Yeah, sorted," she responded.

"Everything OK?"

"Two bottles of lemonade short, but that would be OK, probably not rang in properly. The money matches though."

Smiling, Paul looked a little relieved. They had had their share of 'till dippers'. It was good to know that they had honest staff in at the minute. Paul trusted Sophie implicitly, which made his job easier.

"Listen, clear up the tables and get yourself away. It's gonna be busy tomorrow and you'll sharp make up the work."

"OK, will do." She was a little bored and was grateful for the escape. Things would be better tomorrow when it was busier.

Clumping around with a spray and a cloth, she cleaned up the tables in the lounge. The bar area was OK; she had done that earlier, because as usual, it was the dirtiest. There was another hushed giggle from the loved-up couple as Sophie left the lounge area. Sometimes, when people were whispering, she thought it was about her. From experience, she realised that ninety-nine percent of the time, they weren't, but still, the feeling was there. She looked back at them. They weren't looking in her direction, so she plumped for the idea that it had been a private joke and nothing to do with her. She really would have to get a grip on this anxiety of hers. Waving to Paul, she left the premises. She got onto her scooter. It was one of those large machines, in size more akin to a motorcycle, but with the controls of a scooter. She would have had a motorbike, but necessity dictated otherwise. She put on her helmet and gloves, kicked off the stand and turned the engine on. It roared into life, the noise belying the size of the vehicle.

Weaving down the road toward Easington, which was three miles east of Loftus, she made her way home. Pulling onto the drive, she came to a halt. The engine's roar became more apparent when it was switched off, because of the sudden auditory vacuum. Skilfully kicking the stand out, she leant the scooter onto it and dismounted. As she walked to the bungalow, she took off her protective gear. She stuffed the gloves and scarf into her helmet. Before she entered the building, she let out a sigh in preparation for what was to come next. She struggled to unlock the door at the top of the steep steps with her bulky jacket, holding her helmet and trying to lift her prosthetic over the threshold all at the same time. She was sure it was on purpose to annoy her. Her mother's excuse for not moving to a more accessible house was because she and her husband, Sophie's father, had bought it when they had first got married and so she was reluctant to let it go. She didn't want to live in some dingy council bungalow. She was a bit 'Mrs Bucket'. Finally getting through the door, she pivoted on her prosthetic and kicked the door shut. It did slam a little too heavily and she winced a silent apology.

Her mother, as always, was sat in the living room. Jeremy Kyle had just ended. The older woman looked up as her daughter entered. She didn't hide her disdain of the biker gear. Her brother, Sophie's uncle, had died in his early twenties in a motorcycle accident. The family had blamed the fact that he had been on a motorbike, rather than the incompetence of the man who was behind the steering wheel of the car that had done the killing. It was really the fear of the vulnerability of her daughter that she resented. Her daughter had her father's rebelliousness. Everything was a great adventure for them, but created a constant state of anxiety for the family. How could someone so vulnerable take so many risks?

Getting up from her seat, Anne walked passed Sophie, conspicuously not looking at her motorcycle wear.

"You're early?" she said, as she entered the kitchen.

Sophie followed, whilst trying to find an available place to plonk her gear. Anne picked up the kettle and proceeded to fill it at the sink.

Sophie hung her jacket on the back of a kitchen chair and put the helmet underneath the same. "Paul let me go, things were a bit dead and he said I could make up for it tomorrow."

Anne raised her eyebrows. "Make it up?"

"You know, for someone who's so strait-laced, you're awfully suggestive," replied Sophie indignantly.

Blushing a little from the rebuke, but still smirking, Anne continued making the tea. Minutes later, they were both sat in the living room sipping from steamy mugs.

"There's nothing between us you know." Sophie referred to the earlier conversation. She added, "He wants out of the pub business."

"Have you considered it, or do you think it would be too much for you?"

"I have, I would do it more for the community than money, unlike Paul. There's not a lot of money to be made from the pub industry these days."

Falling silent for a while, both considered their next words. "So, what exactly are you going to do with yourself? You can't be sat working in a pub all your life."

Sophie, looking at her tea, replied quietly, "I don't know, I just don't know."

They both fell into silence again, until Anne said, "Well, what are we going to eat?" Anne got up from the comfy seat, proffered her hand for Sophie's empty cup and then walked back into the kitchen. Sophie was left in silence. The TV had been turned off when they had re-entered the room earlier. Why did her mother insist on making her feel uncomfortable? One moment she resented what she did and then complained when she didn't do anything. Sophie suspected that the reason was because her mother felt insecure. After all, she did ride around on a dangerous motorbike and was thirty-nine years old and without a proper job or solid relationship. Yes, she got disability benefit, but that was for subsistence, which wasn't exactly having a life. What was she going to do, watch Jeremy Kyle all day and keep half a dozen cats?

Feeling a little tired, she got up to help her mother in the kitchen. She walked in to see her being industrious, peeling the vegetables.

Anne said, "Set the table and fill the condiments."

Sophie bemoaned, "I was a volunteer, and now I'm a slave." Smiling to herself, she set about completing the tasks at hand. She rattled through the cutlery drawer and clanked the implements on the bare table. She set the places facing each other. She then went to the cupboard and got the salt and pepper cellars. She filled them, using the tubs from the next cupboard. "Well, watcha makin?" she enquired.

"Cod loin and veg," came the taut reply.

"Well, bless the lords of blandness and the mighty angels of boredom," said Sophie sarcastically.

"You don't have to eat it, you can always get a take-away; you could get a good return on your shares–" equally sarcastic.

They both smiled. The banter was good and showed that although they had wildly differing viewpoints, they still loved each other and were, despite everything, friends, as well as family.

When tea was over, Sophie went to her bedroom and her mother put the dishes away. Sophie showered and brushed her hair. She watched the TV that was sat in the corner of her room until she felt tired. She switched the TV off. The only sound was that of distant traffic. Easington was a quiet village, near a quiet town. The traffic that passed through the village generally went to Whitby in the east or towards Middlesbrough in the west, tourists, most often. The street lamp outside the house moved slightly, with the coastal wind, which moved the shadows in the room. The curtains fluttered slightly. Sophie stared into the middle distance, thinking about her situation. She didn't want to take advantage of the fact that she had a disability – many did; she wasn't going to be one of them. She reviewed her life, as the wind outside grew progressively stronger. She was intelligent, reasonably good looking, she had some money, but not enough to do anything substantial with. She was independently minded and strong willed. On the flip side, she dressed, tomboy fashion, she came across as arrogant and aloof, but most of all, she was overly defensive. She put it down to her disability and what she perceived that others made of it. She would put people down, before they would do it to her. This made her lonely. She had read many self-help books about positive thinking and happiness, but they all made little difference. The wind blew slightly harder outside and the curtains moved. So, she got up. Standing, she let her nighty fall back into place and then shuffled around to the window. As she went to close the opened window a thought occurred to her. What she really needed was a sense of purpose. Getting back into her bed, she soon fell asleep; as she nodded off she thought, what the hell was it going to be?

It was early morning. The clock said 6:32. She hadn't set the alarm. Work was to start at three in the afternoon. She sat on the side of the bed. Her hair, which hung down to the back of the shoulder, was like a rat's nest. Looking across the room she saw her image in the long mirror, on the cupboard door. She couldn't see the half leg. For a moment, she thought, 'normal'. Then, looking down, the half leg was visible, or not as the case may be. Mixed feelings rose within her. If she had had a full leg like everyone else, she would have been 'normal'. The question was, what exactly would she have gained if she was? Of course, there would be full mobility and with a smile she thought, a bigger motorbike. Or would there? She might have ended up as one of those girls who are always up their own arse, constantly taking selfies and asking to look at them on Facebook. She shuddered at the thought. But no, she was a half woman, who had led a full life instead of vice versa. Was that how she felt? To be honest, she didn't know. This was probably the reasoning that led her to realise that she needed something more. Leaning over to grab the prosthetic, with a little resentment, she strapped it on. The prosthetic, at this moment, represented the life that she had not had, but equally, it was part of the woman that she had become.

Standing, she made her way to the shower and undressed before stepping in and washing away the negative thoughts she had accumulated. Having finished, she stepped out and grabbed a towel from the radiator. Wrapping it around herself, she then decided that she really did feel refreshed. Going back into the bedroom, she got some clothes and went for her usual affair of jeans and T-Shirt. Trainers completed her attire and so, she was ready for the day. She clumped her way downstairs, then along the corridor and made for the kitchen. The clock on the wall showed 7:13. Her mother, unsurprisingly, was sat at the table, reading her paper. Sophie walked over to the kettle, which was still hot and poured. Minutes later she was sat with her mother at the table, eating toast.

"What time are you starting?" asked the older woman.

"Three-thirty."

"Good, you can come shopping with me."

Sophie sighed.

Sophie stomped around the supermarket, behind her mother. She wasn't exactly sulking, but she wasn't exactly cooperative either. Anne was in her flowery skirt, white blouse and high heels, looking like a typical middle-to-late aged woman. She turned and looked at Sophie in disdain. "Will you please stop acting yourself, you're thirty-nine for god's sake."

Sophie was pretending to look at items as she trailed behind, but it was obvious that she was being purposely awkward. Sophie looked up in an exasperated way, making out that everything was way too much trouble. She clonked faster and decided she was going to milk it. "Do you make a habit of picking on disabled people?"

Anne, wise to her daughter, replied, "Is that physically or mentally, because with you I'm not sure either way!"

Sophie smiled, so did Anne.

"I've got one leg, so that means I can only go half your speed," said Sophie.

Anne quickly retorted, "The same with the brain too!"

Both chortled to each other as they went down the aisle.

"Can I have a ride in the trolley?"

"I wouldn't get you through the metal detector at the door."

"Woah, Mam, that was bad."

"It's OK, dear, I didn't mean it, I was just pulling your leg." Then after a moment's pause, "In the singular."

Sophie, by this time, was creased.

Anne smiled and pushed the trolley. Looking back at her daughter she said loudly, "Come on, hop to it."

Sophie was soon behind her, with exaggerated hopping. Anne had to cover her mouth to stop herself from laughing out loud. Of course, by this time, other customers were looking their way. Both women were used to it and carried on as though no one else was there. They were a sight. A prim and proper housewife and a leather/denim clad one-legged woman following, ribbing each other. Sophie's mother knew things were getting out of hand when Sophie loudly announced that her mother beat her with her prosthetic, at those odd times when she wouldn't do as she was told. At this point, her mother literally grabbed her and frog stomped her to the till, where the groceries were half loaded.

"If you don't pack it in and start packing, it will happen for real."

The clerk behind the till smiled and shook his head, he had seen the performance many times. He liked these women.

"She's a bitch," he said to Sophie, nodding toward her mother.

Sophie winked at him. He felt his ear being grabbed.

Anne stage whispered into his ear. "That goes for you too. I'll use her leg to hit you!"

He bowed his head and dealt with the groceries.

As Sophie and Anne walked out of the supermarket, Sophie happened to glance at the customer noticeboard. It wasn't that she wanted anything, but more out of curiosity. The usual furniture was for sale and a lawnmower. She then noticed an A4 sheet with a picture of a motorcycle. As she looked closer, it came to her attention that the first recruitment drive was to be at the 'Angel' on Sunday at three PM. Frowning she thought, 'I know nothing about that, I'll have to have a word with Paul.' Catching up to her mother, who had by now opened the car boot, she helped her load the groceries. They got into the car and went home. Once home, it wasn't long before Sophie got herself fed, watered and ready for work.

She arrived at work. She parked in her usual spot at the back of the building and went in to face the daily grind. She put her gear away in the staff cloakroom and went to the bar to see how the land lay. The part-time barmaid saw Sophie and smiled. When she saw Sophie, she knew her shift was just about over. Sophie returned the smile and asked where Paul was. The barmaid pointed him out; he was across the lounge. He was stood talking to a customer. He seemed relaxed, so it can't have been a problem. She waited politely for him to finish and when he had, she called him over.

"Paul, when I was at the supermarket, I noticed a sign advertising a meet for a bike club in this place. Do you know anything about it?"

"Oh yeah, a black guy came in, seemed like a good bloke, didn't seem to be any bother, so I said they could come in at three on Sunday, when it was quiet. The place will be dead, so it'll be good for business."

Having her answer, she seemed almost deflated, a bit disappointed that she hadn't been kept in the loop. Seeing her concern, he said, "Look, it's not a surprise, the notice has been up for the last three days." He gestured toward the front door and the noticeboard behind it. She nodded, satisfied that the situation was in hand. But she had a funny feeling that something was going to come of it.

CHAPTER 7

23/07/17

The clock showed two-thirty on the wall in the 'Angel' pub. As expected, all was quiet and empty, except for John, in the corner of the lounge, in his usual spot. Since his wife had died, he had become a regular. When she was alive, she wouldn't let him drink. Now that he had the opportunity, he actually didn't bother that much. But, as an act of defiance, he had two half pints and a bag of cheese and onion crisps in the Angel every Sunday afternoon. He then went home to an empty house to sleep it off. He was doing what he always did, staring out of the window. Because it was Sunday, there wasn't exactly an awful lot to stare at! He looked down at his glass. As he went to pick it up, a loud roar of an engine shattered the silence. John looked up with a vague interest, identifying that it was a motorbike, then he carried on drinking. Approximately a minute later a large ginger-haired man walked through the door. His long hair was tied back, which exaggerated the receding hair at the front. He had already unzipped his jacket and a large aproned belly hung over his jeans waist. Stomping towards the bar in his large boots, he raised his hand to get the barmaid's attention. Sophie gave a muffled response – that she would be there in a minute.

A few seconds later, there was another rumbling sound, which coughed to a stop. Moments later, another biker, about five feet ten, let the front door close behind him. With his helmet still on, the biker walked forward and took off his gloves. Darren watched the figure approach and turned to face him.

As he did so, Sophie gave a fake cough and asked, "Can I help you?"

Darren turned to her voice and clamped eyes on her. Momentarily, both of their eyes locked and they both purposely averted their gaze. Darren blushed and mumbled that he wanted a lemonade; as an afterthought he explained it was because he was riding. He turned back to the biker who had just walked in. As he did, he saw a black man before him.

A little taken aback, Darren held his hand out and simply stated "Darren". The man understood the gesture, took his hand and replied "Brendan".

Darren, with a questioning tone asked, "Drink?"

"Orange juice please, riding and all that."

Darren smiled and repeated the order to Sophie. Darren noticed that she walked with a limp. He had a funny feeling that he was going to be noticing her a lot more in the future. Turning back to Brendan, Darren said, "Sorry if I'm rude, mate, but you don't seem to be from around here?"

Brendan looked at him for a second or two, deciding if he was the aggressive type, then said, "Originally no, I'm from London. I work at the accountants across the road." He nodded in the direction of the offices above the supermarket.

Darren said, "I've never seen you before; then again, if you're working nine to five, I wouldn't. I work for my mother at the baker's factory."

Nodding his acknowledgement, Brendan asked, "Are you here for the bike club?"

"Yeah, seems like a good idea, nowt better to do. Do you know who's organizing it?"

"Yeah, me!" As he finished his reply, Sophie shouted for their attention. Darren paid and then passed Brendan his drink. They both said cheers in unison and clinked glasses.

As they sipped from their glasses, two more motorcycles arrived. One immediately after the other, the engines switched off. Darren and Brendan looked at each other.

"This could be promising," said Brendan.

Two people walked in, one in open-faced helmet, the other in a turban. They shook the hands of the newly arrived and introduced themselves to each other.

Darren asked, "Gentlemen, can I get you a drink? We're having soft because we're riding – do you want one?"

They both said yes and made their orders. The conversation went on about how they had found out about the meeting. After a while, they noticed that it had got to quarter past three and so it was about time they started to organize things.

Brendan asked Sophie where the best place for them to talk would be and she led them to a little used back room. Thanking her they filed past and went into a slightly dank room.

Sarcastically, Malika said, "We really are starting at the bottom."

Each got a chair from the stacks around the room and they found a place around the table, looking at each other a little apprehensively.

Brendan finally spoke. "Well, gents, we've all done the intros so there's no need to go into all that. My reasoning for this club, is more of a social thing. Make friends, have a few drinks, go on rides and maybe get a bit of fresh air."

Each of the others gave a small nod of ascent. Brendan was about to speak again, when there was a knock on the door. Brendan got up, being the nearest and answered it. Opening the door, Brendan was greeted by an Asian man in his twenties, probably Pakistani.

Speaking in a mixed accent of Pakistani/Yorkshire, the man asked, "Is this the bikers' meet, mate?"

"Yes, I suppose it is," replied Brendan.

"I wanna join, if that's OK, sorry I'm late."

Stepping back to let the man in, Brendan said, "Come in, grab a chair and find a space at the table. Lucky for you, we've just started."

Looking relieved, the new guy squeezed past and looked sideways at the others as he grabbed a chair. He then pulled up between Darren and Mike, who both shuffled apart to let him in.

"OK, we'll have to do the introductions after all," sighed Brendan, as he sat down again.

Just as he did so, the door was knocked again. Only this time, the door opened and Sophie, who pointedly did not look at Darren asked, "Does anyone want another drink, before you start?"

"I do," said the new guy. "Lemonade please."

Nodding, Sophie left.

"OK, right, where were we?" said Brendan, hoping to reset the meeting.

Again, another knock at the door. "For god's sake," muttered Brendan.

Sophie appeared again. She walked around the table and gave the new guy his drink. As she walked out, she suddenly stopped and said, "Can I join?"

Everyone looked at each other. Darren blushed, and without making eye contact he said, "Can for me."

Sophie smiled at that and blushed herself. Each of the others nodded. Smiling broadly, she got a chair and sat opposite Darren.

"Aren't you working?" asked the new guy.

"It's not busy," came the curt reply. "Sophie, by the way." All smiles.

"Muhammad," said the new guy.

"Are we done?" asked Brendan. "Maybe we can get started now. I hereby call the first bikers' club meeting of Loftus to order.

"The first point of order, should be the simplest, what do we call the club?"

Each of the new members looked at each other. They were under the impression that the club was already formed and named.

Muhammad spoke up. "You mean to tell me, that we're just making a club up?"

"Yep," Brendan responded.

Speaking next, with a little concern in his voice, Darren said, "I thought we were going to be a new chapter of a club, like the Hell's Angels or something."

Brendan put his hand up in a placating gesture. "No, like Muhammad said, this is from scratch. I can't see a problem, a few friends get together for socialising and a few bike rides, what's the problem?"

"I think what they're trying to say, is that they thought things might be a bit more, well, organised," answered Sophie. "The impression I get, is that you all feel the same way as me and want to be involved in something special and different from your usual humdrum lives, am I right?" The little speech came across as maybe a bit too impassioned, but the point was made. There was silence for a moment or two, but eventually, Sophie added, "I'm in."

This was followed by each of the others with a nod of ascent.

Brendan looked pleased and smiled. "Thanks, I almost thought we were dead in the water before we'd even started." Pausing, perhaps for effect, he then continued, "Loftus and this area in general is a dead-end backwater; we all know it. We can change it, even if it's just for us; we are effectively creating an escape route from our lives. We have to build a level of trust between ourselves and to work for something that's bigger than each of us individually." He stopped for a moment to gauge each one of their reactions. It seemed that he was hitting the right spots. "I suppose we have to be like a secret organisation. No one will be allowed to join without a nomination and a second. I suppose it will be like the freemasons." There were some smiles and someone snorted. He wasn't sure who it was, but at this point, it didn't matter. "Shall I continue?" Again, he received nods and he thought he saw some understanding of how serious the situation should be taken.

"OK, we're back where we started. The first thing we should think about, is the club name – what should we call ourselves?"

Muhammad, who already was seen to be cynical, piped up, "How about, the Loftus Losers?"

A ripple of dissent came from the rest of the group almost immediately.

Muhammad explained himself: "Well we're supposed to be anti-establishment and it would show that we're past caring anymore."

Darren said sarcastically, "Yeah right, you can imagine it, can't yer: who are you with, one biker to another, some would say, I'm an Angel or a Slave, whereas you would say, I'm a loser! Sounds about right."

Muhammad looked embarrassed and went quiet.

Malika spoke next and suggested, "How about the Back-wood Bikers?"

Brendan said, "Better, but boring, we need a name with a little spice, even snappy."

Sophie looked deep in thought. Mike hadn't said a word at all and Darren was drumming his fingers on the table, which was annoying the rest of them. The fingers stopped and Darren suggested, "The Back-wood Barbarians." In saying this, he was acknowledging Malika, whilst putting an edgier feel to the name. Malika agreed. Muhammad was still sulking from the earlier rebuke and didn't say anything.

Sophie blurted out, "The North-East Barbarians." By stating a general area, it indicated where they were from, whilst retaining the edginess of Darren's name.

Brendan raised his voice a touch higher. "We're trying to be a little more specific; the North-East is too generalised."

Malika gave a 'Hmmm' sound and Darren resumed drumming his fingers, Muhammad continued sulking and Sophie concentrated some more. After five minutes of silence and no suggestions, Brendan prompted, "Well, anything more?"

Mike raised his hand. Because of his previous silence, everyone looked in his direction with interest. "What about…" He looked around at the group, feeling anxious, now that he was suddenly the centre of attention.

"Well?" asked Sophie expectantly.

"What about, The Guardian Angels?" finished Mike.

They all looked at each other. It was immediately apparent that they were impressed with the new suggestion. Mike, however, was simply relieved to have said something and not to have had any negative feedback.

Brendan looked around. "Well, do we have an agreement – is it going to be the Guardian Angels?" Brendan had noticed that everyone had stopped concentrating and had a look of relief on their faces. The name was to be the intention of their new personas and the question of locality, well, they can't get more specific than the pub that they were sat in! "OK, it seems to be unanimous, Guardian Angels it is, do we have any objections before it's carried?"

There were smiles all round. Good, thought Brendan, the first step has been taken. Already, the group seemed to be gelling; this might work.

Sophie stood and said that she had to go and see if the bar had any customers. She squeezed past a couple of the guys and made her way to the door. As she was about to walk out, she stopped. The guys wanted more drinks and so she took their orders. She didn't moan about it. It could justify her being away from the bar, if she was still getting business. The meeting had only taken ten minutes so far, so no real loss. She made her way to the bar. John was still sat in the corner, next to the window, eyes still looking out. She walked over to him and picked up his empty glass and crisp packet. She looked outside and saw the five bikes belonging to the guys in the back room. She guessed Darren's was the biggest.

"Nice fella, that Darren," said John.

"Mmm yeah," she replied almost subconsciously. She glanced in his direction, blushing slightly.

"Half pint please?" he said.

"OK," she replied as she walked back behind the bar. She drew the drink and went back to where he was sat and handed it to him. With the other hand, she took his money. Looking up at her, he met her gaze. "You could do a damned sight worse." He took a sip and put it on the table. "Joining the club will be good for you."

"How do you know?" she asked curiously.

"I can read–" nodding towards the noticeboard. "Don't worry, I'll be here for half an hour, I'll keep an eye on the bar."

She looked at him thankfully and went to the backroom with the lads' drinks, to finish the meeting. As she entered, she heard Brendan talking. "OK, I suppose that was the hardest part of the whole meeting and I'm glad it's over with." Feeling as though they were making some sort of headway, the group steeled themselves, ready for the in-depth part.

"The first rules being the where and when of meetings. I propose that we have our meetings here, at the Angel, until we get our own place. I would also propose, bearing in mind that we all made it, that meetings be held at three PM each Sunday. The only exception being a religious holiday." There were nods around the table, so the first rules were passed. "Secondly, we rotate the positions of responsibility on an annual basis, starting with Chairman, Deputy and Treasurer, so that no person has more power than any other. Thirdly, I propose the rules can only be proposed if they are seconded and both persons, the proposer and second must be present at the vote and of course a majority is given." Once again, this was passed without dissent.

The meeting went on like this for about an hour longer, without much controversy. The first sticking point came, when finance arose. Brendan broached the subject. "Of course, there will be things to pay for, such as rent. This will happen, no matter where we reside, unless we buy a place. This can only be done through recruitment and club activities."

It was then, the rest of the members understood the extent of commitment that would be required. There was a moment of silence; they all looked at each other.

Brendan seized the initiative. "Look, this is the reason we've had this meeting. No matter what club you join, whether it's a swimming club, the scouts or the freemasons, it will cost money. If you want it so that we just have regular bike rides, that's great, but it won't have any sort of permanence or security. Personally, I wanted a club that was bigger than me, if you see what I mean."

His openness seemed to strike a chord with them all.

Muhammad then said, "We're obviously going to have to talk figures. Some of us, with a genuine respect, might not be able to afford it."

Again, a momentary silence. Slowly each person agreed to continue in principle, with the proviso of a disclosure of the costs.

"So, now we have a general idea of the principles of what we're supposed to be doing, the question is, how are we going to do it? We're now going to have to decide as to how to get things going. I'm an accountant, so in the first set up phase I can get a bank account and set up the financial methods that we will use. Who is going to set up the catering?"

Darren raised his hand and said, "I reckon I could get discounts at various places, especially at the baking end of things."

Brendan wrote this down and then said, "Alcohol and drinks next?"

Muhammad put his hand up. "I have access to alcohol, but that might be a problem, bearing in mind where we are at the minute."

"I can help Darren with the catering," offered Malika.

Darren nodded at Malika in acknowledgement. Sophie volunteered her services with the alcohol and drinks. That left Mike. Quietly, Mike said, "I can offer discounts to club members on bike maintenance. It would make a good selling point when recruiting and good for business."

Smiling at everyone around the table, Brendan said, "You know what, this might just work."

Everyone looked at each other and nodded their agreement. By having set tasks, each member began to feel a sense of belonging and joint purpose. Each of them, at this point, felt as though they had made the right decision.

Suddenly standing, Sophie exclaimed, "Oh my god, I've left John out the front." She hurriedly left the room and went to the front bar. John was still sat where she had left him. He faced her as she approached. "Sorry, John, I didn't realise the time," she explained apologetically.

"It's OK, I wasn't going anywhere; besides, no-one's been in."

A little relieved, she said, "Would you like another half on me?"

He considered it for a moment and said with a smile, "OK, since you're paying."

She smiled and went to the bar. She rustled about in her pocket and found some change and then poured John his drink. As she did so, the newly formed biker club filed out of the room. Malika and Muhammad were in conversation and so were Brendan and Mike, who followed the first two. Darren came out last, quietly shutting the door behind him. The first four waved to Sophie as they left. Darren hung around at the back, silently. Sophie knew he wanted to talk to her.

She felt apprehensive, frightened and excited all at the same time. She knew he was going to ask her out. But, she felt she would miss the solitude she had. It was strange that she had a need to belong and yet also the need to be alone. She began to blush – and he hadn't said anything yet. Darren was quiet. He looked in her direction, but couldn't find the courage to say anything. For someone as obviously strong and as large as he was, he felt remarkably small and vulnerable. He sensed that she knew why he was there. He tried to ask her out, but instead came out with, "Can I have a lime and lemonade please?"

He sat at the bar, considering his options – what was he going to do to get around this problem? Glad for the diversion and not having to look at him directly, Sophie went to the back of the bar for some lime cordial and then to the pumps for lemonade. She looked up and asked, "Ice?" He shook his head. Once the drink had settled, she walked over and placed the drink in front of him. Without looking up, he handed her the change. She rang the till and put in the money. Then silence fell over the bar again. The silence was awkward. Sophie walked up and down, suddenly aware of the stomp of the prosthetic. To stop herself moving around, she pretended to occupy herself with the tidying of the shelves.

Darren broke the silence. "A good meeting, wasn't it? Went better than I thought it would." Sophie nodded, trying not to respond. Suddenly, Darren felt a hand on his shoulder. Looking behind, John was smiling at him.

"You're a big lad."

More curious than anything else, Darren slowly nodded.

John said, "I'll bet you're not frightened of very much and no-one bothers you?"

Darren replied, "No, they don't, but I keep myself to myself and don't bother people either."

"If you're so big and not intimidated by anyone, how come you haven't got the balls to ask her out?"

Darren was taken aback, not knowing what to say. He turned and looked at Sophie, who was, by this time, bright red. Darren turned back to where the old man was, who was now walking out of the door, chuckling to himself.

Brendan, Malika, Muhammad and Mike all walked into the bright, cool afternoon. It was now just after four-thirty. Each of them held their helmets. Muhammad said to the others in general, "I think they have something going on." He nodded back to the pub, referring to Darren and Sophie. As he said it, the old man who had been sat in the lounge came out of the Angel. He looked at them, smiled and doffed his flat cap. "Afternoon, gentlemen." They all nodded in return.

They all got onto their motorcycles and as they did, Brendan said, "Well guys, that went well, are you all up for next week?"

One at a time, they each agreed that they would return.

"I think the other two will be, somehow," said Muhammad, smiling.

Malika held his hand up in farewell and said, "Until next week then." He started his engine up, which was then copied by each of the others. Two then paddled backward with their feet, to get onto the road, while the other two rode straight off. Just one bike remained at the front of the pub – Darren's.

Brendan went down the back alley to his house and dismounted. With a bit of a struggle up the small step, he managed to get his bike into the back yard and then into its shed. He locked the shed and then entered the house by the back door. He took his helmet and gloves off and flicked on the kettle. As it came to the boil, he removed the rest of his bike gear. Before long, he was sat with a mug of tea and a copy of MCN at the kitchen table. He paused and thought that today had been a good day. There weren't that many people, but they all seemed like a friendly bunch. OK, so there was going to be a few things to iron out and a few teething problems, but that always happened when you did something new.

Mike chugged down the high street toward his garage. He didn't have far to go. Muhammad had passed him a big hurry, almost as soon as he had gotten on to the road. Mike thought, he was a young one, maybe a little spoilt. How else would someone who lives with their mam and dad be able to afford such an expensive bike? After five minutes, he arrived at the garage. Stopping in front of the main doors he turned his engine off. He then unlocked the doors and pulled the right-side open, with enough space to get the bike in. Turning back, he then pushed the bike through the gap and into the corner of the garage. Once satisfied that he had it in the right place, he went back out and locked up. As he took his helmet and gloves off, he walked around to the back of the building, to his flat entrance. Opening the door, he was met with a smell of muskiness, suggesting the corridor didn't get much fresh air. Why did he smell it this time? He didn't normally. Stomping up the stairs, he went into the spare room and dressed into shorts and T-shirt. As he did so, he smiled to himself; he was looking forward to next week.

Muhammad streaked past Mike's BMW. The Hayabusa was a fast machine. Muhammad was a fast guy. He had gone to the meeting expecting to be rejected, because he was a 'Paki'. Surprisingly, he found an old Indian guy, a stuffy black guy and a disabled white woman. It felt like a multi-cultural cliché in action, but somehow, even though it had only been one meeting, he felt a certain affinity and belonging. He smiled as the bike's engine tone lowered aggressively. The Subaru had been good, but the 'Busa' was exhilarating. The exhaust popped with a little backfire and then purred as Muhammad came to a gentle stop. He dismounted the burbling machine and opened the gate to the back yard. Unlike Brendan, he got back on the bike and slowly rode it over the low step. The sound of the engine echoed around the street, because of the enclosing walls of the yard. He killed the engine and removed the keys. His father came out to greet him.

"How did it go?"

"Great!" came the enthusiastic response.

"Will you be going again?"

"Yep," he said. He tossed the keys into the air and caught them as he walked past his dad and into the back of the shop. His dad followed him in, smiling and shaking his head.

Malika rode home to Saltburn, the long way around. Instead of going through Brotton and down the bank, he decided to go via Liverton Mines and along the moor road. As he did so, he made a point of sticking to the speed limits and being as defensive as possible. It had been a long time since he had ridden his motorcycle. The Honda purred along; the lack of any traffic was making the ride a pleasant experience. As he rode, he thought of the group he had just left. None of them seemed in any way aggressive, not even the big ginger man, Darren. That might have been because he was distracted by the girl, Sophie. At no time did he feel intimidated or belittled. That was a good start to this club. After giving the matter a little more thought, he decided that he was going to go back again. The money side may become an issue, but somehow, he didn't think so.

Darren and Sophie were now the only people left in the Angel. Both felt a little uncomfortable and awkward, especially after John's comment. It wasn't particularly warm, but Darren was sweating.

"Well?" asked Sophie.

"Well what?" replied Darren, knowing what she meant, but trying not to answer.

"Are you asking me or not?"

Darren looked at her.

Sophie continued, "I am a peg leg you know."

She tapped her prosthetic leg with her knuckles.

Darren, unfazed, said, "Yeah, and I'm a fat git." He grabbed a handful of stomach that hung over his belt.

"Does that mean you're asking me out, or are we trying to see who's the most disabled?"

He looked a little embarrassed. "Yeah, OK, where would you like to go?"

Rolling her eyes, she said, "That's romantic!"

"Well I haven't done this too often you know." Accompanying the limp smile, his facial expression showed an apology. After a moment's thought, he said, "When do you finish?"

Answering, she said, "About seven tonight."

"Fine we'll go for a ride out," he suggested.

"A ride out?" Bemused, she nodded and said, "About eight OK?"

"Eight it is then," he replied, smiling. He got up to leave, turned back, smiled, grabbed his helmet and walked to the front door. When he opened the door, he thought, it's been a good day today. Glancing back one more time, to see Sophie watching him go, he flashed a smile and stepped out.

CHAPTER 8

23/07/17

It was 6:45 and Sophie was nowhere near finished at the Angel. She still had all the glasses to pick up in the lounge and Natalie was out the back having yet another tab. Sophie had told Paul not to employ anyone under the age of thirty-five because of mobile phones and especially not a smoker. They always take twice as many breaks as anyone else. She was getting tense, she wanted to be home to be getting ready for her first date in over five years. Darren was obviously spoilt and maybe a little too laid back, but he was a nice guy and yeah, smirking to herself, she thought, she fancied the pants off him. Where was that damned girl? Just as she thought it, in walked Natalie, mobile phone in hand. She was frowning at the device. It was obvious that she was more concerned about what was going on with Facebook, rather than what she was doing in her job. Giving her an acidic glare, Sophie waved a glass in front of the girl's face and pointed to the lounge. Looking up, Natalie returned the glare and put the mobile into her pocket. She then stalked round the bar and began clearing up. Sophie served a couple of people and began to put the collected glasses in a crate behind the counter then racked them for cleaning. Paul appeared behind her, making her jump.

"Listen, get yourself away."

Sophie turned his way and said, "Thanks." He knew she was on a hot date and sympathised with her position. He didn't want her to feel the way he did at the minute, with his recent divorce. She stopped what she was doing and said with a hint of contempt, "You know, you could make the place a damned sight more efficient if you didn't employ half-wit bimbos."

As she said it, it was obvious that Natalie had heard her and gave Sophie a dirty look. Paul noticed and told Sophie to make a quick exit to prevent an escalation. Thanking him, Sophie stomped out of the bar and went to the cloakroom, grabbed her gear, got ready and got on her scooter. Her sense of anticipation was building. She hoped it was going to be worth the hassle.

It was 7:15, Darren was sweating. It wasn't the heat or the effort of getting ready, it was his mother. She was more wound up than he was. She was running around like a mother hen. She hadn't got changed from her work clothes when she found out that her son had a date. She was more excited than he was.

"So, how are you going, do you need the car?"

"No, Mam, I'm going on the bike," Darren said quietly. His frustration was beginning to show, despite his best efforts.

Pausing, she looked at him with dismay. What sort of girl was she going to be? "You mean to tell me that you're taking a girl out on the back of that bloody thing?" Maureen was desperately hoping he wasn't.

"I'll ask her, but I doubt she'll get on." Maureen looked a little relieved at that. "She'll probably be going on her own bike. She's very independent, a bit like you. Maybe Freud was right in people being attracted to their opposite sexed parent!" Maureen looked horrified. "Just winding you up; besides, I could do a lot worse than have a woman like the number one lady in my life."

His mam blushed and gave him a hug. She said, "You're my treasure and I worry about you."

"I know, that's why I haven't moved out at forty-four years old."

"Go on, get out." His mother was getting a little choked and knowing this, her rather large offspring, bent down and kissed her on the forehead. He walked out of the front door and went to the garage. He clicked the fob and the automatic door opened, revealing the Volvo and Darren's pride and joy. He sat astride the Rocket. He always felt better in the saddle, it gave him a sense of freedom in a way that nothing else did. Turning the key, the engine came to life. He moved forward approximately six feet and then stopped. He pressed the fob and the garage door closed. He noticed his mother stood at the front door. She looked distraught, but then again, she always did. He waved, more for encouragement than as a goodbye and then he pulled away to see the new woman in his life.

Darren pulled up outside of the semi-detached house. He didn't go onto the drive; he regarded it as bad manners. He dismounted and removed his helmet, then walked up the steep walkway. He lightly knocked on the door and waited. It wasn't long before the door opened and there stood a rather strait-laced looking woman, probably in her mid-sixties. Tilting her head back slightly, despite Darren standing two steps below her, she said, "Can I help you?" in a clipped business-like tone.

"I've come to pick up Sophie," he replied, feeling a bit intimidated.

"You're Darren I suppose."

In the background a voice shouted, "Mother, pack it in, let him in."

Looking him over with faux critical eyes, she smirked and took a step back. "Come in," she said, trying to sound reluctant.

The height difference became more apparent when they stood next to each other in the hallway. In a more relaxed tone Sophie's mother said, "I'm Anne, Sophie's mother."

Proffering his hand, he said, "Hi Anne, I'm Darren."

Smiling, she shook it. Unexpectedly, Anne shouted up the stairs, "Sophie, hurry up, he's here, hop to it."

Darren cringed. He then heard Sophie's voice: "Mother, I swear to god."

Anne nudged Darren and pointed down the corridor and said "Kitchen" in the previously used clipped tone. Darren complied and walked in the direction that she had pointed. Once in the kitchen, he sat at the table. As he did, he heard stomping coming from upstairs.

Anne walked in and asked, "Tea, Coffee?"

Darren politely declined. Shrugging, Anne put the kettle on anyway and made one for herself. A few moments later, he heard someone coming down the stairs. Clump, tap, clump, tap, the noises made it obvious that it was Sophie. She entered the kitchen. She was in her leathers. Darren couldn't help but look appreciatively at what he saw. Reminding himself of his manners, he stood up.

He said, "Your sister's been looking after me." He nodded in Anne's direction. Sophie smiled and Anne blushed.

Anne said, "He looks rough, but talks smooth, doesn't he!"

"Mother!" Sophie chastised.

Anne then said, "You'd better get going or I'll borrow the bike instead."

Sophie retorted, "You don't like bikes."

Anne, looking at Darren, said, "I can see the appeal."

Feigning disgust, Sophie, sounding exasperated, replied, "For god's sake, Mother."

The two of them went to the front door. Sophie walked slightly ahead trying to fasten her jacket. After a minute of cursing, she finally managed to zip up and took her helmet off Darren, who had patiently waited for her.

"Thanks," she said. "That was a bugger to do for some reason."

Her mother stood at the end of the corridor, in the kitchen doorway, her arms folded. "She not normally all fingers and thumbs you know, you must be better than the other boyfriends that keep coming and going around here, you're making her nervous."

Darren couldn't help but smile and Sophie barked at her mam, "Will you stop it!", trying to chastise her, but she knew from experience that if she said anything, she would be worse. Sophie looked at Darren, trying to get him on side, but he only shrugged.

"He's a smart one, knows when to keep his mouth shut – perhaps you could have a few lessons."

Without answering back, Sophie turned and opened the front door. She was, by now, in a state of high anxiety and she could do without her mother trying her best to show her up. As he closed the door, Darren waved to Anne and said, "Was nice to see yer, see yer later."

"You better go," replied Anne, trying to sound ominous. The door shut to and he pushed the handle upward to make sure it was shut properly and then followed Sophie up the drive. As he reached her, she was lifting the garage door. In the middle of the garage, stood Sophie's scooter. It was bigger than he imagined it would be.

"I like your mam, seems very friendly, likes to wind you, up doesn't she?"

Sighing, Sophie explained, "It's a front really, she does care, it's really banter, to keep me on my toes."

"Not like my mam, she's always serious. She's been like that since my dad left us. She runs the bakery and has a lot of responsibility, so I suppose it's pretty much expected."

Looking at Darren, she explained, "My dad died when I was six, I think that's why we go on like we do, better laughing than crying."

Changing the subject and not wanting to get too deep on the first date, he returned his focus onto the machine that stood in front of them. "Nice scooter, quite big, isn't it?"

She walked around it. "It's an Asprilla SRV850, fastest scooter in the world and has a max speed of one-hundred and twenty-four miles per hour, automatic gear box and a V-ninety-degree twin four stroke, with an eight-hundred and thirty-nine CC displacement." Glancing his way, she looked a little embarrassed. "Sorry, sad I know."

"Hell no, I think it's great to meet a woman who hasn't got her face constantly in Facebook or her head up her arse!" replied Darren, full of admiration.

Sophie looked visibly relieved.

"So, how often do you get out on it?" he enquired.

"Roughly once a fortnight, for a good run, but I do use it for work too. To be honest, that's the main reason I wanted to join the club, a good excuse to get out more!"

He really did admire this woman. He was beginning to like her, as well as fancy her. To his eyes, she was gorgeous, particularly as she was now. All leather, long auburn hair. She wasn't the skinniest of girls, that's because she was obviously a real woman, who lived a real life and did real things. Not an internet fantasist, constantly demanding attention, with the impression that the world owed them a favour. She did, however, look after herself enough to keep trim and acted in a feminine way without being flouncy or giddy. It suddenly occurred to him that he was full of admiration for her, but what would she be thinking of him? He became self-conscious about his weight and appearance, so decided to change his train of thought.

Looking at his watch, he said, "Listen, do you think we'd better make a move, it's getting on a bit."

"Yeah, you're right."

She grabbed her helmet and put it on. He followed suit as he walked down the drive toward his bike. She pushed the scooter out of the garage and closed the door. As she did this, Darren turned around and asked, "I thought you might want to come on mine, with me?"

"I can't." She bent over and tapped her prosthetic through the trousers. "The straps and what have you get uncomfortable astride a bike seat, that's why I got this."

Darren blushed. "Sorry, I just thought..." He trailed off.

"I know what you thought. Don't worry, I'm not one of these feminazis, I simply can't sit on a bike seat for more than a couple of minutes." After a moment's pause she said, "Besides," lightening the conversation, "I think deep down you know you can't keep up with me, so having me on the back of your piece of junk eliminates the competition."

Darren smiled broadly. "Is that so?" He then added, "Mein Fuhrer!"

He walked off before she could respond. She grabbed the handlebars and pushed the scooter off its stand. By the time she had sorted herself out with the helmet and gloves, Darren was astride his bike and was adjusting his own helmet and gloves. Once sorted, she started up the engine. A second later, she heard Darren do the same. As Sophie was about to set off, she noticed something out of the corner of her eye. Pausing, she looked left and saw her mother waving. She wasn't waving at her. When she looked down the drive she saw Darren waving back. After a moment or two, her mam smiled in her direction. Sophie pointed at her in a warning gesture, pretending to be annoyed. Her mother's smile broadened. Shaking her head, Sophie went down the drive and clicked on her indicator. As she approached, Darren turned and gave her a questioning thumbs up. She nodded in response and then waited as his thunderous machine began to move off. He looked over his shoulder and moved into the road. With a glance, to check for traffic, Sophie quickly followed. Sophie watched Darren's back as he moved down the road. He filled the bike, but because of the size of the bike, he didn't look out of proportion. She did fancy him, she thought. He was a big cuddly lump and she could see in his face that he genuinely fancied her. Too many times, she had been on sympathy dates or she was the last to be asked out, when she was with her friends. This was her time. For once everything felt right and she intended to make the best of it. The weather was good, although perhaps a little on the fresh side, but you know, it was already a good night regardless.

Sophie watched Darren ride down Loftus High Street. They had just gone through the marketplace and passed the Angel, where it had been decided that the club would hold its meetings. They made the descent down the bank, past the dying shops. They arrived at the main crossroads, where the only traffic lights in Loftus were situated. Darren was indicating left, so she did likewise. She thought to herself, why is it that the lights take forever, when you have somewhere to go? After what seemed like an interminably long time, the lights finally turned green; ironically for Sophie, Darren, being in no hurry, slowly set off.

They both turned the corner and quite unexpectedly, Darren indicated left again and went down another small bank, which led to Rosecroft Lane. The road curved up onto a steep bank and at the top, there was a small hump, which indicated the presence of a railway bridge. On the left, they passed a new housing estate, where Rosecroft School used to stand. On the right was a wood. As they continued, the road became more undulating and they left the town of Loftus behind them. The road narrowed and began to twist, until it came to a junction. The road they were about to leave met the road that Sophie thought they would have been on in the first place. Bemused as to why they had taken the detour, she mentally shrugged and followed Darren onto the main road. There were a few farm buildings either side of the road, which soon disappeared behind them. Although the road straightened, it was still very undulating, which made it more fun to ride on. Darren sped up to about fifty, when they left the thirty zone, and Sophie easily kept up. After two minutes of comparatively fast riding, they got to the junction, which was an entry to the moor road that led to Whitby in the east and Guisborough in the west. Darren was indicating right and then rode uphill again. Within a quarter of a mile he was indicating left. The road he was going onto, led to small village, known as Danby. Danby, from this perspective, was the gateway to the North Yorkshire Moors. As would be expected, the road to Danby became twisted and even more undulating and as they approached Danby itself, it became very steep. At the bottom of the twisty road, they turned right onto the road to Hutton-le-Hole. As the junction was at the bottom of the valley, the only way was up. With a twist of the throttle, Darren climbed the hill easily. With the smaller engine on the scooter, although it kept up, the power difference was significant, and the sounds of the motors gave away the effort that each was making. After climbing the hill, the two of them settled back down to a steady pace. Darkness was beginning to descend and so their main beams came on. They continued down the road. What they could see of the countryside was dotted with the odd tree and outcrops of rock, but mainly, it was a place of brown hills and valleys, which was occupied by the occasional sheep.

In the distance, a black dot would move, probably a car or truck. The last of the sun sat low and made everything orange and somehow more open. The feeling of freedom made the ride even more enjoyable and so Sophie smiled to herself in contentment. It was worth coming out. If it had been any later in the year, the experience wouldn't have been the same. This continued for about another ten minutes, until Darren indicated left and exited the road. They entered an empty picnic area. All that was there were four bench tables and a couple of bins, which seemed a waste of time, given the amount of rubbish on the floor. Slowing to a rumble, Darren brought his machine to a halt, near to one of the tables and put his feet down. He then stopped the engine and put his kick stand down. Pulling up next to him, Sophie did the same. They both took off their helmets and smiled at each other. The wind was quite gentle and surprisingly warm on their faces, which was a relief from the sweaty interior of their helmets. Sophie rubbed her hair to try and dry it out and then went and sat on a table, resting her feet on the seat. She opened her jacket to let the air in and to cool down and then looked around to take in the scenery. It was breathtaking. The orange of the sun was beginning to fade into blackness; she thought that it was like a painting.

Darren walked behind her and sat on the seat, next to her feet. The whole bench rocked unsteadily as his weight was placed on the furniture. Sophie steadied herself.

"Sorry," apologised Darren.

"It's OK, just unexpected–" dismissing the apology. "You picked a nice place, good weather too," Sophie said appreciatively.

Darren said, "I come to places like this, because I find it hard to socialise. My size means that there is invariably some toe-rag with a little man syndrome, who spoils it for me – you know the type, trying to impress their friends."

At that moment, Sophie realised that the very thing that she felt would give her a sense of security, was also the very thing that gave him his greatest vulnerability. They were at the opposite ends of the spectrum, but both had the same problem. His size made him a target, which in turn made him lonely, whereas her disability made people ignore her or at best patronize her, which made her lonely. It is said that Birds of a feather flock together. Giving it a passing thought, maybe that's the real reason why each of the club members ended up where they had this afternoon. They both sat in silence for a while and watched the last glimmer of sunlight fade away. As the light ebbed, so did the heat of the day. In the distance, on the other side of the valley, a car came toward them and then suddenly the headlights turned away. It wasn't completely dark; a poacher's moon lit up the sky. It was only a sliver of light, but enough that the couple could see each other's face. Feeling the chill, Sophie zipped up her jacket and shuffled off the table. Her bum was getting numb on the hard wood anyway. Not standing on ceremony, she gave her backside a good rub to get the blood pumping round. Darren smiled at her with a wide grin. She looked back at him and grinned.

"It is getting a bit chilly, isn't it?"

He replied, "Yeah, it is."

Having got the blood back into her posterior, she sat next to him, a little wary about bench movement. Darren didn't know quite what to do. The talk these days was all about women's independence and liberation, so he didn't want to be too forward. Sophie looked up at his face. The moonlight made her appear vulnerable somehow and he wanted to protect her. He wanted to put his arms around her, but dared not in case of insinuations and giving the wrong impression.

"You're not too bright, are you?"

Taken aback he looked at her quizzically.

"I said it was cold and I've sat next to you, so what's next?" she asked.

"Err," he responded meekly.

She then prompted him, "If I'm cold and I want to get warm, do you have any suggestions?"

He silently put his arm around her. His smile was warmer than his body. She snuggled in, smiling too. Darren thought to himself, this is a romantic moment; I like romance. He squeezed her a little, enjoying the contact. She snuggled in more, enjoying the warmth and the closeness she hadn't felt for such a long time.

Without looking up, Sophie asked, "So, what exactly do you do with yourself?"

He considered his response. "Well, I'm officially a logistics manager at my mother's baking factory. Most of the time I do deliveries myself, but now and again, I do some paperwork and help her run the business."

Probing further: "So if that's officially what you do, what do you do unofficially?"

This time he paused even longer before giving his answer. When he spoke, it was almost like a cathartic admission, something he didn't want to admit to himself, but knew if this new relationship was to work, he had to be honest with her as well as himself.

"I'm a mammy's boy with no ambition and whose mother gave him a job to keep him out of trouble and to have some pocket money at the age of forty-four." He felt dirty and ashamed, but conversely, relieved. Feeling the need to redirect the conversation he asked, "So what about you?"

"Oh me, I'm a Crip without a future. Don't get me wrong, I've been given opportunities, but I'm sick of being patronized and being overlooked, so I've got to the point where I just don't care anymore."

Darren felt even more uncomfortable. He started to move, but she stopped him. "I'm getting warm, stay still." She knew he felt awkward and so tried to consider her words a little more carefully.

"I was born with a missing leg. Mother had chicken pox when she was pregnant. Zolam Globular, the antidote for unborn foetuses wasn't that well known about, back then. There's people a damned sight worse off than me." Taking a breath, she ploughed on. "I've had loads of jobs, most of which I packed in, but I have been sacked a couple of times because of my attitude. You know how my mam and I go on, most people don't understand that's all really defensive banter." Her voice became monotone. She had thought these things so many times but had had no one to talk to. It was a relief. Even if the relationship didn't work, at least she would have got it off her chest. Continuing, she said, "You know I work at the Angel, well Paul the boss wants out of the pub business. It's because his wife left him and he wants to do something on his own. But that means, when he sells up, I'll be jobless again. I love the job. I feel as though there is a sense of community about the place and for once, I'm part of it."

The two of them had confessed. The confessions were more to themselves; they had to have been spoken aloud. Each had been a sounding board for the other. They both felt better and for a moment they let the sound and movement of the wind blow away their problems. They had both opened-up – the fact that neither had criticized the other made them feel an affinity. It was a closeness that they both craved, both physically and mentally.

Darren looked up and noticed that the clouds had moved, leaving the moon completely exposed. The satellite loomed large and bright, showing the two of them the desolation of the landscape, which made them appreciate that they were together. After a few moments of silence, Sophie looked to where Darren was staring, to see what was distracting him. As she did so, he looked down. Her eyes were wide, probably because of the darkness, but he thought they looked deep and fathomless. He wanted to dive into those pools and connect with her, not in a sexual way, it was more than that, but to explore her soul and become part of it. He had never felt this way before. It was then he noticed her looking back at him.

"You really are thick."

He smiled in response.

"Kiss me," she said. He craned his neck downward and she rose to meet him. They kissed. It wasn't a spectacular movie kiss, but the moment and the meaning of it wasn't lost on either. A cloud moved across the moon and the picnic area was plunged into darkness. The change of lighting reminded Sophie of the change of temperature –

despite Darren's warmth, it was getting colder. After the kiss, they stood up.

"It's about time we got back, I'm up early, five o'clock."

Nodding, Sophie walked to her scooter. "I'm glad I came," she said in a slightly hushed voice.

"Me too, we'll have to do it again, you know, another date," said Darren with hope in his voice.

"Yeah, definitely." She smiled enthusiastically.

CHAPTER 9

30/07/17

The following Sunday was a bit overcast, when Brendan arrived at the marketplace. He pulled up alongside Mike who had already arrived. The gang had agreed through the week, that they were going to have a ride out together and they were to meet at the marketplace at ten AM. Brendan took his helmet off while he stayed astride his bike. He killed the engine and then pulled off his gloves.

"You know, I forgot how much I love this, nice morning for it," said Brendan.

"Yeah, not bad. It's not supposed to rain and the sun shouldn't glare too much either." Mike continued, "So where do you think we should go?"

Brendan said, "I was thinking of keeping it simple to start with. Go to Whitby for coffee at the 'Whistlestop Café', then go across the moor road to Guisborough and then back through Skelton."

"Sounds OK to me," agreed Mike.

As this was said, they heard a high-pitched roar as an engine rapidly descended through the gears. Brendan and Mike looked at each other, smiled and said in unison "Muhammad". No sooner did they say it, when a blue and white bike appeared over the crest of the hill that led up to the marketplace. Within seconds, he was alongside the other two. The throbbing engine was switched off. Sitting upright in his perfectly matched leathers, Muhammad removed his helmet. A big smile appeared and Muhammad said with a silly grin, "Forgot how much I love this."

The other two shook their heads. All three of them decided to dismount and have a walk around and then they sat on the bench next to a bus stop, twenty yards down the road. After a few minutes' chat, a soft but unmistakeable bike noise made its presence felt. Malika materialized over the brow of the hill and made his way toward them. Sedately, he parked up next to the other three bikes and turned off the engine. He didn't have to remove a helmet; instead, he wore a turban. He had, however, wrapped a bandero around his mouth and nose, to protect his face and he wore a pair of goggles, which were now situated on his brow. As he approached the others he pulled down the bandero to reveal a neat moustache, beard and a wide grin. "You know–" As he said it, the others laughed and finished his sentence: "I forgot how much I liked this." They all smiled. The four strangest group of bikers sat laughing when again, the air was filled with a deep throb of a large motorcycle, accompanied by a whine of a smaller one. Muhammad grinned and said what everyone was thinking: "The love birds." Brendan nudged Malika and grinned; he nodded over to the oncoming noise. They all looked in the direction they had come from earlier and a large figure on an enormous bike dominated the left side of the road. This scene was closely followed by a large black scooter. The scooter had no problem keeping up. The previous arrivals all looked equally impressed and bemused by the quality of the bikes and the contrast of size between them. The huge triple came to a halt and the thunderous sound stopped when it did. In comparison, when the scooter stopped, it was almost stealth-like. Both Sophie and Darren removed their helmets. Sophie ruffled her hair and shook her head; Darren did the same. At this, Muhammad stood up and shouted, "Oi Darren, what's all this?" He then pretended to flick and ruffle his hair. Grinning he said in a faux camp accent, "Hey guys, did the sun catch my golden locks?"

The first group walked forward to greet the newly arrived. They were all smiling, even the figure of fun that was Darren. Darren pretended to lunge toward Muhammad, who nimbly jumped back a couple of steps and then again pretended to flick his hair as though the movement had put it out of place.

Everyone began to settle down and formed a loose circle, so they could hear each other.

"OK." Brendan got everyone's attention. "I've talked to Mike about this, so, Mike I apologise for repeating myself." Mike shrugged. Brendan continued: "The general idea is for us to go to the Whistlestop Café in Whitby and then over the moor road and through Guisborough." There were nods of agreement and so Brendan went on, "Now, we are a club and that means we stay together as a group. If you're gonna race ahead–" He looked pointedly at Muhammad– "Then the point of a group ride is a bit of a waste of time." Again, nods of agreement. "I think that we should each go our own way, once we return to Skelton on the way back. Does anyone have any questions?" There was no response. "Does anyone need fuel? We're going approximately sixty miles." Again, nobody spoke up. "So, is everyone ready for the first official Guardian Angels bike ride?"

Brendan held his hand out. The others looked at him, confused, until Malika put his hand on top. Realising his intention, everyone else followed suit. Breaking away from each other, each walked to their respective machines. They all stood and put on their helmets, gloves and scarfs. They mounted their bikes and started the engines. At first the noise was deafening, but then settled into a low rumble. As they prepared to set off, the few pedestrians who were about stared at the spectacle. A few cars even slowed to have a look. They did, after all, look a bit of a strange assembly.

Brendan set off first. He looked both ways, checking for traffic and went down the bank that led towards the old bus station on the opposite side of the valley. Mike was next, then Malika. After a moment or two, because his bike was a little harder to manoeuvre at slower speeds, Muhammad followed next. The slight delay with Muhammad had given Sophie the chance to prepare her prosthetic on the scooter and so she quickly followed. Darren was purposely last. He wanted to watch his new girlfriend. Besides, his intimidating form made sure that other road users would be more careful when passing. The group snaked their way past the bus station and then left Loftus proper for their first ride out. The roar of the engines faded into the distance.

Darren watched the others, playing the sentinel at the rear. He waved and thanked people as they let them pass and smiled at a small group of kids, who waved frantically when they saw them. The journey itself wasn't that far. It was only fifteen miles, but the roads were twisty and undulating, with a lot of speed restrictions through each of the villages that they passed on the way. The only expected difficulty was Lythe Bank, which was extremely steep and had a few very tight turns near the bottom. Surprisingly, no one struggled. Despite not having ridden a bike for so long, they all showed quite a high level of competence. It may have been because each was trying to show off to the other, or perhaps it might have been that they had already developed a faith in each other that gave them confidence. Once they had negotiated their way through Lythe itself, which involved a small, tight, single lane hump-backed bridge on a very twisty road, they rode up the coast road. A handful of golfers were walking around, in the sea breeze, as the newly formed gang cruised by. They approached Whitby proper, then entered a suburban speed limit of thirty miles per hour. The reduced speed meant that the gaps that were between them closed. The buildings around them echoed the sounds of the bike engines, making their presence known. They rumbled along the road until they went downward to the town centre. Finally, they ended up at the Whistlestop Café next to the railway station, within sight of the river Esk. Parking up next to each other, in front of the Café, one by one, the engines were switched off and they all dismounted. They made their way into the café.

Locating an empty table, they sat down. It was a counter-service café, which meant that one of them was going to have to take the orders from the rest. Sophie looked at each of them with a menacing glare. It was pretty much decided there and then: she wasn't volunteering, she did enough of that at work. Sighing, Brendan got up, followed by Muhammad. They took the orders and then stood in the queue. As the others sat and chatted about the journey, the other two looked around. It was a clean place and seemed cosy enough. There were a handful of bikers in the place, most of whom were 'weekend warriors'. The type of biker who spent all week at work and then spent the weekend blasting around the North Yorkshire Moors. These were the people who kept the local emergency services busy. In the corner of the café were two proper bikers. What gave them away were the waistcoats and the dishevelled look. They talked to each other intermittently, but mainly looked disinterested in what was going on around them. After a small while, the two Guardian Angels were served and they took a tray of beverages over to the other four. They dished them out and then took their seats. The chatter increased and it soon became obvious that the group felt comfortable in each other's company. After fifteen minutes, the café door opened. It was then that the group was reminded of the two 'proper bikers', who had been sat in the corner. The bikers looked at them with a curious and not quite menacing stare. Pausing for a moment, they walked out, letting the door close behind them. The Guardian Angels all looked at each other. They all knew instinctively that something wasn't quite right. The chatter didn't die off completely, but it had quietened somewhat. They all finished their elevenses and then picked up their helmets from beneath their chairs. There were a lot of scrapings of chairs. Sophie, Muhammad and Mike all went to the toilet as the other three went outside.

The three of them mounted their bikes. While they were sat, Malika said, "That thing with those bikers was a little strange."

Darren nodded and Brendan replied, "Yeah, it was, I wonder what that was about?"

It wasn't long before Muhammad and Mike came out and then mentioned the same thing. They discussed it a while and then not being able to fathom it, they put on helmets and gloves. Sophie hurried out, complaining about having to wait in the women's toilets. Moments later, she was ready to go and they all started up their engines. Like before, they kept the same order in which they had arrived and made their way out of Whitby. Despite the sun, the wind was picking up and, although not too bad, there was the occasional strong gust. This made riding a little more difficult and so they were once again forced to keep their speed down. They made the steady climb out of Whitby and began their journey home. As they ascended the long bank out of Whitby, that was the start of the moor road, the wind became progressively stronger. The six of them kept a good distance between each other, in case the gusts forced them to waver across the road, which, on occasion, it did. As they reached the top of the first bank, Brendan, who was in the lead, noticed the silhouette of the two bikers that they had seen in the café. As they got closer, he managed to confirm it was them. When the group approached, the two bikers sat on their bikes and they turned their heads as they passed. It felt quite intimidating, but they didn't stop the gang's progress. Once they had all passed, the bikers who had been watching them, fell in behind, but leaving a substantial gap. Matters stayed the same for about five miles or so. Darren noticed that they had been there awhile in his rear-view mirrors. As the group approached Ugthorpe Caravan Park, Darren vigorously flashed his light. He realised that he been seen, when Brendan's right indicator came on and then each bike behind did the same. The road was clear on the approach to the junction, so they all followed each other straight in.

There was a big turning circle in front of the Lodge Hotel and they all manoeuvred so they faced back the way they had come. All removed their helmets to discuss what was going on.

"Did you see them?" asked Brendan.

Darren nodded. "Yeah, they followed us until just before we turned off."

They all looked a little nervous.

"Look, we haven't done anything, maybe they think we're going to cause bother or something?" said Muhammad.

"I'm not going to deviate from what we're doing," said Malika defiantly.

"Hey, at the end of the day, there's only two of them and six of us," said Sophie. Everyone turned and looked at her. "Well, bollocks to 'em," she continued, then realising that perhaps she sounded a little too aggressive, she fell silent.

"Well we don't have much of a choice but to carry on. The only other option is to call the police or something, but what do we report? Oh Officer, we think that two bikers, who looked at us, might be after us, oh yeah, and they've disappeared to boot," said Brendan.

Having put it that way, the gang started to feel a little uncomfortable and embarrassed.

"Personally, I think they are watching us and our instincts are right, but as it is, we can't do anything about it, so as Malika and Sophie said, let's crack on." Brendan looked at them all. He had laid it on the line. There were mixed feelings, they did feel intimidated and at the same time acutely embarrassed. Brendan continued as the rest of them put on their helmets. "We continue as we have been. Keep each other in sight and keep your eyes open in case they appear again." They all acknowledged that they had heard him and put their thumbs up in confirmation.

Brendan put his own helmet on and led the way back out of the caravan park drive way. At the end of the drive they had to wait for traffic and then, one at a time, they continued down the road toward Guisborough. They settled back down into a convoy. They covered the distance to Scaling Reservoir, with no sign of the bikers. They then made their way up the hill, passed the Liverton Mines turn off; as they did so, they saw the bikers just arrive at the junction at the brow of the hill that they had just started to climb. Brendan made a point of nodding in their direction. That was the usual greeting between bikers of all types. The greeting was not returned and as before, the two bikers waited until there was a large gap and then followed the gang. The road went down a steep bank and then undulated, progressively went back uphill, until they reached the car park, just before the bank at Birk Brow. As before, they all pulled in. Unlike before, the bikers went straight past and didn't look in their direction. Again, like in Ugthorpe, they had a meeting on their bikes. They removed their helmets and although they wanted to speak about what was going on, they didn't really know what to say.

Brendan spoke. "Well it would be a weird coincidence if they weren't following us."

"That seems to have put a dampener on things, doesn't it?" said Mike, pointing out the obvious.

Brendan, taking charge of the situation, said, "Let's do what we planned, finish the trip down to Guisborough, turn right toward Skelton and then split up from there to wherever home is. I don't think there'll be any bother. It's probably because we're new in the area as a group of bikers and they're checking us out. But still, to be safe, when each of you get home, text me and if there's any bother, we'll go from there."

They all nodded. There was little else that they could do. Once again, they set off and made it to Guisborough roundabout. They never saw the bikers again. Once they approached Skelton, they peeled off at their relevant junctions and made their way home. The whole ride had taken about two and a half hours, including stops and had been quite eventful, even if the events were imagined.

Brendan arrived home and went through his routine of putting his bike away. As he did so, he started to receive text messages on his mobile to say each of the gang had arrived home. None of them reported anything out of the ordinary. Brendan finally entered the kitchen and flicked the kettle on. Well it hadn't gone too bad, even if we did panic unnecessarily. In some ways, it had gone quite well. They were reasonably disciplined, they got on well and most importantly, they had stuck together. He couldn't wait for next Sunday – it might prove to be interesting.

CHAPTER 10

06/08/17

The mist was lifting when the gang met outside the Angel. It was nine AM on Sunday morning and they were getting ready for their weekly ride out. The initial fear of the stalking bikers had faded somewhat and so the group was calm and eager to take their next trip. It had been decided to go for a longer trip out, hence the earlier time. The tour was to go to Whitby as before, but then cut across to Helmsley, where there were a couple of biker-friendly cafés. Everyone was there, except for Muhammad, which was a little strange, as he was normally one of the first. The five decided to give him another fifteen minutes before they set off. Brendan and Malika were deep in conversation, so were Darren and Sophie; Mike just sat, fiddling with the controls on his bike, without dismounting. Five minutes later, the high-pitched whine of Muhammad's sports engine broke the quiet atmosphere of the marketplace. Doing what he normally did, he raced up to the parking bay and put his brakes on at the last second, much to the annoyance of everyone else. He looked around at everyone and they could all tell he was grinning, despite wearing his helmet. He killed the engine and then dismounted the sports machine. He then took off his helmet and gloves and rubbed his head. Having stuffed his gloves into his helmet, he placed it carefully on the floor.

He took off the rucksack that he had on his back. The rest of the crew were watching the new arrival with interest – after all he had been quiet during the whole process up until now, which was very unusual for him. Putting the rucksack on the floor, he then proceeded to unzip it and extracted some items of clothing. The clothing was plastic bagged for protection. Once the rucksack had been emptied, Muhammad un-bagged one item to reveal a leather waistcoat. It was meant as a biker jacket. Everyone glanced at each other questioningly. No-one had even mentioned clothing. It just seemed a little early in the day to be dishing out uniforms. They couldn't help but look at the newly produced jacket. Muhammad held one up to show everyone. He was grinning from ear to ear.

"There, what do you think?" he asked enthusiastically.

He twirled the waistcoat, which was a dark leather. There was some sort of design on the back, but because he waved it about so much, no-one could make out any detail.

Mike, who was still sat on his bike, shouted, "Well, let's have a look then."

He held out his hand expectantly. Muhammad, still beaming, walked over and handed Mike the jacket. He retreated to the neat pile of jackets, which were on top of the rucksack. He picked them up and dished them out to the rest of the crew. Each person extracted the jackets from the bags that they had been given. They checked the stitching and quality. A couple of them tried them on. But as expected, most interest was directed to the design that was on the back. There were a few frowns and even a nod of approval.

Still smiling, Muhammad asked, "Well what do you think?"

He wanted positive responses. He received a couple of 'It's OK's and a couple of nods, but they didn't show the enthusiasm that he had hoped for. Muhammad, a little disappointed, let his smile slip a bit. On the plus side, there were not outright rejections.

"I know it's a bit out of the blue, but I thought it would be a cool idea."

Brendan, Mike and Malika had theirs on already, trying them for size. Muhammad walked over to Darren.

"Sorry mate, I told the supplier that you were a bigger guy and they didn't have anything big enough, so yours should be regarded as a sample. I'll have to go back with your measurements."

Darren handed it back to Muhammad. "It's OK, we'll sort it out once we get back from the run."

Smiling because of the assumed approval, Muhamad took the waistcoat back and asked Sophie what she thought.

"I wouldn't mind a more feminine cut if that's OK," she said.

"Yeah sure," replied Muhammad, enthusiastically. Muhammad raised his voice so everyone could hear him. "When we get back, like Darren said, we can go over things like measurements and whatever else; these are really samples. If you can think of any issues with these, tell me then I'll get it sorted." The other five nodded. "Oh, by the way, what do you think of the design, is it OK?"

On the waistcoat backs, the design showed an angel in battle dress, usually regarded as Archangel Michael in a battle pose. In a circle, around the picture were the words, 'Loftus, Guardian Angels'. Its simplicity made it very effective.

Muhammad explained, "I asked my father to come up with a design. He said he wouldn't be offended if it had to be changed, it was just a starting point, we have to start from somewhere."

Again, the group nodded in general agreement. The idea was sound, the implementation might require a little rework. The four smaller men kept their new jackets on, Brendan, Malika, Mike and of course Muhammad. Size and style prevented the set to be complete, but still, it was a good start, with no real dissent. Muhammad at least felt as though he had made a good contribution to the team and, because of that, he felt as though he was a part of it. His enthusiastic smile returned as he gathered up the plastic bags and put them in the rucksack, which he put back on, ready for the ride out. Mike and Malika were looking at the design more closely and seemed a little undecided, but not objecting.

Brendan, as always, was ready for the off first and switched his engine on. He got everyone's attention when he did so. One at a time, the others followed suit. The mist had begun to clear and so the second official outing of the Loftus Guardian Angels began. Going the same route, at least until they got to Whitby, the gang stayed together. Brendan first, Mike, Malika, Muhammad, Sophie and then Darren. The sea breeze had dispersed the remaining mist and the sun smiled down on the entourage. The noise of the bikes echoed as they went through each village, heralding their arrival and announcing their departure. Once again, they descended Lythe Bank without any incidents and snaked their way along the roads to Whitby. This time, they were to turn onto the moor road without stopping and then continue along back roads in a roundabout way to Helmsley. As they arrived at the start of the moor road, unexpectedly, Muhammad overtook Malika and then Mike, then hung on behind Brendan. Malika and Mike gestured to each other, wondering what was going on. As neither of them knew anything, both just shrugged and carried on. Muhammad's riding seemed a little erratic, but not dangerous, just edgy. The group remained in the new order until they went over the last roundabout before the moor road opened-up properly. It was then Muhammad's bike gave out a deep roar and the Hayabusa launched itself up the straight road. The whine of the engine soon faded as the gap between the missile of a bike and the group increased. Brendan was shaking his head. He glanced in his rear-view mirrors and gave a questioning hand signal. As before, Malika and Mike gestured their ignorance. By now, the Suzuki was a tiny speck on the horizon. The rest of them stayed together and kept a steady pace. Once they reached the turn off for Lealholm, they left the moor road and entered the winding roads of North Yorkshire. The road went downhill almost straight away and so the party slowed to a crawl. The very steep bank, along with the sharp bends, impeded their progress, but despite this, they made a good time. As they approached the bottom of the valley, it was then that Brendan saw a blue and white Hayabusa lying on its side. Brendan quickly realised it belonged to Muhammad, so he came to a halt on the side of the road. Everyone else followed suit. All the engines were stilled and they all got off their bikes. Brendan walked over to the 'Busa' and looked at it. It seemed it had been pushed over, or perhaps it had fallen over because of the uneven surface. His suspicion was that it had been deliberately pushed. Muhammad was too proud of his bike to do something as stupid as to let it fall; besides, he would be here trying to stand it up.

Whilst he was thinking about the bike, Darren shouted the gang over. He was stood at the edge of the other side of the road, looking down a steep decline. He was waving everyone to come over where he was. They all gathered in the same place and looked down. Muhammad was holding his helmet as he traversed the steep climb. At the final approach, he said between gasps "Hi y'awl"; he spoke almost nonchalantly. Walking straight past the other five, gasping, he went to pick up his bike. "Give us a hand please." It took three of them, Brendan, Muhammad and Darren, a good bit of effort to right the bike, made all the harder by the gradient of the road. Once sorted, Muhammad explained what had happened.

"When we approached Whitby, I had the bright idea of having a quick blast up the moor road and then wait for you at the junction." When he said it, he pointed to the junction at the top the hill that they had just come down. "However, when I got there, two bikers were waiting there. Being the kind of guy I am, I said hello. They asked me if I was in an MC, so I answered, 'what?'. They told me it meant a motorcycle club. So, of course I said yes and told them who we were. They then asked if we had asked for permission to make a club. I asked them, who would we ask? They then said, we had to ask them. Of course, at this point I told them to 'do one'. That's when the tussle started. Luckily, I had my helmet on. The one that did most of the talking, pushed me over while I was on the bike. Then, while one held me, the other took my waistcoat off and tore it up. Between the two of them, they then threw me down the bank. Then I heard them ride off."

Once again, an Angels outing had taken a turn for the worse. Malika asked what seemed to be the most obvious question on everyone's mind: "Do you think it was the two guys that followed us the last time?"

Muhammad shrugged. "I don't know to be honest. We didn't see their faces the last time, so I can't say for sure. Anyway, thanks, guys." He nodded toward the bike. "That's gonna be a good six or seven hundred quid to get that sorted."

The fairings on the side that it had fallen on, had cracked, but otherwise, luckily, the bike seemed sound. Muhammad looked at the others. "Look, you guys carry on, I'm gonna have to go home and sort this out."

Brendan spoke. "Two things: firstly, don't go off and do your own thing like that again, and secondly, we stick together, we'll all go back."

The others nodded in agreement.

"Hey guys, I'm really sorry about this," apologised Muhammad. His demeanour showed that he meant it and his voice reflected how humbling the experience had been. They all returned to their bikes and mounted up. The engines were started and they continued down to the bottom of the valley, making their way across to Danby. Passing through Danby, they made the ascent to the junction, where they had had the previous encounter with the bikers. As they approached the junction to the moor road, they caught sight of whom they believed to be the two bikers in question, but the distance didn't allow them to make a definite identification. The party made its way to the junction that headed to Liverton Mines and turned for home. Muhammad's bike seemed to be fine, other than the cracked bodywork. It had been agreed that this had been a warning from whatever gang it was. They were going to have to do some research on how to resolve the issue, if they were going to continue as the Guardians Angels.

Muhammad arrived at the back yard. The engine was turned off and silence befell the back street. He dismounted and opened the gate.

He pushed the bike in, instead of the usual riding in, then put it on its stand. Closing the gate, he took a few steps back and looked at the bike. It wasn't that bad. The bike had been pushed over on the one spot, so there were cracks and no scrapes. A rock had pierced the fairing, causing a small hole. If you didn't look closely, you would find it hard to see any damage at all. His leathers on the other hand were scratched and scruffy. The knees and elbows had green stains from the grass and when he removed his helmet, he saw a gouge and a few scrapes. He thought it was just as well that he had been wearing it. If he hadn't, he would have had a serious injury. He opened his jacket to cool off and as he did so he sighed, more from the relief of stress than the ease in temperature. Letting his shoulders drop, he shook his head and wondered why he was putting himself through all of this. Was it worth it? He heard some shuffling behind him. He was greeted by his dad, putting a couple of bags of rubbish in the wheelie bin.

"Hi son, thought it was you."

Smiling wanly, Muhammad looked at him and then back to the bike.

"Hmm, fallen off?"

Muhammad knew his dad knew otherwise, so didn't argue, instead answering sheepishly "Sort of".

"A bit like Middlesbrough?" His Dad reminded him of the jealousy that the other teens had for him, when he turned up in his new car all those years ago. "Perhaps, son, you're trying too hard again?"

Not wanting to argue, Muhammad said, "No Dad, it's not like that, really. The guys who did this had nothing to do with our club." Muhammad put his hands on his hips in contemplation, considering his options on how to get the fairings fixed.

His dad, persisting with the conversation asked, "So what exactly is the problem?"

Staring in his father's direction, trying to explain that he didn't want to be pressed too hard, by means of body language, he said, "We think it's a rival club. We have research to do to find out exactly what the problem is, but it could be a territorial issue. We're new to all of this, so we don't know for definite. I was caught on my own, in a quiet place. It could have been far worse. We think this was a warning."

Pausing and letting it sink in, his Dad nodded sagely. "Is the aggro worth it?"

"In a way, but you know what, nothing ever comes from not trying, does it?" said Muhammad defiantly. They smiled at each other. How many times had his father said the same thing to him, when he had been at a low ebb?

Directing his attention to the bike, Muhammad's father asked, "So, how are you going to get this sorted?"

Rubbing his chin in thought, Muhammad said, "You know, I think I'll ask Mike."

Frowning, his father asked, "Who's Mike?"

"He's one of the guys in the club, who's always serious. Well to be fair, he's not always serious, just very focussed. If there's anything mechanical to deal with, he's the go to guy. I doubt anyone knows as much as him." As he said this, he realised that he felt loyalty and respect for Mike, that feeling of belonging and a faith in someone else had begun to replace the emptiness that had plagued him before. What surprised him, was that his feelings did not require economic or religious ties. It was simply a case of being with like-minded people, who shared a common goal. He believed that was why he had wanted to join the club, to defy the status quo, to be who he wanted to be. When all of this occurred to him, he had a renewed respect for his parents and why they had moved away from the intense influence wrought by their upbringing and background. A well of emotion rose-up in him. This was his path. He saw his parents in a new light. He walked over to his father and hugged him. His Dad, a bit shocked, returned the hug and smiled. He wasn't quite sure what had instigated the action, but seeing it as a positive, he didn't question it. Releasing his hold, he stepped back and said to his Dad, "I get it now, thanks." Completely nonplussed, his father said "OK". Returning his attention back to the bike, Muhammad reached into his jacket and brought out his mobile phone. He rang Mike and asked if he could fix the bike. Mike being Mike, said in a roundabout way, that he could. He would do it 'at cost'. Satisfied, Muhammad thanked him and put the phone away.

His dad was watching and decided that he seen a change in his son. It was a good and positive change. He had found his way and a sense of purpose. The funk of depression had left him.

"Listen, son, I have to get on, places to go and people to see."

Diverting his attention back to his father, he smiled. "OK, see what she wants."

His dad patted him on the shoulder. "Get cleaned up, tea's soon, you know what will happen if you're late."

His dad left him. Life had changed. The push over by those bikers had done him the world of good. He had fallen from a position of selfishness. The others had come for him and they were now helping him to get back on his feet. The whole incident had been caused by impetuousness and impatience. He hadn't been judged, just helped. Because of this he felt loyalty and more of a willingness to get involved with the club. He had wanted to be part of something that was bigger than himself; he had found it. Feeling like he had had a good day, despite the setback, he pushed the bike into the shed. In the past, he would have simply got the bike repaired and sold it on, as though he was disgusted with it being sullied and less than perfect. But now, it was something that had helped him reach and experience something personal and profound; it was now part of him. It would be repaired and they would be together forever, if it was within his power.

Today had been a shock for everyone. He supposed, most of all, for Muhammad. He supped his tea and put the mug back onto the table. Muhammad had been stupid to race off on his own like that, but still, he shouldn't have been assaulted, regardless. A lot of questions were racing through Brendan's head right now. He felt responsible – after all, he had set the whole thing up and seemed to be the de facto leader. Taking another sip of the tea, he pondered on how the issue should be approached. They didn't even know who these bikers were. So, how were they supposed to put a stop to their problems? He stood up, feeling frustrated with the situation. This was supposed to be a social thing, with a few people getting together and riding about. He started to pace up and down the kitchen. His annoyance was beginning to build. The thought of other people dictating what they were going to do, was an anathema to him. OK, first things first. Picking up the phone, he rang Muhammad.

"Hi Muhammad, how's it going?" he asked with a deep concern.

"Fine, boss, just the shock of it all, took a while for me to get my head round it."

He certainly sounded like he was OK. Brendan then asked, "So, what's the problem with the bike?"

Strangely, Muhammad didn't seem too bothered when he gave his reply. "The fairing's damaged, as expected, but otherwise it seems OK. I've called Mike, to see if he can sort it."

The conversation paused, then Brendan asked, "Look, Muhammad, if you don't want to stay in the club, that would be fine, I would understand. In fact, I was thinking about asking everyone if they want to disband. I don't want to go out and be constantly looking over my back; I wouldn't expect anyone else to do so either."

Sounding dismayed, Muhammad cut Brendan off. "Wooahh, I don't think so. The club means a lot to me, believe it or not. Besides, I have this thing about bullies. If we change what we do, then they've won – that isn't happening."

Brendan was silent. Then in a hushed voice, he said, "Thanks."

In an equally hushed voice, Muhammad said, "We're in it together. As we said in the beginning, up theirs."

Brendan, feeling relieved and grateful, said, "Look, I'm gonna talk to the others and see how they feel. Remember, Mike's autistic, Sophie's disabled and Malika's a pensioner; they might not want the hassle."

"If Sophie packed in, I would have thought that, in all likelihood, so would Darren and/or vice versa."

Again, there was silence between them as they considered the possibilities. Breaking the impasse, Muhammad said, "Whatever we do, we have to do it together regardless and we won't know what direction to take things until we've talked about it. So, I would suggest you get cracking and have a chat with each one, then we talk about it on Sunday."

Next, Brendan rang Malika. The conversation went pretty much the same way as it had when he talked to Muhammad. There was an air of defiance when Malika spoke.

"You know what, Brendan, I have had enough of being told what to do by people who don't have a clue themselves. I might be a little cynical with my life's philosophy, but these people are frightened to be themselves and are obviously following the crowd, whatever crowd that might be. I will not be told how to live my life. That's the reason why I joined the club, to do my own thing. Nobody is going to dictate to me."

Brendan was stunned into silence by Malika's anger. Then, smiling to himself, he said, "So, you're still in then?"

There was a "Harrumph" down the other end of the line. His smile broadened when he heard Malika say, "Bring it on!" If anyone else had said it, he would have shrugged it off. As it was, he had to stifle a laugh to prevent a serious situation from turning into a farce. Well, I guess that's three of us still in, he thought. Three to go. The call to Mike was a little more stunted. Mike didn't like being on the phone, because he couldn't see the person he was talking to. But the general conversation was pretty much like the previous two. Mike made his indignation of the situation known and agreed that he wanted to stay in the club, come what may. Besides, he said that he needed a bit of a social life. Again, smiling at the way each of them were being defiant, he put the phone down, so that he could make his final call. The phone was picked up at the other end by Darren. Brendan expressed his surprise. "Oh, err, have I caught you at a bad time?"

"No, she's just gone to the loo and we're at her mam's. I only picked up the phone, cos I saw your name."

A little relieved, Brendan continued, "Look, I've rang to see how you two feel about 'the Muhammad situation' and to see if you have any doubts about staying in the club?"

Darren, without consulting Sophie, said outright, "No, I don't think they'll be an issue, definitely not from me and even less of a chance of problems from Sophie."

Brendan was expecting the reply he got, but given the circumstances, he had to be sure. Then, in the background he heard, "Who is it?" It was Sophie's voice.

Darren replied, "Brendan. He was asking if we wanted out of the club."

Sophie raised her voice, so Brendan could hear. "I don't F'ing well think so. Has anyone dropped out?"

Brendan confirmed that no-one had, much to Sophie's delight.

As Brendan put the phone down, he thought to himself 'Well, this is going really well. The team is sticking together, maybe we were meant to be together. It could be that there really are Guardian Angels looking out for us and everything will work out in the end.' He finished his mug of, by now, tepid coffee and went to bed. After today's events, he needed a good night's sleep.

CHAPTER 11

07/08/17

With the hardest part over with, keeping the club together, Brendan now set about trying to formulate a plan to deal with the situation of the mysterious bike club. The two bikers might have been a couple of unsanctioned rogues and that would explain why they had kept their distance and only attacked Muhammad, when he was on his own. However, the possibility was that these people were trying to enforce some sort of code. This could only lead to two results: either there was going to be some sort of confrontation in the future or the newly formed bike club would have to be disbanded. Given the response of the guys on the phone, the former would be most likely. The best recourse was to gather as much information as possible. It would be advantageous to know what they were up against. However, where do you start? How do you find out about an organization that doesn't publicly exist? Brendan sat on the big comfy chair in his living room. The only illumination was from the kitchen. The TV was off and he sat in silence. He waited on a thought that refused to formulate itself. Staring blankly into space, he tried to empty his mind. He momentarily closed his eyes and sighed; the exhalation relaxed him. After what seemed five minutes, he opened his eyes again. It was then he noticed something in the periphery of his vision. Lying on the table next to him, were the pile of biker magazines that had inspired this whole adventure. On the front of one of the magazines was a photo of some sort of biker festival. The thought occurred to him that if these guys were part of the biker scene, then they would be going to these sort of places. Picking the magazine up, he flicked through it and came to the adverts near the back, which expounded various locations and clubs that were holding such events. Grabbing a pen and paper from his desk, he proceeded to go through each magazine. He wrote down the festivals and events in the area, from South Yorkshire to the Borders. Then wrote down all the clubs that had turned up to each. Although, realistically, he was not much further forward, he did have a list of a potential six clubs. The guys in question might be from any of these clubs, but it was a start. They were based in the general area and it would be unlikely that anyone would travel so far afield, just to bully a group of Weekend Warriors.

Brendan turned on his computer and tried to find something out about any of these people. Other than a passing mention on the odd forum, there was practically nothing. Of course, there were a list of names, but that meant nothing without any indication of their activities. So, he started with the most obvious. He researched the 'Hell's Angels' and why they were so 'special' and why they had such notoriety. He needed to talk to someone about what he had found, and Malika sprang to mind. Picking up his phone, Brendan sent a text to his Indian friend, asking if he was available for a chat. Within a couple of minutes, he received an answer. Brendan rang him.

"What's up?" asked the heavily accented voice.

"This incident with Muhammad has got me thinking." Malika politely waited for Brendan to continue. "Well, I've done a bit of research. Other than a list of one-percenter club names, I don't have anything at all. I was wondering if you had any idea as to what we should do next?"

Malika then asked, "What do you mean by a one-percenter club?"

"Well, cutting a long story short, these clubs are, or at least they think they are, the top echelons of biker clubs. These are the one-percent of bikers that cause trouble. They run drugs, prostitution and other illegal activities. They believe that they can bully others into complying with what they say. They have been known to cause so much bother that the police have sent in under-cover officers to get inside intelligence."

Having explained the situation, Brendan waited for Malika's response.

"I know nothing of any of this," said the Indian, with apprehension in his voice.

Brendan explained, "Like I said, I've done a bit of research, trying to find out exactly who we're dealing with. I've got the names of the six most likely clubs, but even they are a calculated guess."

Malika seemed a little quiet. Brendan thought that the older man was having doubts about the whole situation and the possible consequences. But Brendan's fears were dispelled a moment later.

"So, what you're telling me is that what we are potentially dealing with, is a secret society of bullies, with the mental age of fourteen."

Brendan, smiling on the other end of the call, said, "Essentially, yes." This wasn't quite what Brendan was expecting.

"If they are bad guys, as you say, then they will have police records," deduced Malika.

"I would suppose so." Brendan was wondering where this was going.

Malika said slowly, "I have a cousin in India." Brendan let him continue. He could tell that Malika was thinking as he was talking, so he didn't want to interrupt. "My cousin has a son who is very good on computers. I will make enquiries to see if he can help us at all."

Malika was being secretive, but given the train of thought that Brendan believed Malika was following, he considered it a good idea.

Malika then asked, "Can you send me the list of the six clubs and I will see what I can do."

Impressed by the turn of events, Brendan said he would, as soon as the conversation was over. He thanked his friend and then, as promised, sent the list. Picking up the magazines that he had used for research, he tidied them away and got himself ready for a good night's sleep.

While he was showering the next morning, he became overwhelmed with a growing sense of anger. 'Who the bloody hell do they think they are to dictate to us what we do? We only want to have a good ride out and to enjoy ourselves, we're not bothering anyone.' It was these kind of thoughts that he ruminated on throughout the day. Normally at work, he wouldn't even look up from the computer screen. Now, with his renewed sense of purpose, he was clock watching. He had better things to do than crunch numbers for businesses in a place like this. He wanted to be out with his new friends and chewing up the miles on the open road. But, most of all, he wanted to fight the good fight, with the guys.

Valerie kept looking his way. At first, he didn't notice, but as she had been doing it so often, it got to the point where he couldn't do anything but. He caught her at it again and returned the look. She, realising that she had been spotted, averted her gaze.

"Val, what is it?"

Because she had been confronted directly, she had no choice but to answer. "I don't know, you seem different somehow, I can't quite put my finger on it."

Looking hard at her, he debated as to whether he should tell her about the bike club. The boss was out and he was on top of his work, despite the lack of focus, so he decided he would. "A group of us have started a biker club. We get out for fresh air and a bit of socialising – that's probably what you're seeing."

She gave him a shrug. "Maybe, but I don't think so, it seems to be more than that, I really mean it in a nice way."

Returning her shrug, he had answered her without giving away too many details. He tried to continue with his work, but the earlier frustration got the better of him and he turned to her. He felt that he had to get things off his chest. He didn't speak, despite having decided to. Valerie stopped working, seeing that he had something to say. She waited patiently for him to go first.

"We do have a problem." Pausing, worried if he was making the right decision to speak to her. "While we've been out, one of our guys got attacked by another gang, but we're not sure who it is. We're new at this so we can only guess as to why."

Valerie's eyes widened "Oh," she exclaimed quietly. This sounded terribly exciting to Valerie's ears and she suddenly saw Brendan in an entirely new light. She thought he was a suited, staid black man who had been employed because of positive discrimination, but now she saw a wild, tough biker. She was beginning to warm to him, especially now that he had decided to confide in her. She leaned forward and gave him her full attention. She put both elbows on the desk and put her chin into her cupped hands. She was fascinated by this development and didn't want to miss a thing. "Well, anyway," he continued. "The thing is, I rang each of the gang up and asked what they thought of the situation, and given that we're a new club, did they want to disband."

At this, Valerie took in an excited intake of breath. She nodded, with her chin still in her cupped hands and asked, "Well, what did they say?"

With a smile, Brendan said with undisguised pride, "They all, without exception, said 'stuff 'em'." Valerie gave a smile of encouragement. Finishing the story, Brendan said rhetorically, "The problem is, what do we do, where do we go from here?"

Giving a moment's thought, Valerie asked, "Might I give a suggestion?" Focussing his eyes on her, he nodded. "If you haven't already, why don't you get a uniform or whatever it is you wear, for all of you, to show that you are all on a united front."

For a moment, he stared at Valerie. "You know what, you have just answered the question. I think this is territorial, whoever it is thinks that we're upstarts trying to muscle in or something like that. When Muhammad was attacked, the waistcoat had been taken off him and thrown; nothing else was taken."

He smiled at his own comprehension. Valerie smiled too. She suddenly thought to herself, that it might be that she liked Brendan Sykes a lot more than she had originally. He might be an interesting person after all. "Thanks for that. Until you mentioned the idea of a uniform, I never made the link. I thought the waistcoat had just been taken off Muhammad as part of his roughing up, but I get it now."

Smiling, Valerie turned back to her computer screen, as did Brendan. But before settling back down to her work, she gave him one last, unnoticed glance.

When Brendan got home he rang Muhammad. He told him that he thought the situation with him had arisen because of a perceived territorial dispute, which of course, at the minute, was one-sided. Muhammad then asked what they could do about it. That's when Brendan surprised him and said, "Well, if it's about territory, let's sort it out. They can come and get us if they want. Why can't we tell them that we mean business and that we're staying put!"

Muhammad, at this point, was a little quiet. After all, he had been the butt-end of the mystery club's warning. "How exactly, are we going to do that?" he enquired.

"Muhammad, what I would like you to do, is to go and get full leather jackets and waistcoats, with our emblem on – that way, we are making a statement of intent, which should make a point, bearing in mind your last run in with them."

Muhammad considered his response before saying, "This might just become a bit more serious. I'm gonna ring the others for their measurements and tell them what the crack is; it's only right that they know what they're getting themselves into."

Brendan agreed with his friend. "We all wanted change and a sense of purpose, so now we have it. I asked everyone, including you, what they thought and they all came back with a defiant attitude. So now, we will see if they meant it."

Muhammad replied, "I'm not changing my mind, but agreeing on a bike ride is one thing, an all-out confrontation or even war with a territorial bunch of thugs is another."

Brendan said in a quiet, determined voice, "I'm sick of being pushed around by people. I have been since I was a kid, physically and racially. So, I'm pushing back. I admit, it does seem personal and perhaps it is, but you know, this is my thing and it's gonna stay that way." For emphasis, and perhaps melodramatically he added, "Even if it kills me!"

Muhammad, drawing the conversation to a close, said, "I'll call the others. Like I said, I need their measurements and I'll update them."

Brendan simply said "Thanks" and put the phone down.

Muhammad sat, feeling pensive. What he was about to do, on the face of it, was very simple and straightforward. But he knew that the implications were enormous. Firstly, he rang Brendan back.

"You know what it is, you ranted on that much, you forgot to give me your own measurements."

Chuckling, Brendan said, "Yeah, I s'pose I did, didn't I. Sorry about that. It's a large anyway, a forty-four chest and a thirty-six waist."

Muhammad snorted. "I don't think so, more like a forty-four and forty-two."

Brendan was silent, obviously not happy, but didn't argue; reality hurt.

Not wanting to upset his friend further, Muhammad said, "Don't worry, I'll sort it."

After taking notes, he then rang each of the others and while he did so, he explained why he was getting the clothing. Unsurprisingly, they all agreed with Brendan's sentiment and told him to go ahead.

When he got to Mike, the conversation became a little more involving. He asked Mike when he would fix his bike. Mike said it would take a while to get the parts and of course he couldn't guarantee the work. He was a qualified bike mechanic, but his business was only insured for cars. Muhammad explained that the bike was over ten years old and so well out of warranty. He also expressed his gratitude for dealing with it. It was agreed that Muhammad would use the bike until all the parts came in. That way, he had its use and Mike wouldn't have to store it while waiting. Muhammad was relieved – the next closest place that he knew that could deal with the bike, was in Newcastle, which would involve a massive amount of travel and aggravation.

After he got the agreement, Muhammad said, "Listen, Mike, I owe you one."

Mike, being Mike said, "One what?"

Responding, Muhammad said, "A favour."

"How can you owe me favour? It is an abstract concept – you cannot trade in the abstract, unless you are talking about money, which is representative of an abstract."

Realising that he might end up in one of Mike's literal arguments, he cut in and gave his thanks for doing the bike and then asked Mike to ring him when the parts came in. Maybe a trip to Newcastle wouldn't have been such a bad thing!

It was six o'clock on the Tuesday when Muhammad turned up on his bike. Mike had rung unexpectedly, saying that when he ordered the parts, they would arrive the same day, so it might be a good idea to bring the bike for him to look at. He had looked at the bike himself, before he had come round, and all that he could see was that it had damage to the fairings and little else, but then again, he was hardly an expert. Mike, on the other hand, despite what he portrayed, was an expert. In fact, Mike's approach to anything mechanical was beyond expertise, it was obsessional. If anyone would sort it out, it would be him. The roar of the Hayabusa suddenly stopped. The difference between the loud exhausts and the following silence was stark. Anyone around the bike, when the silence befell, had to shake their heads to re-orientate themselves. As the engine noise died, Mike came out from the garage. As with all mechanics, he had a cloth in his hands, scrubbing oil or grease from his skin. The rubbing must have been out of habit rather than cleanliness, because they were as immaculate as his coveralls. He approached the bike as Muhammad dismounted. He cocked his head.

"It doesn't look too bad, but the fairings are going to have to come off. There might be more hidden cracks and by taking them off, I'll be able to see if there is any more damage underneath."

Muhammad nodded. "That's what I thought, but to be honest, if I have anything to do with it, it will end up destroyed."

Muhammad had taken a couple of steps back and let Mike walk around the vehicle. Every now and again, Mike would stoop down and tug at the plastics. After a minute or two of examining the bodywork, he held out his hand wordlessly. At first, Muhammad was confused by the gesture, but then he handed over the keys. Mike could come across as arrogant at times, thought Muhammad. He knew it was his manner and he understood why, but still, it could be annoying. Starting the engine, Mike let it run without touching anything else on the bike. He walked around it, listening carefully. Again, he approached the bike and started flicking on each switch, ensuring they worked. He checked the indicators, horn, lights, brakes and, finally, the alarm system. Muhammad simply stood in the same place during the entire process, with a look of apprehension. Mike looked at Muhammad.

"I think you got off quite lightly, believe it or not. The fairings are beyond repair. Those are the parts that I can get delivered in a day. I don't want to worry you, but I'll have to check the frame. It's unlikely that it's been damaged. These bikes can take a lot of abuse, but it's nice to know for definite. I'll be able to tell you when the fairings are off."

Muhammad was nodding to show that he understood what he was being told. "So, how much do you reckon it'll cost?" he asked.

Rubbing his chin, Mike said, "Round about six-hundred, give or take. It would be a lot more if labour was included, but there you go."

"You know, Mike, I'm really grateful for your help."

Mike smiled in return. Almost as an afterthought, Mike said, "I apologise for going on last night, on the phone. I sometimes forget that most people do not talk logically."

Muhammad went to pat Mike on the shoulder for reassurance but remembered not to. Autistic people generally avoid casual physical contact. So, in a more formal manner, Muhammad stuck his hand out, which Mike accepted and they shook. For a moment, both men considered the paradox. Here they were, two people from opposite ends of the emotional spectrum, one who hated rules and conformity and the other who loved them. What brought them together was a common purpose and now, an unlikely friendship.

"Will you ring you ring me later, with the bad news?"

"Bad news?" answered Mike with a raised eyebrow.

"You know, the actual costs."

Mike said, "How are the costs 'bad news'?"

Cocking his head sideways, Muhammad looked at Mike and smiled. Realising what he had said, Mike returned the smile. Muhammad, forgetting himself, slapped him on the shoulder. Flinching from the contact, Mike said, "Don't worry, I'll get back to you as soon as possible." He then walked back into the garage, leaving Muhammad to stare after him. Leaving the bike in Mike's capable hands, Muhammad walked home, carrying his helmet, thinking to himself, how was he going to manage without his bike?

He pulled up outside the house, but didn't go up the steep drive. He parked the bike up and switched off the engine. Dismounting, he stepped onto the pavement and stood while he removed his helmet and gloves. This time, Darren wasn't quite so reticent when he turned up at Sophie's mam's. He had a good idea as to what to expect. He liked Anne; she was very easy to get on with. He could see where Sophie got her sense of humour from. He looked at the front garden as he walked to the door. It had been paved, probably to save on maintenance. It was most likely that Anne did most of the chores, he thought. He smiled to himself, just like my mother.

He knocked on the door and waited patiently. He noticed some shadowy movement behind the frosted glass and then a few seconds later heard the clicking of heels approaching the entrance. The door opened and Anne's diminutive figure stood in front of him.

"Hello Anne, how are you?" he asked.

She smiled and politely replied, "Fine, how are you?" As she spoke, she stepped back to let in his large bulk. He walked past her and then turned back as she closed the door behind them. He pointed down the corridor with a questioning gesture, indicating the kitchen. She nodded and so he continued down the corridor and entered the hub of the house. Darren politely stood and waited until the lady of the house bid him to sit. Choosing the closest chair, he sat at the table.

"Cup of tea?" Anne enquired.

"Err, yeah, please. Is she gonna be that long?"

"Probably, she's trying to impress, you know."

He looked a little embarrassed. Darren, trying to be the gentleman, also bearing in mind he was speaking to the girl's mother said, "She doesn't need to, I'm more than impressed anyway."

Anne looked at him quite hard. This time, he felt like he was being examined and analysed, whereas last time, everything seemed breezy.

He asked, "Is everything OK?"

Anne continued to put the kettle on and then set out three mugs. She put the tea bags in the mugs and stood the milk, ready on the counter top. Once done, she turned to him and again, gave him that stern look.

At six-foot four, he was normally the one who put others on their guard. However, in this instance, it was him who felt intimidated. Suddenly, Anne sat in front of Darren on the next chair. Despite looking down, he felt small.

"She likes you, in fact I would say, she likes you more than anybody else that's taken her out." Darren was already getting where this was going and felt his face flush as he went red. "What exactly are you doing with my daughter, more specifically, what are your intentions?"

The feeling he had was as though he was quarry, a bit like a rabbit staring at a pair of oncoming headlights. Anne persisted with the emotional pressure. Taking in a small breath, giving himself the room to think this out, he replied, "Anne, I know why you're asking this and to be honest, all I can say is that my intentions are honourable, but what I can't tell you is how we'll end up. I have no intention of hurting her.

As things stand, I want to make something of it, but if I have a potential wicked mother-in-law on my case, it will make things a damned sight harder."

Leaning back from her aggressive stoop, Anne blinked. "She's my daughter and she's not the easiest to get on with, I know that. But, I love her to bits and don't want to see her get upset."

It was then that Darren realised that he had been sweating. Christ, that woman's intimidating. Anne gave him another one of her condescending looks and set about finishing the tea. As she put it on to the table, Sophie walked in. She had a leather jacket on and jeans, instead of the usual leathers, but she still had her boots on.

"So, what were you two talking about?"

"I said that we would get two camels and a mule for you in Saudi, whereas he said we would get three camels."

Looking over at Anne, Darren looked shocked. "You didn't tell me you were offered a mule! I would have accepted a mule."

Anne retorted, "Typical man, doesn't listen." And she got up again and made Sophie's mug of tea.

As the mug was placed in front of her, Sophie said, with a touch of disdain, "You gave him the warning talk, didn't you?"

Anne looked a little uncomfortable. Sophie slurped the tea. Darren was about to speak, to calm the obviously choppy waters, when both women looked at him. Presently, it didn't seem like a good idea.

Anne said, with a hint of an apology, "You're my princess you know."

The curt reply was "A princess almost in her forties". The rest of the mug of tea was drank in silence. When they had finished, they all stood up. The two women glared at each other.

Darren suddenly hugged Anne and said, "It's OK, I'll be fine."

Anne tilted her head back and grinned, then play punched him. "Go on out, the two of you."

As the two of them walked down the corridor, Darren said, "I can't believe your own mother said you look like a mule."

Sophie, half smiling said, "That's funny, cos you sound like an ass. So, where are we going tonight?" Sophie enquired.

"I thought we would head out to eat al fresco and see the city lights," he answered. With a hint of humorous sarcasm, Sophie said, "You mean we're going for fish and chips on Redcar seafront, don't cha."

Darren, looking a little sheepish, followed her out of the front door. As she walked to the garage she loudly added "Ever the romantic!" Darren quietly stalked back to his bike and put his gear on.

This time, Sophie led the way. She went along the A171, through Brotton and down the hill to Saltburn. They went up Saltburn Bank and followed the road to Marske, then along the coastal road to Redcar. Finding a spot to park wasn't that difficult these days. The time of the video arcades had passed, with the advent of the home gaming stations and computers. Despite the council's best efforts in renewing the seafront, Redcar was dying. The town's demise did not detract from the beauty of the flat beach in front of them. The promenade faced east. Any ideas of watching a romantic sunset wasn't a possibility, so they just sat on the benches, overlooking the calm sea, while they ate their fish and chips as the light faded. There were noises of traffic behind them, as well as the usual goings on of a small town, but somehow, it was peaceful. Maybe it wasn't so much the place, but more of who they were with. There was a connection between the two of them. Neither really felt the need to go out of their way to impress the other, but they did anyway, which made the effort more pleasurable. Perhaps it was their age, but there was no urgency or sense of immediacy. This meant that they could just be. Eventually, the light pleasant breeze became colder and after trying to warm up by cuddling in, they gave it up and made up their minds to go home. The ride back was a steady affair, no rushing or pushing the speed zones, just a nice steady pace so they could take in their surroundings.

CHAPTER 12

07/08/17

Malika was tired, surprisingly so. Perhaps it was his age. It was Monday night. He had chased the staff out again and was sat in the semi-dark. He debated about having half a glass of wine, but thought better of it. If he felt tired now, a little wine wouldn't help. He mulled over the events of yesterday. He knew that the others felt defiant, and he supposed he did too. He could understand why Muhammad would; after all, it had been him who had been thrown about and it was his bike that had been damaged. Brendan would be annoyed because, essentially, the club was his baby and the other mystery club was interfering.

He didn't really know why he was sat here in the restaurant – he could do the same at home. Perhaps it reminded him of his father and how they had worked together, to set the place up. Then, after his dad had died, he had worked with Saavi. They had spent most of their time here. His dad had wanted a grandson, but when he realised that none were forthcoming, he decided to make the business his legacy. Malika sighed and looked into the darkness. He felt despondent. The light from the dying embers of the sun shone through the half-closed blinds. Specks of dust hung in the air, intensifying the feelings of stillness. He could hear noises from outside. He guessed that there were teenagers with skateboards outside. The rolling sounds of hard wheels on the paving passed his window every few minutes. The youths seemed to be taking advantage of the absence of pedestrians. There was little traffic. Occasionally, there would be a few shouts and then some laughter. He couldn't hear what was said, from inside the restaurant, but to be honest, he didn't take much notice. Sitting a while longer, he didn't do too much thinking and just absorbed the imagined aura of his late father and his wife. He decided that he didn't really care too much for the place, just the memories.

The noises of the teens outside had died to nothing and so he sat in silence. When the street lights finally came on, he decided it was time to make a move. He couldn't sit here all night. Standing up, he stretched and then walked to the rear of the premises. He looked at the backyard. He secured the tops of the wheelie bins and picked up a couple of cigarette butts. He thought to himself 'I'm gonna have to have a word with that damned chef!' Annoyed, he put the butt ends into the bin and then went inside to wash his hands. He put a few pots and pans away, which should have been done by the staff. Muttering to himself that he was too soft a manager. Completing those tasks, he then went around the windows and locked them or made them otherwise secure. He locked the back door and then went around each room and switched the lights off. The main room was already off, to let other potential customers know that they were shut.

Again, he found himself in the main restaurant. The light had changed from sunset to streetlight. The sense of stillness was more acute and he felt a pang of emotion. He missed her more than he dared admit. He was in a paradox, he didn't want to think of her, erstwhile he would be upset, but then again, he felt that he had to think of her or he might forget about her. A small lump arose in his throat. He wouldn't succumb. He had done enough grieving. Taking a gasp of air, whilst trying to calm himself, he regained his composure. He was glad that he was on his own. He didn't want people to witness episodes such as this. Shaking himself, he went behind the counter and set the alarm. The beeping was loud and intermittent. He had one minute to get out of the door and to lock up. Where had he put those damned keys? Quickly rummaging around he managed to find them. Picking them up, he hurried to the door and stepped outside. He clicked the door shut and then fumbled with the keys. In doing so, he dropped them. "For crying out loud," he berated himself. Feeling as though he was in a movie, trying to stop a bomb, he eventually managed to find the right key. The gap between each beep was getting shorter, reminding him of the urgent need to lock up. The beeps had almost reached a crescendo, when suddenly they stopped. The blue light of the alarm system, above the door, flashed twice in succession and then all was silent. He pulled the key out of the slot and gave an inward sigh of relief. He hated it when that happened. He got himself into such a tizz and then panic would set in.

Taking three deep breaths, he regained his composure and then put the shop keys into his pocket. Now looking for his car keys, he searched his jacket. He finally located them and prepared to walk to the car, which was located on the other side of the street. As he set off he heard the, by now, familiar sound of a skateboard behind him. He turned and saw what he assumed to be a teenager go past. The youth pushed the board with one foot, while the other was on the board. The teen wore a hoodie, with the hood up, so the face could not be seen. He watched the skater go down the path, to the corner of the street. When the hoodie got there, he stopped, then skilfully flicked up the board. He turned to face Malika directly. Feeling suddenly nervous, Malika didn't want to stay and find out what might transpire next. He continued toward his car and as he did so, another similarly dressed individual came into view. This one, however, was on a bicycle, a BMX he believed, which was far too small for its rider. The 'cyclist' stopped near Malika's car. 'Trouble, what the hell am I going to do now?' thought Malika.

The youth on the bike shouted over to Malika, while cocking his head to indicate the Mercedes, "Nice car, mate, not bad for a rag 'ead."

At that moment, a blue flashing light came into view, and both youths ducked down besides cars nearest them. Malika attempted to flag the car down, but it passed at speed, not noticing the panicked Indian. It seemed it was on an emergency call and had no time to stop. Disheartened, Malika put his hands down and as he did so, the youths stood up to reveal themselves once more. The sound of the skateboard hitting the floor, announced the fact that the hyenas were closing in.

❁❁❁

Brendan had finished work at five and he had felt tired. Looking at the computer screen all day had given him a headache. He was sick of looking at PAYE, National Insurance and the HMRC. The only highlight had been the diversionary conversation with Valerie. The two of them seemed to be getting on a lot better lately, which made the working environment much more relaxed. They had even had lunch together, which had never happened before. He wasn't a hundred percent sure, but he thought that he might like her. Walking home, going down the bank from the marketplace, he felt a mental fatigue, but with the fresh air and the light exercise from the walk, he began to feel invigorated and the tiredness was beginning to lift. It was getting cool now; there were only a couple of hours of sunlight left. He wanted to have a word with Malika, to see how the research was coming on. He could have just nipped into the restaurant, but thought it wasn't right to mix club and work business. He had reprimanded himself for talking about the club to Valerie, but then again, she's just an employee, whereas Malika was an employer. Malika had the unfortunate responsibility of having to lead by example, so Brendan didn't want to make things awkward for him. He walked briskly along the same route that he always did and soon arrived home. It had only been a fifteen-minute walk and he hadn't gotten out of breath. The thought occurred to him that perhaps he wasn't in as bad a shape as he had assumed. Following his usual routine, he dealt with the mail, flicked the kettle on and set away his microwave meal. This time, he did it with a sense of urgency, wanting to be ready as quickly as possible to see Malika in Saltburn. Malika had said he would try to knock off early and let his manager shut up shop. Brendan soon had his meal and cuppa, then cleaned himself up before getting into his Cordura. Fully prepared, he gave himself a final check over. Mobile phone, wallet, change and kitchen roll for insects on his visor. He patted each area of this clothing relevant to the item as he mentally ticked off the list. Picking up his helmet, he walked into the backyard to get his bike out. As with all small spaces and large objects, he had a struggle getting the bike into the back alley. Leaving the bike on its stand, he went through the lock up routine in his head, to make sure the house was secure and then put on his helmet and gloves. A minute later, he pulled out of the alley way and began the journey to Saltburn.

Brendan didn't hurry. He made a point of enjoying the scenery as he tootled along. Riding North-west, the sun was quite low, which made it difficult to see, after he crested the hill at Brotton. He flicked down the shades in the helmet and averted his gaze slightly, away from the deep orange hue. The going to the coast was all downhill from here. He relaxed and let the engine lazily tick over. The odd car passed him, some a little too close for comfort, but in this mood, he wasn't bothered. Once he got to the short piece of road, that ran parallel to the beach, he prepared himself for the steep bank that was to come. Saltburn Bank, with its three tight hairpins, has seen many bikes topple so it requires a good amount of concentration, even for those with many years of experience. Uneventfully, he climbed the bank and finally arrived at the large Victorian terrace house that was Malika's home. It was a neat house, double glazed with wooden frames instead of the usual PVC, to ensure the property was in keeping with the surrounding homes. A modernity that retained its past. It wasn't a particularly ostentatious property, but its location was an aspirational neighbourhood, which had an obvious wealth that was subtly understated.

Dismounting his bike, Brendan walked up the path and knocked on the door. He waited, but could see no movement. He stood for a minute or two, when suddenly a head popped up behind the neighbour's fence. "Hello," announced the new face. It wasn't smiling, despite the cheery tone, which indicated the greeting was forced.

"Hello," responded Brendan. "I've come to see Malika; do you know if he's in?"

Slightly surprised that the person was known to his neighbour, new face curtly said, "Car's not here, so he mustn't be in."

Looking down the path, where his bike was parked, Brendan realised that he had missed the obvious. He looked back at the face and said, "You know what, I didn't even notice." Brendan smiled in a self-deprecating way, trying to make light of the situation. The face didn't seem impressed and didn't return the smile. Feeling a little uncomfortable and out of place, he asked "Can you do me a favour please, when he turns up, if you see him of course, can you tell him that Brendan's been, thanks."

The face gave a little nod, but didn't answer. Feeling the gaze of the face following him as he went down the path, he returned to his bike. He put his helmet and gloves on and started the bike. He turned to wave his thanks to the face, but the face had gone already. Pushing off, Brendan made his way back to Loftus the same way that he had come.

Malika had said that he was going to knock off early and he was sure that he hadn't seen Malika's car on the way back, so he thought he would go to the restaurant. He cut through the night, along Loftus high street, the beam from his headlight bouncing off the terrace house windows. The noise of his throbbing engine echoed off the buildings. Typically, the traffic lights changed to red at the crossroads. He sat waiting for them to change. No traffic came from any direction. 'Why the hell do they do that?' he thought with frustration. Once they turned green, he set off up the bank that he had walked down earlier and finally arrived at the marketplace.

On a right-hand corner, he saw a youth in a hoodie and on his side of the road, he was sure that he saw Malika. Glancing toward the restaurant, he saw that it was in darkness, which confirmed that the figure he saw was Malika. He turned the bike in the direction of his friend and pulled up a couple of spaces away from Malika's car. As he did so, he noticed another hoodie in front of Malika. The immediate thought was that intimidation was the intent of these figures and his friend needed help. He thought it might be a good idea to keep his helmet on. As he dismounted the bike, he saw Malika's face – it wore an expression of relief. As it was dark, the two hoodies looked more menacing than they probably were. Somehow, their faces always seemed to be in the shadows, making recognition impossible. Brendan was in his leathers and kept his helmet on, so was well armoured against any possible attack, but that left Malika vulnerable. The yob with the bike, dropped it and then walked to the side of the car toward Malika, just as the skateboard yob crossed the road. Despite Malika's look towards Brendan, the thugs hadn't realised that Brendan was here to help the Indian.

Malika stepped back and came up against his car. Then, to the yobs' surprise, Malika went into a martial arts stance. This was a last ditch effort on Malika's part; he was cornered. It had been a long time since he trained in the art of Kalaripayattu. The last time he had competed must have been at least thirty years ago.

Bike thug, suddenly wary of this unexpected development, stepped back and said with sarcasm, "Whoa, who's this, the turbanator?"

Skateboard giggled like a girl, Bike looked at him to be quiet. Malika's heart rate was going ten to the dozen. 'Any time, Brendan' Malika thought, wondering where his friend was. Just as he thought it, a bus came up the hill, into the marketplace, lighting the whole area. Both hoodies diverted their faces away from the light, to prevent recognition and to retain night vision. The bus came to its stop, but then immediately set off, as the driver didn't see any waiting passengers. Darkness swiftly returned and so did the attention of the thugs. Bike yob took a light step toward Malika, probing his defences, seeing how he would react. Worryingly for the yob, Malika didn't show any sign of nerves. As the yob assessed the situation, his friend yelled at him and pointed down the road.

About a hundred yards away, Brendan had put the yob's bike on its stand, in the middle of the road, at such an angle that when the next vehicle came around the corner, the bike would be hit. Brendan walked onto the path near the bike and leant against the wall, awaiting its destruction. Then he gave them the middle finger. As he expected, they both came toward him, away from Malika. He readied himself for the oncoming onslaught. Both yobs hurried over to Brendan, clearly worried about the bike and its location. When they got closer, Biker yob told skateboard to retrieve his transport, while he confronted Brendan.

"Think yer clever, mate?"

The youth spread his arms and walked toward Brendan with his shoulders back, chest forward and a bobbing head, snarling and trying to intimidate. Through his helmet, Brendan was trying not to laugh and then wound him up by imitating him in an exaggerated manner. As the confrontation went on, skateboard had moved the BMX bike to the other side of the road, out of the reach of Brendan. Seeing that the yobs were now trying to carry out a pincer movement, Brendan thought that it might be a good idea to make a move. It was now obvious that skateboard was the minion in the pairing and biker boy was the lead. Brendan decided that when dealing with a snake, the best option was to cut off its head, so aimed for biker boy first.

Biker maintained his wide stance, whilst at the same time he shuffled forward to close the distance on his intended victim. Brendan thought to himself that the idiot in front of him hadn't had any training and his first impression was correct, he was simply a thug. Narrowing his stance, to reduce his target area, Brendan prepared to strike. Skater boy was also closing the distance between them, which increased the urgency of a decision as to when to strike. A car, suddenly and unexpectedly, came over the hill. This distracted biker momentarily, who was concerned about being recognised. He turned his face away from the oncoming lights. Brendan, using the opportunity, struck. He toe-punched the yob in the groin, who immediately dropped to his knees. As biker fell, he followed through with another kick on the side of the injured teen's head. Brendan could see that biker was unconscious before he hit the floor. Brendan turned quickly, fully expecting some sort of attack from skateboard. But to his surprise, Malika held him in a choke hold on the floor.

Looking up at Brendan, with a wide grin, he said, "Hey, I'm not as strong or as fast as I used to be, but I'm still faster and stronger than this dingbat."

Brendan returned the smile, relieved that his friend was OK. He turned back to the prostate yob on the floor, took off his gloves and checked his pulse. Brendan focussed his attention on the yob who was still in a chokehold.

"So, what's the crack, what's all this about?" he asked.

At first there was silence, but after a few helpful squeezes of his neck, by the Indian, he began to talk. "Our dealers said they would write off our debts and give us fifty quid, if we gave the Indian a slap and a scare."

Brendan and Malika looked at each other, concerned.

"Your dealer, who is he?" probed Brendan.

"I don't know his name, but I know he's a biker, like you lot."

The Angels understood what that meant. The mysterious bikers were putting pressure on them, without showing themselves directly. Malika let the yob stand up.

"Listen to me, young man." Brendan was surprised that the yob did. "We will let you go and we won't tell the police or anyone else what happened, but you mustn't either. Besides, it won't look good if it gets out that you got your arse kicked by an old 'rag 'ead'. You can tell your dealer that you gave us a hard time."

The yob nodded, grateful to get off so lightly. The yob went over to the bike he had put on the far path and with the skateboard, put both on the other side of the wall, so they were out of sight. He then struggled to pick his mate up, who was, by now, beginning to regain consciousness. The two of them hobbled down the bank, away from the marketplace.

Now that the immediate crisis was over, Brendan removed his helmet and walked with his friend, back to the car. As they walked, they discussed the new information that they had just gathered. Malika voiced the obvious.

"Well, it seems, for whatever reason, this gang is worried about us; the problem we have, is trying to work out what they are worried about!"

Brendan nodded his agreement of the assessment and said, "We'll have to think about this and not for too long – the heat seems to be getting turned up." After a pause, Brendan suggested, "Why don't you come and stay at my place, it's just down the road and we can discuss it over a drink?"

Malika said, "You know, I was thinking of having a glass of wine earlier, what the hell."

Malika followed Brendan down the bank from the marketplace and when they reached the traffic lights, they turned up the final bank. Brendan's house was on the left. Opposite Brendan's house, running parallel with the wall that separated the public garden from the street, were parking spaces. Malika found a spot and got out of the car. Meanwhile, Brendan rode further up the road, so he could access the back alley behind his house. After a couple of minutes, a light went on in one of the houses and so Malika walked toward it. The door opened and Brendan, who was in the process of taking his helmet off, gestured for Malika to enter. A muffled "Make yourself comfortable" came through the helmet. Brendan went to the back of the house, with his helmet finally removed, and he began to sort his bike out.

Malika walked into the spartan house. This place had never had a good clean, he thought. Although everything was neat and tidy, contrary to the habits of most bachelors, the house, however, was still essentially bare and dusty. He entered the living room. There was a two-piece suite, as in, two, two-seater settees, and a large leather easy chair, probably a lazy boy. In the corner was a neat office set-up with a computer, printer and other paraphernalia. The TV, usually a talking point in a male's house, wasn't that large or special. It seemed that Brendan wasn't ostentatious at all. He didn't have a car – what would be the point, working so close by – which meant the bike was his private transport; this suggested that the man was pragmatic. Having glanced around the living room, he made his way to the kitchen, which was the next adjoining room. It too was austere, but practical. As he entered, so did Brendan, from the backyard. He had taken off his bike gear, down to the waist and as he entered he smiled at Malika.

"Right, food, coffee and then a drink, what do you reckon?"

"Sounds good to me," responded the Indian.

Brendan asked what Malika wanted and they settled on pre-frozen chicken and chips. Brendan put the kettle on and prepared the cups.

"Right, while that's boiling, I'll get changed, I'll be five minutes."

Nodding, Malika sat at the kitchen table. As he did so, he took his coat off and hung it on the back of the seat. When sitting, he realised that he missed having company and talking to someone. Normally, the only contact he had with people was at work or in the semi-formal meetings of the club. Brendan reappeared. "We'll skip the coffee," he said, brandishing a bottle of red. It would be another half an hour or so before the food was cooked, so Brendan parked up at the table and they drank a Malbec while they waited.

"So," began Malika, "it seems that, like me, you're not from round here – how did you end up in Loftus?"

Taking a sip of wine, Brendan said, "I'm from London, Putney, to be specific." Pausing for a moment, he glanced at Malika. Brendan had already decided he was going to tell him what had happened. "My brother, older brother Josh, was a bit of a bad lad. I was in awe of him, as most younger siblings are and I generally went along with whatever he did and said." Again, Brendan paused; he was deep in thought about his past and Malika could see that he was reliving the experience as he talked. "Well, anyway, I was about thirteen when I went along with

Josh's gang. I didn't know what they were doing or anything like that. Just being with them made me feel pretty good, as you would expect at that age," said Brendan, explaining the justification for the actions he was about to relate.

Malika nodded, following the story.

"Well," continued Brendan, "Josh and his gang, cutting a long story short, asked me to look out for the police on a street corner, which, of course, I did. They all went down the street. It was dark and I couldn't see what was going on, but I heard a lot of yelling and shouting. Then after about a minute or so, the whole gang ran past me." Taking a sip of wine and focussing his eyes, it looked as though he was viewing the scene unfold around him as it happened. Bringing himself back to the present, he continued, "Everyone had passed and hadn't said a word to me, so there I am, stood wondering what was going on. So, I decided to run after them. As we ran, I fell further back, being the smallest. By now, there were flashing blue lights and as I was at the back, I was the first to be picked by the police. I was taken to the station and questioned. Of course, I couldn't answer any questions and so looked guilty of something, but I didn't know what. It later transpired that my brother and his gang had gone on a hunt for a gang member from another area, had found him, then stabbed him." Even though he ran the scenario a thousand times through his head, he still couldn't grasp it. "Anyway, my brother and a couple of others got sent down for it and I was let off. My parents went mad at my brother for dragging me into it, as you can imagine. I was told to buckle down and get grades, so that I would escape that kind of life. I ended up at college and got an accountancy degree and after one job and another, I ended up here."

Brendan had needed to tell someone for years; it was cathartic. He knew that what had happened wasn't his fault, but despite his age at the time, or more likely because of it, he had always felt guilty.

Malika sat quietly. He looked at his friend and took a sip of alcohol. "Nice house by the way." The feigned irreverence of what he had just said made Brendan grin. Malika smiled and asked, "So, do you still talk to your family and have you made up with your brother?"

Brendan looked a little pained. "No, I haven't talked to my brother since Dad died eight years ago and he lives with my mother, so going to see her, which I do on her birthday, is a bit tense, to say the least."

The older man put his glass down and stared at Brendan. "Life is too short, you know," he said, with a tinge of regret, but didn't expand on it.

A ding resounded. Brendan got up and went to the oven. He opened the door and peered inside to see the condition of the food. He pulled out the chips and moved them around a bit, so they would cook more evenly and put the chicken onto a lower shelf. He then reset the oven for a further ten minutes and sat back down.

"Well, what about you?"

Malika told him the story of his father and his wife and how they couldn't have children. He explained how his father wanted a legacy, which Malika didn't provide for him, and the sense of disappointment his father had held. "That's something I will have to live with until I die."

Brendan shook his head. "No, that's something your father had to live with, not you."

His friend smiled wanly and said, "Still doesn't feel right though."

Brendan shrugged his shoulders and said philosophically, "No-one can answer that, except you."

CHAPTER 13

09/08/17

The garage was quiet, the only noise was the clanking of Mike's spanner against the underside of the car. He was busy removing the exhaust on a customer's car. His neck ached a little from having to look upward. Resting for a moment, he rubbed the nape of his neck to relax the muscles. Finally feeling the relief in his neck, he continued with the task at hand. After about ten minutes, he had managed to take the whole exhaust off. He examined it and decided he could save the catalytic convertor, but the other two parts would have to be replaced. Setting aside the convertor, he picked up the other two parts and put them into the scrap bin at the other side of the garage. He then took off the plastic gloves that he was wearing and washed his hands. He retrieved the previously ordered parts from the backroom and put them on the lift, so they could be conveniently retrieved when they were needed. Going back into the storeroom he got some bolts and copper grease and went back to work under the car, replacing the old parts. Other than the sounds of his actions, the garage was silent. Minutes later, he wasn't quite sure how long exactly because of his focussed attention, he heard two motorcycles pull up outside of the building. He reckoned they were Harley Davidsons. That's weird, he thought. He didn't know anyone with a Harley, let alone two people. Shortly after, perhaps ten seconds, there was silence again. Thinking they had gone he returned his attention to the work at hand. Mike, if anything, was fastidious. Each bolt was greased, as was each gasket between each part of the exhaust. He then started to put each part onto the car. As he ratchetted the last bolt, he heard a movement within the garage. With his autism, he felt it very hard not to complete a task and so he chose to ignore the sound until the torque wrench clicked to say that he had tightened the bolt to the correct tension. As he finished, a voice, right next to him, suddenly broke the silence. "Good job!"

The proximity of the voice made him jump. As he stepped back in the enclosed space, under the lift, another voice said, "Yeah, it is, very professional."

The first voice said, "Not many places go to those lengths these days, normally it's bish, bash, bosh, gimme your dosh!"

Mike stood silently, not sure what to do. The two individuals walked away from the lift. Each went to the opposite sides of the work area. As they did so, Mike came out from under the car. He watched them move around. He had difficulties conveying emotions, but that didn't mean he couldn't read or feel them. He could sense the menace in these people and it wasn't the disgruntled teenager type of aggression. It was the kind, where no matter what you said or did, violence was an inevitability. Mike stood at the side of the car lift, with a spanner in his hand. It was only a small spanner and wouldn't serve as a weapon. He was stuck as to what to do. Essentially, he was defenceless and the only viable item that he could use, was near one of the bikers. He thought, logically, the best course of action would be to talk, some form of diplomacy. The only problem being his autism. Diplomacy would involve trying to find some common ground and then negotiation, preferably where there would be a win-win situation. He had no idea where to begin. Logic dictated that he would have to ask them what they wanted and why they were here.

"So, gentlemen," he said loudly. "How can I help you?"

They didn't even acknowledge him. This wasn't going so well. He needed to establish communication; to do that, he had to get their attention. "Are you the two gentlemen that roughed up Muhammad the other day?"

That got their attention. They both stopped their mooching and turned to face him. They closed the distance. Neither made an overtly aggressive gesture, but were clearly confident in themselves. The slightly bigger one, on Mike's right, asked, in a curt tone, "What of it?"

"My response to that is, why?" His following of logic had gotten him a reaction, so now he awaited a response. He had found a common ground, even though it was one-sided and entailed the use of aggression on their part; nonetheless, it was still working. Next, he had to work out how he was going to negotiate. He had to be able to have or have access to something that they require. Given the probable lifestyle and his juxtaposition to the said lifestyle, this may prove to be difficult. Falling back onto logic again, he said, "So, what exactly do you want now, can I help you with anything?" He spoke in monotone; this was his normal speech, but they inferred a hint of sarcasm.

The smaller of the two had long greasy hair and what appeared to be a three-day old stubble. The bigger, also had long greasy hair, but he was clean shaven. They both sported a large assortment of tattoos. Suddenly appearing to lose interest, the shorter one snorted, turned and walked back towards the side of the garage, where he had been looking earlier. The bigger one, with a backward glance at Mike, equally nonchalant, brushed past him and followed his companion. Mike realised that they didn't consider him a threat in the slightest and had made a point of dismissing him out of hand.

The smaller one pointed at the covering that protected Mike's father's bike. Mike began to panic. His stomach was now roiling. As he watched, the two bikers grabbed the cover and lifted it up, revealing the Bellisima. The condition of the machine took both bikers by surprise. The smaller one looked at the taller and whispered, "Wow, she's a beauty." They let the cover drop and then stood back to admire the Italian artwork. Mike, was by now, raging inside. He could feel himself working into a frenzy. He was almost on the verge of having a meltdown. Inside his head, he was repeating the mantra 'this is not good, this is not good'. Physically, he was rooted to the spot. His face contorted as he fought to keep control. He tried to slow his breathing, which helped, taking the edge off. He started to engage his logical thinking again. 'They're just looking, that's all,' he thought. He repeated this new mantra to himself, whilst his breathing came under control. He managed to calm down so he could deal with the reality at hand. Completely unaware of the thought processes that had been going on behind them, both bikers turned and looked at Mike. The smaller one said with genuine respect, "That's some bike you have there."

The coastal wind was picking up as Darren and Sophie made their way down the road from Redcar to Marske. Autumn was on its way, Sophie thought as the gusts cut through her leathers. 'Next time it'll be an extra layer.' Darren was in front; she thought about him too. There was something about him that was different from the others she had met. She could tell that he harboured deep feelings and probably meant it, when they spoke to each other in the loving way that new couples tend to. But, there did seem to be a sense of loneliness about him too. A sort of stand-offishness, not quite aloof, more of a distrust. Despite this, she felt comfortable with him and enjoyed his company. This time she didn't feel the need to act, to fit in with a given situation; everything was easy and natural. She just liked being with him. Every now and again, she had butterflies and her stomach churned, something she hadn't experienced before. She tried her best to supress this new phenomenon for her own protection.

Because of her disability, men tended to be overly sympathetic and tried too hard. This became tiresome. They were thinking of her problems and not her. Then you had the other end of the spectrum, where it seemed they went out with her for a bet. In public, these men were great, but in private, she became a second-class citizen. Neither were conducive for any kind of relationship. Darren, however, obviously took her disability into consideration, but otherwise it came across as being none of his business, in the same way as a menstrual cycle. She smirked to herself with the thought: 'God, I'm a rough chavvy bitch, her mother was right, what the hell does he see in me?'

As they made their way through Marske, they negotiated the speed bumps, which were irritatingly minimally marked and then began the climb up the small hill to the roundabout that led to Marske Road, which in turn took them to Saltburn. She looked at the old coble boat that had been turned into a garden feature as they entered Saltburn properly and smiled; she had always liked that, but that was her all over, she liked being different. Slowly, they descended Saltburn Bank and motored up the windy bank that ran along behind Hummersea cliffs. Eventually, they reached Brotton high street, turned left and finished the climb to their highest point, before descending the bank to Carlin How.

Carlin How was an old coal and steel village, way past its heyday. Skinningrove Steel Works sits across the road from the main housing, which consists of rows of terraced dwellings. The name of the steel works was unfortunate – it referred to the fishing village in the valley below, where its jetty, which was used for transport, was situated. The steel works is a shadow of its former self, its main claim to fame being a provider of materials for the British Navy's HMS Queen Elizabeth. The imposing factory dominates the area. Its grubbiness and rough exterior was a physical reflection of the financial dire straits the district found itself in. This was unfortunate as the surrounding area was blessed with outstanding natural beauty.

The two lovebirds slowed to thirty miles per hour as they went through the village and then descended the steep Carlin How Bank. They passed the scrapyard on the left and slowed further for the hairpin. Having got round the bend, the road, although steep, curved in a long lazy arc, that allowed for acceleration back up the other side of the valley. The bank up to Loftus was equally as steep as the one they had come down, but with the added pace, was easily climbed. They entered Loftus properly. They were immediately greeted with more terraced houses on the left and allotments on the right. Like Carlin How, Loftus is a grubby looking place that has always seemed run down. One of those places that had never had a chance of reaching its potential. It was too far out of the way to be metropolitan, but was on a main tourist route to Whitby and the North Yorkshire Moors. Despite the potential of passing trade, Loftus was never able to capitalise, because of a lack of investment. The two of them passed Muhammad's parents' shop, which was in the first line of terraces and then they went to pass Mike's garage on the right. Looking at the clock on his dashboard, Darren noticed that it was after eight o'clock. Mike was known to be a late worker, but not this late. Frowning, he looked back towards the garage again. He was sure that he had seen two bikes parked outside the garage. They looked like big ones, the type used by biker gangs. He continued up the road and then indicated off and turned the corner towards the community centre. He pulled up without going into the carpark. Sophie soon pulled up along-side. She flipped her front visor up and asked what was wrong.

"Mike's light is on in the garage; it isn't normally on this late."

"So, he's just working late," she responded.

"I saw two bikes outside of the garage, two big bikes, do you know what I mean?" he said with concern. She looked at him sternly. He continued, "It could mean trouble."

She considered what he'd said and then proposed that they go back and look. Looking worried, Darren said, "Right, this is what we'll do. When we both arrive outside of the garage, I'll go in and check and you listen out for anything. If there's any noise or commotion, call the police."

She smiled wanly. "This is bike business, there's no time for chivalry, which I do appreciate and I don't want to argue about equality etc, so we will do this together, end of."

It clearly was. Darren looked doubtful and apprehensive at the same time. He nodded reluctantly.

They put their visors back down and headed back towards the garage. Going down the street as quietly as they could, so as not to draw attention to themselves, they turned off onto the side road next to the garage. Turning off their engines, they sat for a minute, listening out for any indication of what was happening inside, hoping they still had the element of surprise. As no-one made an appearance, they dismounted the bikes. Darren put his hand up as Sophie went to take her helmet off. He shook his head and signalled for her to keep it on. She nodded and refastened it. They both walked toward the chink of light that came from the slightly ajar door. Looking in, they tried to see what was going on inside. They saw Mike's back – he was stood next to the car lift –and just at his side were the two owners of the bikes outside. The two bikers stood next to an old renovated bike and were seemingly talking about it to Mike. The double doors creaked open about two feet. The three occupants of the garage, Mike and the two bikers, all turned and looked.

Sophie hobbled in, lifting her visor and said in a chirpy voice, "Hiya Mike, how's it going?"

Looking a little relieved, Mike gave her a smile. He thought, 'Well, at least I'll have witness to the carryings on.'

Sophie came over and put her hand on his shoulder and gave him a peck on the cheek. One of the bikers, the taller one, quipped "Girlfriend?". Embarrassed, Mike looked down and went red.

"No, he's not my boyfriend, he is." She pointed back towards the door, when Darren walked in. He stood, easily six inches above the taller biker. Both bikers looked a little hesitant; this was now a wholly different scenario from what they had planned.

Darren nonchalantly walked over to the bikers and held his hand out in a friendly gesture. The taller one took it and attempted to give a 'man clasp' and tried to squeeze hard. Darren returned the favour, only harder. When they both withdrew their hands, it was obvious who had won the silent competition. The biker managed not to wince, but there was a slight involuntary contortion to his face, which belied the pain. For a few moments, there was silence. The bikers, considering the change of circumstances, were now having to reassess the situation. They still had to maintain an aura of intimidation, only now they would be conveyors of a message, rather than simply bullies.

"So, what you been doin' this late, Mike?" asked Sophie.

Caught slightly off guard, Mike stammered a response. "I was working a bit late, just catching up with a customer's car, when these two err… gentlemen turned up."

"OK, why don't Darren and I look after these gentlemen, while you pack up – that way you can get sorted quicker."

Mike looked at her with a worried expression. He then said, in a slightly hushed voice, "These are the guys that assaulted Muhammad, I asked them earlier and they sort of confirmed it."

This time Darren spoke: "Well, this changes thing a bit, doesn't it."

Desperately trying to find an opportunity to reassert himself, the taller of the bikers said with what seemed to be forced menace, "Listen, mate." The 'mate' was almost spat out. "This is our territory and we dictate what goes on around 'ere."

Our three heroes all looked at each other, perplexed.

Sophie said incredulously, "Your territory, what the hell's that supposed to mean?"

Tall biker, looking equally perplexed by their lack of understanding of the obvious, gave it a moment's thought. It was then he believed he understood what the problem was. With the realisation, he said with a smile, "Let me take the time to explain something to you. There are different types of bikers. There is an unwritten code that they all comply with. Firstly, there is the hierarchy. At the top, are the one-percenters, us. We dictate what everyone else does; then there are the support groups, which essentially make up the numbers; then there are the 'Weekend Warriors', who aren't really clubs as such, but individuals with no associations and just go out for rides with mates etc. The one-percenters are known as MCs and the others are known as MCCs;

differentiation is important."

Mike interjected and said, "Legally, you have no right to stop us from doing anything we want."

Darren and Sophie nodded their agreement, both of whom had folded their arms, looked at the bikers and awaited a response.

The biker smiled. "Legally, as you put it, you are correct. Bikers are anarchists and operate outside of mainstream society. So, they operate using their own rules."

At this, the three became concerned. Mike, again, asked the question that the others were thinking. "So, how do we know when we transgress and who would we see about it anyway?"

Again, the wry smile accompanied his answer. "You will have to see your local one-percenters, who will give you clearance on your colours – that's the badge you use and where you can operate. You also have to ask permission before entering another MC's territory."

Mike, having listened carefully, gave a pointed observation. "This makes no sense at all. You're telling me that bikers, particularly the one-percenters, operate as an antithesis to society and shun the purported oppression. Yet, you and your cronies dictate without redress as you see fit. That makes you the oppressors. Social laws are meant to protect those that reside in the same society. Surely, if you feel repressed, then your rules must be more encompassing, not aggressive or vindictive?"

Lost for an answer, the biker simply shrugged. By means of explanation, as limp as it was, he said, "That's the way it has always been and if you want to be part of this world of ours, you will have to comply."

Sophie, with contempt, observed, "Ok, I get where you're coming from, essentially you're a type of mafia. I'm just curious as to why you attacked our friend and why you're vainly trying to intimidate us now?"

Tall biker seemed uncomfortable at this, now that they were cornered. "We were enforcing the rules; as I said, you do not wear colours without permission and you certainly do not take group rides through someone else's territory without asking first." Although he did feel embarrassed by what he was implying, he looked and felt justified in saying it and it was also apparent, his belief in what he did, would mean that he would be happy to do it again.

Darren spoke. "For clarity, I take it, you mean the badge we have on our waistcoat, is what you mean by 'colours'."

The biker nodded.

"Ah, so what you're saying is that if we don't wear the waistcoats, we won't get the harassment."

Tall biker said sarcastically, "Simple, isn't it!"

Darren, with a hint of annoyance, retorted, "Only if you're told first."

Tall biker responded with "Would you have complied?".

Sophie came back immediately with "Probably not!".

Finally making his point, tall biker said, "There you go." Silence befell the cavernous garage.

Sophie broke the silence with another question. "So, what now. You've come and said your piece, you've made your veiled threat; does that mean you're going now?"

Trying his best to dominate the situation, tall biker said, "Well, are you going to comply with what I've said? You'll have to ask permission to do everything as bikers." Looking at the people around him, he asked, "Who's the boss here, the woman?" He said it with a contemptuous smirk. He fished around in a small pocket on the front of his waistcoat and fetched out a business card. He gave it to Sophie. "You will need this to contact the Secretary, to get an understanding of the rules and to be instructed as to what to do."

She pocketed the card without a second thought and then took a step forward and said, "I don't think so."

Darren took a step forward too. The actions weren't lost on the bikers.

"Well, it looks like we're at an impasse and that means you have a problem," said the tall biker, with a hint of menace. "Well, you see, the problem is that we have to be seen to have done something, to sort this sorry mess out. Usually it would mean that the people concerned would receive a good kicking. But, given that there is a cripple, a retard and a fat git, that wouldn't exactly help our credibility, if we carried it out." Pausing for effect and glancing around for a reaction, which he didn't get, he then continued. "So, I think we'll tax you instead."

Darren snorted. "Sunshine, you're overstating your abilities and how were you planning on taxing us?"

Looking expansively around the garage, tall biker said, "Well, this is quite neat and there are a lot of very cool tools about, which would be easy to flog, but that would be tedious and time consuming." He said all this, as though he could do as he wished. The three protagonists looked bemused. "However, we'll take the bike instead," he said, matter of fact. He patted the Bellisima next to him.

Mike was beside himself already and now that the bike had been mentioned directly, he was almost frozen on the spot. Sophie could see the panic in his eyes and put a reassuring hand on his shoulder. Although it did calm him slightly, she could feel him beginning to shake under his coveralls. She thought, 'Is he shaking with fear or anger – probably both?'

The smaller biker smiled at this and walked around the bike they expected to be taking ownership of. It was a nice bike, very basic and designed for running around cosmopolitan areas in Italy, in the fifties and sixties. It was quite rare, particularly in this condition. The bike's value wasn't the issue for Mike, it was his dad's. The sentimental value, to him, was beyond price.

"Yeah, we should get some decent dosh for this," said the smaller biker, genuinely impressed.

Taller biker announced it was time for them to leave with a "Right, OK" and proceeded to grab the handlebars and push it towards the doors. Sophie stepped in front of the bike to stop him going any further. It was then that things began to get a bit surreal.

Darren said sternly, "No! Let him have it."

Sophie glanced up at him; the look of disappointment and betrayal that came across her face made Darren feel guilty. Darren then turned to the biker who was pushing the Bellisima.

"Do you want the keys?" Darren asked with an even tone. Everyone in the place looked at Darren, stunned. "I can get the keys for you if you want – it would be a pity to have to wreck the ignition on such a nice bike. Besides, its value would be retained if it had less repairs."

Having heard this, the blood drained from Mike's face and Sophie was appalled. The two bikers, however, felt as though their message had finally gotten through to someone.

"Err yeah, it might be a good idea," said the taller biker. He put the bike back on its stand.

"Give me a moment and I'll go and get them." Darren sounded almost apologetic. He went to the office and rummaged around until he found the keys. While he was out of sight, he quickly wrote in a duplicating pad that was on the desk. Once done, he went back to the waiting bikers. Handing the keys over to the bemused biker he said, "Oh, can you give this message to your boss please. He'll be very interested in what it has to say."

With a look of contempt, maintaining the act of being an aggressor, he snatched the paper from Darren's hand and immediately stuffed it into his waistcoat pocket. Looking forgetful, Darren then quickly closed the distance to the biker and thrust his hand out for a handshake.

"I would like to thank you for not beating us up and to say it's been an honour to meet some genuine MC guys and thanks for the advice too."

Hesitantly and reluctantly, the biker shook his hand. Darren then stepped back and the bikers continued toward the door. Mike and Sophie were, by this time, overtly disgusted by Darren's actions and so just stood and watched in silence.

"By the way," shouted Darren. The two bikers turned to face him. "When can we expect the payment?"

"What?" said the taller biker.

"For the bike," prompted Darren.

Confused, the biker repeated, "What?"

With a smug look, Darren explained, "The paper you have just put in your pocket is a receipt for ten thousand pounds."

Tall biker retorted, "We're not paying ten thousand pounds."

"Oh, I think you are. Firstly, when you walked in, you were on CCTV. Secondly, we have just shook hands after I handed a piece of paper to you, as though a deal had just been made for the bike."

Coming to a complete stop, putting the bike on its stand, he faced Darren face on. "You have no proof of a sale at all." Darren looked even more smug, now that he had their attention. Glancing at his pocket, the biker fished out the piece of paper and opened it up. Sure enough, it was a roughly written receipt for ten thousand pounds.

"All I have to do is rip up this piece of paper and there will be no evidence."

Darren replied, "That is a copy of a receipt, number one rule in business is, keep a copy of everything. Also, the handing of the bike, keys and receipt was all done on CCTV." Darren pointed into the direction of a dark corner of the garage ceiling. They all looked, but couldn't make anything out, but there was no reason not to believe what he said.

The biker then said, "I can just go in the office and smash up the recorder, where will you be then?"

Expecting this response, Darren replied calmly, "The CCTV is live-streamed to ADT security services, there are no recorders on this site, for that very reason." Suddenly, the tables had been turned. Moving in for the kill, Darren said, "There are a couple of other things you haven't considered. How were you going to take the remaining bike?"

Replying with a feeble voice, "We'd just collect it later," the biker knew he was on to a loser, but persisted anyway.

Darren, now in the dominant position, stated: "This is what's going to happen if you take the bike. I will go to court to pursue the money. If you still don't cough up, I will engage the services of some bailiffs whom will no doubt be accompanied by the police, when they know who they will be collecting from and where it will be. This will be easily done, because you have given us the address."

By this time, Sophie was grinning broadly and was waving the card that she had been given earlier. Moving in with the coup de grâce, Darren said, "When you leave, your bike or his, whichever is left, will disappear. If you hadn't noticed, you're in a garage; it will be stripped in about two hours. If you think you could report it as stolen, you will see on the receipt, it was given in part-exchange and the V5 documents were to be given later." Darren held his hand out, waiting for the keys.

The biker stared at him. They had been outwitted, that was true, but they could always become violent; then again, they had the CCTV to consider. After a few seconds, Darren shook his hand, perhaps a little smugly, to remind the biker it was there and prompted, "You could still take it, but I have a funny feeling that being kicked out of your one-percenter club would be the least of your problems."

With obvious reluctance, the biker handed back the keys, leaving the bike where it stood and walked out. The sound of retreating engines faded into the night.

Mike looked at Darren and said, "I don't have a CCTV!"

Darren smiled at him and said, "They didn't know that!"

Sophie squealed and hugged her hero.

CHAPTER 14

13/08/17

It was a damp morning. It wasn't a very good day for tourism in North Yorkshire. At about ten AM, Darren and Sophie's bikes pulled up outside the Angel. Normally they would have sat and chatted awhile on the bikes, but with the weather and the seriousness of the impending meeting, they didn't hang around. Dismounting, they silently took off their helmets and went inside. The building was mostly in darkness, except for the bar lights. Customers weren't expected to start coming in for at least another hour for their Sunday meals. There was clattering in the back room, where the chef and his assistant were working, but other than that, all was quiet.

"I'll get the coffee machine out," said Sophie. This was to keep herself busy and to give her an excuse to look around the place.

As she wandered, Paul saw her. "Oh hi," he said in between yawns. He stretched his arms up. "You in for a meeting?" he asked.

"Yeah, just looking for the coffee machine."

He put his arms down. "You know when I said I wanted to sell up?"

She stopped what she was doing and looked at him intently, her interest suddenly focussed. "Yes," she said, her expression urging him to carry on.

"Well the brewery, who I bought the place off, said they would be willing to buy it back, with a ten-grand loss on my part. So, I'm putting it out there. If you know anyone who can rustle up the money to cover my losses, they can have it. I'm not bothered about a profit, I just don't want a load of debt around my neck when I go."

Sophie thought about what she was hearing. She could scrape fifty-grand herself from the money her dad had left her. She had another five-grand in a savings account and perhaps she could get a loan for the rest. She would ask Darren what he thought after the meeting. He's done business stuff before, so he might know where to look and what to do.

"Anyway..." Paul sighed as he walked away to get on with whatever he had to do.

She looked at him as he went; maybe, just maybe, she thought. She continued to look for the coffee beans and milk, having already located the machine. She took them through to the meeting room and then went back for the cups, flicking the light on as she went back out. As she left the room, she heard the front door open and shut, then the sound of Darren's voice greeting whom she assumed were two of the others. As she made her way to the bar to fetch some cups, she waved to Brendan and Malika, who returned the gesture. She arranged the chairs in the meeting room and then went back to the group at the front, which had grown in number, with the arrival of Mike. They chatted awhile about what had happened in the last week and decided that they were going to have to discuss the matter at length in the meeting. This wasn't to be for another fifteen minutes until Muhammad arrived. When he did arrive, he looked dishevelled and harassed.

"You know, I'm bloody sick, it's like my arm's been cut off without the bike."

Mike interjected and said, "It will be ready in two days. I had to wait for the plastics, they're very hard to get hold of."

Apologising, Muhammad said, "Sorry, mate, I wasn't having a go."

"Well it seems we are all here," said Brendan in a loud voice, to draw attention to himself and to calm the situation down. The group was tense with all the activities that had occurred over the last few days. Brendan acknowledged the stress that they were all under and said it might be a good idea to formalize any actions and comments to avoid further confusion and backbiting. "Right everyone, I think it might be a good idea to go in and settle down a bit and have a think about what we are going to do."

With that, the motley crew made their way behind the bar and filed into the now, bright and airy meeting room. Each of them took the seats they had taken on the first meeting. It seemed that the team had found their natural pecking order with each other and were comfortable with it; they had a good dynamic. The next thing came the coffee – each gave their order and Brendan duly passed them out. Once everyone was settled, Brendan announced that the meeting was about to begin. The tension in the room was palpable; each wanted to speak, but knew they had to restrain themselves if they wanted to be heard.

"OK, lady and gentlemen," said Brendan as he opened the meeting. Sophie offered him a wan smile for the lady reference. Everyone's attention was now focussed. "Over the last couple of weeks there have been a few incursions, by, what do you call them again, Sophie?" Producing the card that she had been given, she passed it to Mike, who was sat next to her, he in turn, passed it to Brendan. "Oh yeah, the Beezlebubs," he said, as he glanced at the card. "So far, Muhammad has been flung about and had his bike damaged." The rest of the gathering looked sympathetically at Muhammad. Brendan continued, "So, that's a cost for the repairs to the bike and leathers, then Malika was targeted by a couple of thugs, sent by the Beezles, and finally, Mike was also targeted as well. It seems that the Beezles have a problem with us, for being in 'their' territory. The first thing that needs to be discussed is, is everyone wanting to stay in the Guardian Angels? Now before we get carried away with peer pressure, I have something to say about this. I am not saying the following to put you off, but we must look at the situation realistically. Each of us do not owe anything to any of the others for anything at all, no matter what has been said or done in the past. So, to that end, if anyone wants to back out now, before any real trouble starts, then they can do so without any recriminations or shame at all. We are all here on a voluntary basis."

He paused, looking for a reaction. The gang all looked at him stony faced and with the expectation that he would carry on, he obliged. "We are going to have to decide, individually first, if you are in or out; these people obviously mean business. They were willing to beat up an old man – no disrespect, Malika – and steal a motorcycle. I think, so far, we should think ourselves lucky that we have got away with the things we have. My guess is that they will be back to cause more bother, unless we do something. That means, whoever is here, must be able to rely on the others without question."

There was silence. Each of them considered what Brendan had just said. Brendan gave it a minute to let his words sink in. Breaking the silence, he said, "We'll have a show of hands to see who is staying."

Mike, on Brendan's left said, "Well I'm staying. Firstly, because I feel like I belong in this club. Socialising is hard for me, so on that basis alone, I will stop. The other night, Darren and Sophie helped me, when they didn't have to; no-one has done that for me before." There were smiles all around the table, which made Mike embarrassed, but he smiled too.

Sophie, who was next to Mike spoke next. "I don't like being told what to do at the best of times, I'll be damned if a few thugs are gonna tell me how it is now; besides, I have another reason to stop!" Muhammad tittered when she said it. Sophie dug him in the ribs with her elbow. He winced, but smiled.

Muhammad was next. "They damaged my bike and flung me down a hill, I owe them payback."

Malika paused before he spoke. "I will not be humiliated by random thugs, outside of my own business. Thanks to Brendan, it was avoided. Thugs like that only respond to one thing; I'm going to be there when it happens."

Everyone stared at Malika – this wasn't what they expected from him. Looking back at them, he gave a thin smile and said, "Perhaps these feelings will soften with time." Then he looked down at his hands and contemplated the situation.

Darren was next and he said with heartfelt conviction, "I like who I'm with." Which got smiles all around. "I don't want to sound flippant, but I need a sense of purpose and this club gave it to me, so yes, I'll be hanging around."

Smiling at everyone, it was, of course, Brendan who was last to speak. "I started all of this, so I feel responsible. Like you all suggested, I want to be part of something that is bigger than myself. There is, of course, the issue of bullying. From what I can gather, each of us has been subjected to it in the past." They all nodded in agreement. "Well, I'm not expecting things to be straightforward or work out exactly as we want, but I think, if we stick together, we can make something of this club." Continuing, Brendan said, "Well, this is it, now that we have decided, we need to formulate a plan so that we will be left alone, whether we have to fight for it or come to some sort of arrangement."

Brendan then said, "OK, now we're all singing from the same hymn sheet, we need to work out how to do this. Does anyone have any ideas?" Malika raised his hand and everyone faced him. "This is down to egos. We are here for social reasons and enjoy to each other's company. They, on the other hand, are trying to express their machismo. They are trying to demonstrate that they are a group of alpha males and they are stamping their authority in their territory." Listening intently, no-one interrupted. "It would be very unlikely that they would have the wit or foresight to be able to negotiate in such a way that gives long term benefit to all parties; they will have to believe that they have the upper hand in any event, whether that be Mentally, Financially or Physically."

Muhammad then interjected, "So, how do we do things in such a way, that we get what we want, while at the same time, allow them to think that they have the upper hand?"

Darren responded, "Well, it's not a direct answer, but something might come of it. If I explain the rules, according to the thugs that visited us and with some research that I've done. Apparently, in the first instance, an approach must be made to the local one-percent club before setting anything up. I'll explain what they mean by a one-percent and its relevance. In the US there was a bike rally and trouble ensued. The police said that bikers were nothing but bother and in response, the American Motorcycle Association said that it was the one-percent minority and not the majority that caused bother. Like a bunch of aggrieved teenagers, the troublesome clubs declared themselves separate from the whole biker scene and, in effect, became a mafia-type community. They simply bully others to take territory and control. They deal in various nefarious activities, such as drug dealing, prostitution and other things of that nature. To create a veneer, there have been attempts to romanticise the freedom that these people seem to enjoy and the idea that they are social rebels and misfits with a strong sense of loyalty, which is why we are sat here. But, like most things, they are not as they appear. They are simply nasty people, who enjoy the reputation.

Mike, with a frown said, "It seems that the most appropriate analogy of the way they carry on, is like Klingons in Star Trek, where the ego is all, thinly disguised as honour." The rest of the gang smiled at his nerdy comment, but it also created a joint 'aha' moment. Continuing with his analogy: "What that means, is that we have to do something that will, either, give us respect or diminish theirs, preferably both. We could go to their place and pick a fight with the biggest guy they have or do something for them, that they themselves wouldn't have the gumption to do."

Sophie, having heard all of this, said, "What about something the other way around? We could humiliate them in front of other one-percenters and gain respect that way?"

Brendan said, "No, it would have to be a show of prowess somehow, to humiliate them would be against their 'warrior code', which means we wouldn't get respect either; in fact, we would most likely be resented and pursued further."

Darren brought the conversation back on track and said, "The first thing that we need to do is show that we are sticking together and mean business."

Interrupting, Brendan looked pointedly at Muhammad. "Muhammad, get those waistcoats sorted properly – can you get them for next week?" Muhammad nodded. "OK Darren, carry on, sorry."

Nodding his acknowledgement, Darren continued, "We have to be realistic, we cannot fight these people directly, so we are going to have to go through their processes, as much as we baulk at the idea." At this, the rest of the crew looked sullen, but they had nothing to counter with. "We were supposed to have asked permission to wear colours before doing so; however, I would suggest that by wearing them and the fact that we got away with the various incursions and add to that that act of going to their place to sort everything out, will get us a little respect, however begrudged, because of our defiance."

They were all silent.

Brendan looked at his group of bikers, and yes, they were his, he had started this and because of it, he had a pang of guilt.

Malika was watching his friend and said quietly, "Brendan, don't worry, we're in this together and as corny as it sounds, it will all work out."

Brendan gave a thin, thankful smile but contradicted the Indian. "Look, until this is resolved, we are effectively at war; in the first instance, we will sue for peace. Like Darren said, we will have to go to their place, but in the meantime, we need to form a battle plan, shore up our defences and think of a method of attack. We have limited resources and an acute inability to literally fight back. That's the reason for my stress."

When they had arrived, there was a high anxiety level and a lot of excitement. Now, however, the anxiety was still high, but the atmosphere had become very sombre. The time for quippy remarks and smart comments had come to an end. The focus was now on survival, possibly in the literal sense.

Muhammad leaned forward and sighed. "Why must we go to their place and make ourselves vulnerable, especially with the way they've been carrying on?"

Darren replied, "Because it's a show of strength, it demonstrates that we are not afraid of them. Of course, it's a risk, but that's the whole point, they'll know that too."

Mike then said, "They key to this whole thing is to find out exactly what they want."

Malika leaned forward, catching everyone's attention, then placed a plastic folder on the table in front of himself. The gang looked at him. Malika sighed, then in silence proceeded to open the folder. In a hushed tone, Malika explained, "In the first instance, before we do anything, we gather intelligence, then once we have it, we have to define its usefulness."

The club members were all quiet while Malika continued to take out sheets of paper from the folder. He passed each sheet out one at a time, firstly to Muhammad, who then looked at each of them before passing it on down the line. On each sheet was a mugshot of each known member of the Beezlebubs. Along with each picture was a list of details, such as name and address, close relatives, bike registrations and a general synopsis of their actual, probable and suggested criminal activities. After looking at the sheets, the crew looked at Malika, amazed. Furtively, he looked back at them and by way of explanation said, "I have a very clever nephew in India" closing the statement with a sly smile. "Of course, I have examined these things quite extensively–" referring to the papers that he was by now putting back into the plastic folder. "It seems that the Beezlebubs are essentially a bunch of drug dealers and this is the reason why they are so uppity about their territory. They have this area for their profit margin. We are, from their point of view, a threat of their lucrative business."

It was then that the rest of the crew realised what they were going to be taking on. This could potentially be a very serious situation. Malika sensed that he had just increased the anxiety level another notch or two.

Mike asked, "Shouldn't we just tell the police?"

Brendan snappily retorted, "What, what would we tell them, that we hacked your system because we were harassed by a couple of bikers? Besides, they have the info already, obviously." Brendan couldn't hide the stress that he was feeling and looked pained when he asked again, "Is everyone still in?" This time there were no words of revenge or loyalty, but they all nodded.

Sophie said, "Now we understand the situation, we're still left with the problem of what we do and more to the point, how?"

Muhammad suggested, "Perhaps we could harass their families, you know, general stuff, like cars and houses being vandalized, a bit like guerrilla warfare."

Darren pointed out: "That would simply escalate things. Like I said before, we need to make a gesture that shows credibility."

"To be honest, credibility shouldn't really be an issue, given that they are drug dealers. They aren't separate from society, they're just anti-social," said Sophie, with disgust.

Brendan interjected: "Look, we need a plan, not philosophy or opinion." He couldn't hide his frustration. The gang quietened again.

"I could arrange it, so that all their bank accounts are closed down." Everyone looked at Malika incredulously. "Well, I did get this lot–" he gestured at the file. Continuing: "They can't launder money if they haven't got an account. I mean, look at the trouble they'll have with their suppliers and dealers. If they can't pay the suppliers, they'll be cut off and if they have debts with them, they will have a lot of problems. Also, they will have a lot of problems with the dealers if they can't collect."

"Oh, I like that. That would be bitchin'. I would have thought that we would have a lot of respect if we did something like that," said Muhammad admiringly, smiling broadly. Everyone else was smiling at this too.

Still, the prospect of facing down an established biker gang with a bad reputation, who also happened to be well-known drug dealers to boot was an ominous thought. The fact was, the people around this table were misfits in society because of circumstance and not choice, they were here because they only had each other and no-one else. So, whatever they did, they had to do it for each other and altogether.

Brendan took a deep breath and interrupted the renewed animation of the team. "As I now understand it. All of us are to go to the Beezlebubs' clubhouse and tell them that we know all about them. They are to leave us alone or we will shut them down."

The seriousness returned. There were no smiles, but everyone nodded. It seemed, Brendan thought, a game was afoot.

CHAPTER 15

20/08/17

It was late on Sunday evening when the gang met up at the marketplace. There was a light rain and nightfall had arrived. It had been a miserable day and was turning into a miserable night. One by one, the Guardian Angels turned up. This time there were no effusive greetings, just nods. The engines were left running and they sat on their steel horses until they had all got together. Muhammad came last, his Hayabusa fixed and looking like new. The leathers were the only giveaway of the violent experience that he had suffered. When they were ready, they set off in the order that they had become accustomed to. As they travelled, they wound their way through the little villages and onto the main moor road as they had before. Once they arrived at Whitby, they continued to follow the A171 to Scarborough. The drizzle didn't let up, each rider feeling more miserable as they continued, getting soaked to the skin. They stopped for a refuel at Burmiston, just outside of Scarborough and had a quick coffee, to help stave off the, by now, chilly wind that was building in strength.

As they were drinking the coffee in the forecourt, next to the bikes, Muhammad said, "I hope this is worth it, this isn't my idea of a jolly jape across the County of North Yorkshire."

Malika, looking particularly pathetic, with his turban all soaked, shrugged his shoulders. Mike was quiet, pacing up and down. Sophie approached him.

"Are you OK?" He nodded, but didn't say anything. Sophie said with concern, "If you want to wait here, you can you know."

Mike glanced at her. "No it's OK, I was just thinking about my dad. I shouldn't think about the past, but the bike thing got me annoyed."

"That's understandable," she said sympathetically. She asked if he had had a coffee and he said no. "Perhaps you should, it'll pick you up and give you a little more clarity and focus."

He mulled it over for a moment or two and said, "OK." Having decided, they walked with each other to the kiosk, chatting as they went.

Darren was sat on his bike seat as he watched the two of them walk across his field of view. He felt sorry for Mike. He must be feeling insecure at the minute. The thugs had gone to where he lived – that must be disconcerting. He took a sip from his cup. As he did so, Brendan came and stood by him. "So, what do you reckon, boss?" Darren took another sip and waited for an answer.

Brendan looked at the gang, paired off with each other. He felt an affinity and a bond with these people that he hadn't experienced before. There was an intimacy and closeness between them. He was hopeful and somehow, he knew everything was going to be OK. But he replied, "I would say, fifty-fifty. We're going into the lion's den and going to give it a kick in the balls, you know what I mean."

Darren spat his coffee out and coughed on the remaining liquid. He smiled, despite the apprehension that he knew they both felt. The drizzle, as persistent as it was, was now almost unnoticed by the crew. Darren said with a touch of pride, "You know, it's weird how we all just, got on. Take Malika and Muhammad for example, normally Sikhs and Muslims hate each other and look at them, they're always together. Then here's you, a black guy in the North East. Probably one of the most inward looking, working class, white male areas in the country and yet you're in charge of a biker gang. Then there's Mike, Autistic, not the best socializer, now one of the core founder members. Then, of course, there's Sophie, well we'll leave it at that..." He smiled to himself.

Brendan put his hand on his shoulder and smiled too. Brendan said, "What about you then, perhaps a spoiled mammy's boy, who did nothing but think of himself, now protecting his friends and the less fortunate. That wasn't a dig by the way – like you said, it is extraordinary how this has worked out."

Darren looked up at him and proffered his cup. Brendan did the same with his; they silently clinked cups and nodded. Brendan was right. It wasn't just because of Sophie that he was here. Darren spoke rhetorically, "You know, I think this is how these other clubs started out, with a need for each other, but then greed and ego took over."

Brendan considered the statement. "You're probably right, most people start with good intentions and it usually goes downhill when reality bites. I'm sure that happens in most jobs too, like the police, social services and, most definitely, politicians."

Making a joke of it, Darren said, "I'm sure you're stretching it a bit now!"

Brendan, smirking, said, "Yeah, you might be right."

A loud laugh broke across the forecourt and the two of them looked toward the sound. Muhammad was laughing hard and Malika stood smiling. Only the two of them knew what the laughing was about, but it didn't matter. Brendan thought they needed a bit of levity before the oncoming confrontation. Mike and Sophie were smiling as they were talking; perhaps it had been the coffee, but more likely, Mike had felt the need to talk to someone. Sophie was good company, in fact, the whole gang were. None were judgemental but accepted people for who they were, which made for a comfortable and easy-going atmosphere.

Darren drank the last of his coffee and went to the rest room, as Brendan walked over to the others, telling them it was time to go. Just before they set off, they had another group meeting.

Brendan spoke. "Now, this really is the last chance for any of you to back out, again, with no recriminations." As before, they all stood silently. Nodding his satisfaction, Brendan continued: "It's about another twenty to thirty minutes down the road. I've Google-earthed it, it seems to be a run-down industrial estate. It would be, wouldn't it" he added sarcastically. It implied fewer prying eyes, thus less chance of witnesses. "I'm going to say this and you might not like it, but it has to be sorted before we go. I'll do the talking; does anyone have a problem with that?" As expected, there was no response. "Malika, do you have the files?" Malika nodded and patted his jacket to indicate where they were. "Now remember, we are going to show solidarity and resolve, there should be no need for physical confrontation." At that, he looked at Darren and Muhammad – both shrugged their shoulders and looked at each other with a thin smile. "OK, so if you're ready, let's do this."

Turning to their respective bikes, they put on their helmets and gloves and mounted the motorcycles. The engines were all started rapidly, one after the other. Once again, Brendan gave the thumbs up and so began the last leg toward an event that none of them were likely to forget in a hurry. They filed onto the road, heading south. The wind had built up and the rain had increased in intensity. It was harder to stay warm. The troop made its way through to the industrial estate and then they came to a halt. Brendan held his hand up and gestured for them to stay where they were. He dismounted and looked at the fading site map on a billboard before remounting. They set off again and worked their way further into the unknown.

Eventually they arrived outside of an anonymous looking industrial unit. They knew they had reached the right place because of two parked bikes. The bikes were Harley Davidsons. From the outset, the gang could discern that the bikers were trying to be the same as each other, which seemed a little ironic for people who were allegedly different. The gang didn't pull up next to the other bikes, but went across the road into another unit's parking area. Partly to separate themselves from those that they were visiting and to help keep a distance, if there were going to be any entanglements with the bikers.

The rain had dissipated slightly, but the wind's speed had increased. Some of the bikes rocked on their stands. Everyone had taken off their helmets and gathered together. Brendan shouted against the noise of the wind. "We need someone to stop with the bikes. In case they fall over or someone interferes with them. Does anyone want to volunteer?"

No-one spoke, until Mike raised his hand. "I'll do it, we need the bikes to be OK so we can get back; besides, I'll probably say something out of turn and land us in trouble."

Brendan nodded and thanked him by patting him on the shoulder. Mike, uncomfortable because of having the body contact, flinched, but was equally grateful for the acknowledgement. He smiled and then put his hood up from the collar of his jacket and went and stood in the lee side of the roller shutters, as partial shelter from the intensifying wind. The others waved as they moved over to the Beezlebubs' clubhouse. Mike waved back, frightened for his friends and feeling guilty for staying. As they walked through the lashing rain, they noticed the movement of shadows, through a door which was next to the main roller shutters. As they approached, they fell into single file. Brendan being at the front, knocked on the door. After they had stood for about a minute, there was still no answer. The rain lessened somewhat, but the wind became stronger and made it harder to communicate with the others. Brendan guessed it was probably the same reason why those inside hadn't heard them.

Brendan leaned over and shouted into Malika's ear, "I'll go in first and tell them we're here."

Malika nodded, but showed concern on his wind-swept face. Turning to the door, Brendan entered. He closed the door after him and walked down a short corridor and passed through a second door. He entered a large, spacious but dimly lit clubhouse. It was exactly as he imagined it would be. There were four sofas scattered about. A pool table in the centre, a juke box against the left wall and at the far side, under some upstairs offices, was a well-stocked bar. As per any cliché, there were two bikers in T-shirts with leather waistcoats, playing pool. Neither one looked particularly interested in the black man in biker gear. They had noticed him, but were more concerned about finishing their game.

Brendan stood politely and waited until they had finished. He then walked over and introduced himself. "Hi, we've come to see your boss, whoever that might be and make a deal."

The two bikers looked at each other and then at Brendan. "We, what do you mean by we?" enquired the biker on the left.

Brendan replied, "Well, there are four others waiting to come in and one watching the bikes."

"OK, give me minute," said the biker on the right. He walked to the door that Brendan had come in and went to see the others outside. He opened the outside door and gestured for them to come in.

The rain, by this time, had stopped, but the wind had increased in ferocity. The others looked over at Mike through the window, who looked particularly sorry for himself. The wind was ripping at his clothes and he hunched his shoulders, tucked in tight against the doorway.

"Listen, go and get him, he'll catch his death out there. He can stand in here and watch the bikes where it's warm," said the Beezlebub, almost sympathetic. Nodding and smiling his gratitude on behalf of his friend, Muhammad ran across to Mike. At first, Mike wouldn't come, not trusting the situation. But, after Muhammad explained that he would still be watching the bikes, he relented. Finally, the door shut and other than the rattling of the roller door and their heavy breathing, all was quiet.

The silence was quickly broken by the chirpy voice of the Beezlebub. "OK folks, come in."

They all filed in to see Brendan talking to the other biker.

"If you'd just wait here please, I'll go and see the boss." The biker lengthened his stride and half ran up the stairs and knocked on the door at the top.

The atmosphere of the greeting had taken the gang by surprise. It wasn't threatening or tense in the way they had expected. In fact, it almost seemed civilised. The five Angels looked around and made the odd positive comment on their surroundings. The biker who had remained with them, then said with obvious pride, "Yeah, we like it. It took a while to get sorted, but yeah."

After a minute of this they heard the clump of heavy boots coming down the wooden stairs from the office. The biker who had left them, walked over and said, "Well, I've had a word and told the boss you were here. Of course, you have to be searched for unwanted items."

Sophie raised her eyebrows and exclaimed, "Unwanted items, what do you mean?"

With a knowing smile of one who had seen it all before, the biker replied, "Knuckle dusters, knives and any other weapons, listening devices and anything else of such a nature."

Brendan immediately said "Fair enough" and then stepped forward. They were asked to remove their outer clothing, down to their base layer. One by one they were padded down and what surprised them was when it came to Sophie's turn, they asked for a witness to show that they hadn't done anything of a sexual nature. Once the searches were over, everyone got redressed.

Brendan then asked, "What about Mike, in the corridor?"

The response was "As long as he stays in the corridor, he'll be fine. If he needs to be in, he'll be escorted."

Knowing that his team was OK, Brendan asked, "OK, what's next?"

"The boss said that he had a couple of things to attend to and that we should make you a warm drink, if you wanted one."

At this, the Guardians were perplexed. This was the gang that had gone to great lengths to give them a hard time and here they were, offering tea and biscuits!

The hot drinks were passed around and, despite the circumstances, were received gratefully. Darren sat with Sophie on one of the leather sofas, Malika and Muhammad both sat on an adjacent seat and Brendan sat on his own. He looked over and picked up a magazine from the coffee table, which was in the middle of the seating arrangement. Smiling to himself he noted the cover said, 'Back Street Heroes'. He flicked through the pages, whiling away the time. The two bikers returned to the pool table and set up a game. For the next twenty minutes, the only sounds were the clinking of pool balls and the odd gust from the dying winds against the roller doors. After a few minutes, there was knock at the door and Mike popped his round the door and announced, "I've finished, can someone get this please." He proffered the mug that he had drank from. One of the bikers went to retrieve it. "Thanks, mate," Mike said with a smile. The biker returned the smile with a nod and took the mug. Mike retreated into the corridor. As he did so, there was a loud "OK, next" from the upstairs office.

The five Guardians who were present stood up. The first biker, who had initially talked to them, put his hand up and said, "Sorry, but I've been instructed to tell you that only two people can go up – don't worry, the boss is on his own, it's not a trap or anything."

Looking at the rest of the gang, Brendan said, "It's OK, Malika and I will go up." Acknowledging the plan that they had previously arranged, the other three sat back down and the two nominees went up the stairs. Glancing around before knocking, Brendan saw the other three looking up at them and the two bikers had resumed their game. Brendan knocked on the door and received a loud "Come in". He opened the door and entered, with Malika closely in tow.

The office was small, but enough to accommodate a large desk, two chairs in front of it and a large sofa. The walls were adorned with all sorts of badges and pictures from other clubs and memorabilia from past activities. The voice belonged to a large man, who looked quite intimidating. He had a large, veiny, bald head, which was decorated with tattoos. He wore the usual regalia of a biker, T-shirt, jeans and waistcoat. He was obviously overweight, but moved fluidly and with an easy strength. He was undoubtedly strong, but undertrained. It was assumed that the rest of his body, like his arms, would be covered in tattoos. Almost comically, he wore a pair of small reading glasses.

He got up from behind his desk and approached with an open hand and shook each of theirs. He looked as though he was smiling, but it was hard to tell, because of his large grey beard. "Please gentlemen, have a seat." They both obliged and he went back to his own, behind the desk. "First, let me apologise for making you wait, I had an important phone call to answer."

In return, Brendan said, with equal friendliness, "It's OK, your lads make a cracking cuppa."

The boss smiled. "They're prospects, if you hadn't noticed – they don't have any colours on their waistcoats." Brendan and Malika looked at each other and raised their eyebrows. Continuing, the boss said, "They're here on guard, so to speak, we have people here, twenty-four seven." He had said that to make a point – they are a well organised club, with structure. He looked at the newcomers and asked, "So, how can I help you?"

Brendan, feeling apprehensive said, "Look, we've come to see if we can have some sort of arrangement, in respect of leaving us alone with our own club."

The boss said, "OK, first things first, my name is John and you are?" he asked.

"This is Malika and I'm Brendan, our club is called 'The Guardian Angels."

Giving Brendan a stern gaze, he said slowly, "I know," the hint of menace in his voice unmistakeable. John arose from behind his desk and stood in front of the window, overlooking the club.

Brendan, trying not to sound defensive or weak said, "I really don't know what the problem is, we're just a few guys riding around on bikes."

Turning back to face the two visitors, John sighed and weighed them up. "This may take a little while to explain, I know you're both intelligent men. You, being an accountant and you, being a business man of long standing." He gave a pause to let the information sink in. They realised that he had been researching the Angels as much as they had been researching the Beezlebubs, which meant that the Beezlebubs still had the upper hand. "Let me continue with my explanation. I think it was Eric that talked to some of your guys about how clubs should operate." Brendan and Malika both nodded that they understood. John spoke further. "The issue, as you have probably gathered by now, is territory and power. The thing is, ironically, it isn't done to be better than anyone else, it's more of a case of maintaining the status quo. If we don't patrol and enforce our territorial boundaries, others will do it for us. The rule of thumb is that you can ride around in your colours in pairs. Anymore, means that you are 'in force'." An emphasis was put on this last statement, to mean that such actions would be dealt with as a threat. He paused again, to let the new information sink in.

Malika interjected and said, "It seems paradoxical that people who operate outside of the law, dispense their own."

John almost laughed, "You're right, it is, isn't it? The problem you have–" He emphasised the 'you'– "is that you are entering a world you know nothing about. This isn't 'Easy Rider' or 'Sons of Anarchy'. The general practice is that a member of a club will break away, after seeking permission for the different things involved, such as colours, territory etc. In doing this they take with them the general knowledge of how to go about things. They may have their own management style, but essentially, they stay within the accepted bounds."

"So, why can't we just be left alone and let us do our own thing?" persisted Malika.

John seemed to show a little frustration, but made the effort to humour his guests. "Perception. If other clubs saw what we had done, or not, then we would lose respect and credibility. Of course, we can't allow that to happen." John sat back down on his chair and gave the two a considered look. "You could declare yourself as one of our support groups."

Brendan and Malika gave a quizzical look and Brendan asked,

"What do you mean by that?"

Leaning forward and resting against the desk, he said, "You will become a junior club to the Beezlebubs, you will support us in certain things, such as patrols on our behalf and carry out tasks that we ask. In return, you get invites to events we hold and, of course, we look after you in case of any incursions, into your area of responsibility."

Malika then added, "And of course, you will need a regular payment, shall we say as a franchise fee, or maybe a tax?"

John smirked, cocked his head to one side and shrugged his shoulders and said, matter-of-factly, "C'est la vie"

"What if we say no?" asked Malika.

Putting his hands behind his head, John leaned back onto his chair and said, "Well clearly, we have a problem or should I say, you do."

For about thirty seconds there was silence. Malika said it, but Brendan was thinking it too. "We're not going to be your bitches."

Again, as before, there was a conscious effort on the part of John to restrain his temper. "I can't give you any territory. To be honest, when we realised you were amateurs, we only leaned on you a bit. We were hoping that you might just go away. I have to admit that it took a good bit of courage for you to turn up here and even more, wearing your colours." Pausing again, to consider his next words, he suggested another idea. "If you disband, as in drop the name and no longer wear the colours, what I can do personally, is to have you as guests to our events and you won't get any more hassle, being colour free. I'm trying my best to accommodate you, whilst maintaining the status quo."

Brendan and Malika both shook their heads. John rolled his eyes in exasperation, then shook his own head.

"I admire your commitment and tenacity, but you really are on thin ice. As a gesture of good faith and to give you time to talk to your friends, downstairs, I will let you walk out of here with your colours on. If, however, you don't come up with some form of satisfactory arrangement, then the next time any of us see you in your colours, either in a group or otherwise, you will get a good kicking. I have asked politely for you to comply; after all, we do, so it's not something I'm asking you to do, that I wouldn't." John took his reading glasses off and folded them neatly in front of him. He placed both of his hands on the table and bowed his head. "I'm really sorry I've had to speak like this, but unfortunately these are the rules we abide by; I have to make sure that you do too." Again, he sighed. The two visitors knew that he meant it when he had apologised, but they also knew that he would carry out the threat.

Brendan and Malika looked at each other apprehensively and nodded. They both realised that they had reached the point of no return. As soon as they uttered their next few sentences, it would be the beginning of the end. They both looked at John; he returned their gaze with a curious expression.

A bit confused, he asked, "What is it you want now, I'm getting tired of this?"

Brendan gave the go-ahead to Malika, who then proceeded to unzip his jacket. He then gave the file to Brendan. John had, by now, become curious. He shuffled slightly forward in his chair with anticipation. Brendan methodically opened the file and extracted the paperwork, which he then gave to John. Taking them, he then put them on his desk and flicked through a few sheets. After a moment or two he stopped and put on his reading glasses. He then examined the literature properly. He smiled as he worked his way through and when he came to the end he said with an air of contempt, "Is that supposed to scare me? The criminal offences have already been served, so it's already in the public domain and the others are suspected, so therefore not proven. In fact, two things can come of this: one, the police could be prosecuted for malicious prosecution; and two, which would be most interesting, you could be prosecuted for hacking their system." Pausing before speaking further, he gave a sardonic grin. "I'll tell you something, you've got balls, I'll give you that. You came in here and gave a threat to one of the biggest one-percenter bike clubs in the UK, in their own HQ. I have every reason to smash your face in before you leave this room, let alone the club house." It was obvious that John was now having great difficulty in restraining his temper.

Brendan and Malika sat quietly and said nothing. Contrary to the stony-faced exteriors, their insides were roiling, almost to the point of being physically sick. They both knew, if they didn't remain calm over the next few minutes, then their days would be numbered.

John glared at them. "So, what next?" he asked angrily.

Brendan, choosing his words carefully and trying not to show any fear, replied, "This is just to prove that we can cause damage too. OK, it might not be physical, but you know as well as we do, it would be a lot more devastating."

Just as angry, but getting a grip on his emotions, John asked testily, "How's that?"

Making sure he controlled the timbre of his own voice, Brendan explained, "You might suddenly have a County Court Judgement on your credit rating, with a paper trail to prove it, which might mean you losing your motorcycle or even your house." For dramatic effect he added, "Probably both."

John drummed his fingers on his desk, considering what to say, but Brendan pressed on with the attack. "It could be that all the club funds suddenly disappear. We know what cash you have stashed too, but after a couple of police raids, that would disappear as well. I suppose, the coup de grâce would be if the press were to find out that you had been running a paedophile ring, where would your reputation be then?"

At this point, John was doing all he could from killing these two arrogant pricks on the spot. He stood up again, taking a deep breath and put his hands behind his back, looking like a Sergeant Major. He looked out of the office window for a moment and then turned to the guests. This time, he had a look of vengeful viciousness in his eyes. "Even the other club presidents wouldn't say something like that to me and, believe me, they've had plenty of reasons to do so."

Malika, adding his tuppence worth said, almost smugly, "If stuff like that got into the press, no-one would speak to you at all."

Brendan then said, like an after-thought, "I have something to show you." He reached into an internal pocket and pulled out his wallet. He opened the wallet and pulled out a piece of paper. He then handed the same to John, which was snatched. John opened the paper and then looked at Brendan. On the paper was printed two numbers, one was the account number of the club's bank account and the other was the sort code.

Brendan locked eyes with John. "Yeah, I'm sure you guys could give us a right good kicking and we would all end up in hospital, sucking through tubes, for what, three to six months. That would take you about ten to fifteen minutes dependent on the level of resistance. However, your three hundred thousand, six hundred and sixty-eight pounds and seventy-six pence would be where it is now, for about five seconds. That money would help some street urchins in India, while you would be dealing with some not-so-popular criminal offences. Even if you managed to prove it was all dodgy and a set-up, which would take, at best, two years, your precious reputation would be in tatters and the local stray dogs wouldn't piss on you."

John was seething, but he knew they were right. Calmly, which surprised John himself, he asked, "So, all you want is to play bikers in your area and wear your colours?"

Brendan, sounding more confident than he felt, replied, "Pretty much."

John sat back down and said to them, "As you can imagine, I have some thinking to do. If you, gentlemen, would be kind enough to wait downstairs, while I make a couple of phone calls. Oh, don't worry. I won't set you up. When you see some guys come in, you won't come to any harm."

Brendan and Malika rose from their chairs and filed out of the office. They made their way down to the other Guardian Angels. The prospects were still playing pool and glanced at the two of them as they went and sat down.

The negotiators sat with the others, who gave expressions of curiosity. The two of them shook their heads, to quell the questioning. Now was not the time to have a question and answering session. After about half an hour, two more Beezlebubs arrived. They entered the clubhouse with an air of confidence, which suggested that they had some sort of rank, which was emphasised when the two prospects stood erect and nodded as they passed. The new arrivals looked aggressively at the guests, but never spoke. They made a direct line for the steps to the office above. At the top, the first gave one knock and they both entered.

The Guardian Angels sat on the sofas without speaking. Brendan was reading the 'Back Street Heroes' from where he had left it before the meeting. He was trying to look nonchalant, but his stomach told a different story; luckily, only he and Malika knew. After about fifteen minutes, the office door opened. The three head bikers emerged from the office and clumped their way down the wooden steps. After reaching the bottom, they approached the sofas and gestured for the gang not to get up. John perched sideways on the arm of the sofa that Brendan was sat on and folded his arms on his lap. The other two stood and watched.

Craning his neck, John said to the prospects, "You two, go and get some coffees, will yer."

They understood that it meant to clear off out of the way; what was to be said was not for their ears. The prospects were watched as they walked away. As prospects, they were continually watched, until the club was satisfied that they weren't undercover police or spies for another club. When they were far enough away, one of the two bikers who were stood, nodded to John, who was by now more relaxed, unlike the Guardians, who were on the edge of their seats.

"OK, gang, we've decided to explain something to you, some of which you might have heard before. Oh, wait a second, Gregg, do me favour and get the guy in the corridor for me please."

One of the two bikers nodded and went to the door and went in for Mike. When Mike came in, both Gregg and he were smiling and Mike was chatty, which was unusual for him, especially with a stranger.

John said, "It's only fair that you're all here for this." He paused long enough for Mike to settle and then he said, "As I said to your guys here–" He nodded toward Brendan and Malika– "I'm most impressed that you had come here at all, that took some doing, but added to that, you came and issued a threat, which again, deserves respect." He smiled as he said it, but the seriousness of the situation wasn't lost on any of them. "What was stressed to me, was that you guys just want to have a bit of a mess about on the weekend and wear your colours." Each of the Guardians nodded and agreed with him. "But, as you will know, when a bike club gets to a certain size, it has no choice but to expand, otherwise there will be no resources for those present and so this would cause friction." He was referring to the profit margins from their illegal activities and how they would diminish with a larger group. However, he again received nods of understanding. "To maintain order, there has got to be a set of governing rules; these rules reduce friction. Although, what I have said does not seem to make sense on the surface."

At this point, Mike interrupted. "What you're saying is that our club is not conforming and if it expands, there will be issues to resolve. You're saying that, to co-exist, we have to follow the rules."

Smiling that he had got his point through to at least one of them, he continued. "As you won't accept being a support club, we assume therefore, that you are a rival MC, which we are obliged to subjugate." The gang looked at each other nervously. John continued further. "We recognise your determination in being recognised as an MC, which has been borne out by your threat." At this Brendan and Malika looked at each other, worried about what was coming next. John saw the look in their eyes and smiled. "To avoid any violence, whilst at the same time complying with the rules, we have decided upon a solution, so that you can share some of our territory and have recognition, like a sister club if you like. We will be able to access each of the other's areas without hindrance."

Brendan retorted, "You mean, you'll still have access to your various activities and profits, while we play bikers."

John shrugged his shoulders. "Life is full of compromises."

"Now, all of you understand business." As their names were mentioned, he pointed at each of them. "Mike, you have a garage. Brendan, you're an accountant. Sophie, you're a pub manager. Darren, you're a major shareholder in a large bakery. Malika, you own a restaurant, and Muhammad, you run a shop. Clearly, none of you are stupid and just like you, we like to turn a profit. So, what we are suggesting, is that you get us some drugs." He smiled as he said it. However, the gang didn't. "Well, you wanted to play with the big boys, this is how the game goes," said John.

"You want us to buy you some drugs?" asked Sophie.

"No, no, no, don't misunderstand me. We want you to go and get them. Be mules for a day. We have a problem with access to the Middlesbrough drug trade. For some reason, each time we place an order with our supplier, a certain individual turns up and takes everything, both drugs and money. Because you're an unknown entity in the area, you should be able to get by without any problems."

Brendan, looking wary, said, "So, how much and how?"

John looked at his two cronies and smiled – this was obviously his idea and he was playing it quite well. John, focussing his attention on the Guardians, said, "We're looking at a Kilo." At that, the Guardians started to babble amongst themselves, until John held up a calming hand. "The reason why we have decided on this course of action is because, if you were to be given use of some of our territory, then you will have to be seen to be paying homage, that way we can avoid any confrontation and we can each have what we want. I have discussed this with my two lieutenants and we have agreed, assuming you get the gear, you can have, North of the A171, from Marske to Whitby. Both of our clubs will be able to travel along the moor road without any hindrance, but if more than two of each want to enter either territory, then they have to ask permission. Are we agreed?"

Brendan asked, "Is there any other way?"

John said, "I do like your courage and I would be willing to have you as prospects, otherwise, no." They all baulked at that and John stood up. "Given that it's such a big decision, these two and I will go upstairs and have a chinwag, you lot can have half an hour to decide, otherwise, clear off, it's getting late."

The three bikers walked off and mounted the stairs; there was some clumping of boots and then the office door clicked shut.

Darren, exasperated, said, "For Christ's sake, we're as bad off as we were before."

Malika sat with his arms folded, deep in thought. Brendan sat back on the sofa, with his legs crossed. Mike and Muhammad were muttering to one another. Sophie simply sat on the edge of her seat. Time went on and before they knew it, twenty minutes had passed.

Muhammad then asked the question, to no-one in-particular, "What are we going to do?"

Brendan suddenly sat up and announced, "We're going to do it." Everyone stopped talking and looked at him. "Are we a club or not? We can either set off a very short-lived war, which we have little chance of winning or we can do this one off job." He then emphasised, "I think we should." The gang were all looking at him; he thought that they seemed disappointed. "You're my friends and I don't want to see any of you getting hurt, also we have to consider that they know about our lives, where we live and work, which also means other people we know and love. Do you want to see their businesses or lives disrupted because of our hobby?"

Darren said, "When you put it like that, we have little choice."

Brendan nodded and rose from his seat He walked up the steps and knocked on the door. One of the lieutenants opened it and stepped aside to let Brendan in.

"Well?" asked John.

"We'll do it, but I have a question. How is the money side of things being dealt with? It's illegal to be caught with money over five-grand and as well as that, we don't know who and what we are dealing with, so we wouldn't know if we were being seen off."

John replied, "Don't worry about that, you just need to collect, it's all been prearranged."

There was something about the way John spoke that Brendan didn't like, but as he was new to the situation and had no direct evidence to substantiate the gut feeling, he went with the flow.

"The next question, what are the collection arrangements, once we have the goods?"

John gave a thin smile. Brendan had a feeling that they wouldn't be getting to that stage.

John said, "The guys who saw Muhammad will be waiting in the same place that they saw him last. Be there for about sixteen hundred hours, but no more than two of you – any more will bring unwanted attention."

After his briefing, Brendan went back down the stairs and walked straight for the door; the rest of the Guardians, wordlessly, followed him out.

CHAPTER 16

27/08/17

A week after the events at the Beezlebubs' headquarters, the Guardian Angels met up at the Angel. This time there wasn't much banter. What conversations there were, were muted. As they took their seats, the meeting room became silent. Each looked at the other. It seemed that the reality of their predicament had hit home and had become far more serious than any of them had expected.

Brendan looked at the sullen faces. "Well, here we are." Nobody smiled. "I must have said this at least ten times now, but again, if you want out, especially in the given circumstances, there will be no shame in it." No answer. After another glance at his team, he said, "OK, now things have changed."

Mike said sarcastically, "That's an understatement."

Brendan retorted, "We're British, that's what we do!" The whole team smiled at that. At that moment, Brendan thought, 'Humour, we need it, it's in desperate short supply.'

Getting the meeting going, Brendan said, "The idea is that we are to simply collect the gear and the Beezles have made arrangements to pay these people later." He looked for any reaction or comments, but didn't receive one, so he plodded on with the plan at hand. "What we will have to do, is post look-outs at each end of the street, just park up without dismounting. The look-outs will be in pairs. Then, I and one other will go to the house and do the pick-up. Does anyone want to volunteer to come in with me?"

This time, unlike before, there wasn't a flurry of hands. After a few seconds, Malika said, "I'll go. There's a good chance that someone will recognise Muhammad, Sophie can't run, Mike will have a meltdown and Darren looks too intimidating."

Brendan asked, "Is everyone OK with that?" There were grumbles, perhaps because they felt ashamed for not volunteering or perhaps because of the reality of the practicalities, which Malika had so bluntly pointed out.

Brendan continued, "After we have done the pick-up, we will make our way to the garage on Longland Road, just along from the James Cook Hospital. There, we will have a coffee to calm down and go to the loo etc, because, I don't know about you, but I'll be bricking it by then." There were a couple of smiles and nods of acknowledgement. "After about twenty minutes or so, we'll follow the A171 through to Saltburn, Loftus and up to Grinkle Park. That is where we will part company and four of us will return here and wait. Malika and I will continue up to where Muhammad had his run in with the Beezles and we will get rid of the gear." Brendan then produced a red rucksack. "I picked this colour, so that you guys can see it easily. We don't want to be losing fifty-grand's worth of drugs."

There were nods of agreement at this. He was about to stand up, when his mobile phone rang. He fumbled in his jacket, which had been zipped up, ready to go. Eventually, after much cursing, he managed to extract it. As he did so, it rang off. Decoding the device, he looked up who had rung. "Listen, you guys get ready, I'll be out in a sec, I have to take this."

The rest of the Guardians filed past him as he dialled the number.

Outside, the crew mounted their bikes and prepared for the

journey. The engines idled as they waited for Brendan. He came out of the Angel. As he did so, he put on his helmet and gloves as well as the red rucksack. Quickly starting the engine, he then gave the customary thumbs up and they set off. They left Loftus and went up Carlin How Bank. Just as they mounted the crest of the hill, they noticed a police car on the left. It didn't move and Darren, who was at the back, periodically looked in his mirrors to see if it was following. The team went through Brotton and then Skelton, until they reached the by-pass that took them passed Guisborough. The team then saw another police car. Again, they went through the same process, with Darren keeping an eye out. Once more, the police car did not follow. They didn't see any cop cars after that, much to their relief. The sightings of the cop cars wasn't helping to release the tension and anxiety, which by now was at boiling point.

They slipped onto the A174 and then onto the A19. They followed the dual carriageway until they turned onto the A66 and into Cannon Park. Winding their way through the terrace houses, they finally came to a stop. The bikes were all running, but only Brendan dismounted. He walked back to instruct each of them one more time. As a slight change of plan, he told each of them that once Malika and himself were out of the building, they were to disperse in different directions and meet at the rendezvous. Each nodded that they understood what he had said. He remounted his bike and continued a little further and indicated onto one of the non-descript terrace rows. As they made their way past the parked cars, he looked in his rear-view mirrors. He noticed that there were three bikes following him, which meant that the last two had stopped back; so far, so good. He then slowed to a stop, with Malika stopping beside him. The final two bikes slowly rode past and stopped just before the end of the street. 'Good, the basics are in place,' he thought. He took off his helmet and gloves. He wasn't sure if the sweat he saw on Malika's brow was because of the unseasonably warm day, or fear. He knew his sweat was because of fear.

The two Guardian Angels looked at each other apprehensively; the gravity of the situation weighed heavily. The moment they knocked on the door, their lives would be changed forever. At that point, there would be no going back and all six of them would be fatefully entwined in the others' destiny.

"Well, are you up for it?" asked Brendan.

The Indian in front of him smiled and gave a cock-eyed expression. His appearance and demeanour gave the impression that he was an upright citizen and a responsible member of the community, which belied what he was about to take part in. Malika said, "Exciting, isn't it?"

Brendan grinned broadly and replied, "Yeah, it is."

He turned and knocked on the door. It was a few moments when they heard rustling behind the tatty door. Seconds later, a large black man opened the door. He stood almost to the top of the frame and wore a dirty, white vest with a pair of black tracksuit bottoms and some scruffy trainers. "Yeah, what do you want, no sales, so don't try?"

Brendan gave a steady gaze and said, "The Beezlebubs sent us."

At this, the man looked them over and said, "You don't look like Beezles."

To which Brendan said, "We're couriers."

The unshaven man looked them over again and then grunted as he stepped back to let them in. Once in, the door was shut, giving a finality to their decision.

Brendan and Malika followed the big guy down the corridor. The place was neat and tidy, but in every other respect it was run down. The place hadn't been entertained by a decorator for years and there was a smell about the place, a kind of mustiness, most likely from never having had a whiff of fresh air within its four walls. It was apparent that no one lived here and it was purely for business purposes. They walked into a backroom, presumably what would have ordinarily been a dining room. Brendan guessed that most meetings took place here, out of the view of the front window, whereas the rear room's privacy was enhanced by the back-alley wall. There was an old desk with an equally old, but mismatched office chair behind it and two old armchairs in front. Big guy proffered the seats and the two visitors reluctantly sat. The seats were filthy and smelled accordingly. The big guy said gruffly, "Wait here." He then walked out, leaving the two of them on their own.

Once he had gone, Brendan said, "Could do with a good clean, that's for sure."

Malika agreed and said, "I'm going to wash my clothes when I get back." After a minute or so Malika added, "I'm starting to feel itchy, I think I'll have an anti-septic bath too." He moved his body around on the seat for emphasis. Brendan smiled and watched his friend. Eventually, Malika stood up and rubbed his arms. "For god's sake," he mumbled as he tried to reach behind his back to scratch. Brendan chuckled, until he too began to itch. A few minutes later, the two of them were stood and refused to sit back down.

While they were waiting, they heard shuffling upstairs and a low murmur of voices. After a few minutes, big black guy returned, except this time he had an accomplice. His new companion looked to be of Pakistani descent. The new guy gave Malika a look of contempt. He was a man with an obvious grudge against Sikhs. Malika chose to ignore him in return. Given the circumstances, that was probably best. Big Guy said gruffly, "You need to be searched." Rather than going to the lengths and detail that the Beezles had, they were simply patted down and told to lift their T-shirts to ensure there were no listening devices. Brendan thought, it seemed to be an after-thought. After all, if anything was to have happened in a violent way, it would have been before now.

When the search was completed, Malika said to the black guy with humorous sarcasm, "Those chairs have fleas, they're terrible, I'm itching like hell."

To their surprise, he responded and said, "Yeah, I've been on about getting rid of them for ages, it doesn't do the place or our reputation any good, but the boss says no."

Malika responded sympathetically: "Typical management."

The Pakistani guy who had searched Brendan had said nothing at all and only gave Malika the odd glance. It seemed that his working environment wouldn't allow him to say what he thought.

Black guy said, "It'll be a little while before you can be dealt with – would you like a tea or coffee?" Brendan and Malika looked at each other. If the place they were sat in now, was a reflection of the food and drink, then they certainly wouldn't want to consume anything. They both respectfully declined, so the two hosts left. Seconds later, the guests heard two sets of feet clumping upstairs; they surmised that the clumping belonged to the two who had just left.

Malika said to Brendan in a quiet voice, "Well, they seem friendly enough."

Brendan replied, "Looks can be deceiving, you should know that by now."

Malika then asked, what he thought was a rhetorical question. "I wonder why the Beezles were as friendly as they were, even though we threatened them?"

Brendan raised his eyebrows at such an obvious question and said, "We're not a threat and we're clearly being used. All that would have happened if they had beaten us up and what have you, is their own reputation would have been tarnished for beating up a few harmless misfits." Brendan continued, "All that would have happened, if we had carried out what we said, would be that, after everything had settled down, we would be killed off one by one. It might've taken years, but they would have done it. Whereas this way, they gain more."

Brendan walked around the room. He noticed details about the place. The wallpaper that had light on it from the unclean window, was faded and dried out. Just about every piece of wallpaper was curling at its edges. The whole room had been neglected. Looking up, there was a plaster rosette in the middle of the ceiling and all the white paintwork had become a faded yellow, possibly from the effects of smoking. In the middle of the plaster feature, hung a light bulb similarly yellowed.

The fixture didn't have a shade. The fact that the room was so spartan emphasised the infrequency of its use. The desk that stood in the middle of the room was bare. Brendan surmised that the reason for this set up was so that no clues could be garnered about the operations within the house.

Brendan rubbed the glass that looked onto the backyard. Just like in the house, the yard was tidy, neat, but dirty. Moss covered the concrete. In the middle stood a metal bin; it had scorch marks and ash around it. He deduced that it was most likely for burning evidence and anything that might incriminate the inhabitants of this house. Whoever ran this place was very pragmatic. Turning back toward Malika, he noticed the Indian was on his mobile phone. He raised his eyebrows at this and said, "That's weird, I would have thought our mobiles would have been taken off us."

Malika looked up and said, "I think they have some sort of suppressor, I can't get a signal. I bet it really annoys the neighbours, not that they'll complain. It'll also explain why we've been put in this room, it's featureless."

Brendan smiled sardonically at that and began to pace. In his small circuit, he was about to approach the doorway, then, much to his surprise, he met, whom he supposed, was an Indian woman, in a sari. She stood at approximately five-foot tall and was bedecked in jewellery. She appeared to be about sixty years old.

"Please excuse me, gentlemen and I apologise for the delay." She stepped into the room and made a bee-line for the office chair behind the desk. She plonked herself down and said quite unceremoniously, "What can I do for you two fine gentlemen?"

The two men manoeuvred themselves into her front view. Malika then made a slight bow to her and said in Gujarati, "Good afternoon, madam, I am delighted to make your acquaintance."

Brendan looked at his friend, a little taken aback, because the woman had smiled at his gibberish and nodded. He then asked Malika, "Do you two know each other?"

Malika said, "No."

Brendan looked back at the woman; if he wasn't mistaken, she was blushing. She said, "Don't worry, my black friend, I understand that you will be doing the negotiating."

Brendan nodded. She then said, "We are observing some minor cultural doctrine, which I haven't had the pleasure of for a number of years." Again, she smiled. "Would you gentlemen care to take a seat?"

Malika replied in English, "I'm afraid they're not clean enough and making us itch."

"Oh, I'm sorry, I get so busy that I don't have time to look at such minor details," she said sarcastically. She was a woman who seemed to have seen most things in life, most of which belonged to the dark underside of society. She came across as being intelligent and educated. She had a cynical hardness about her, which made her aloof. It was also very apparent that she was a dangerous woman.

"So, I understand that you're here on behalf of the Beezlebubs in North Yorkshire." Both Brendan and Malika nodded. "It has also come to my attention that the Beezlebubs are wanting a short-term line of credit. As you can imagine, this sort of thing doesn't normally happen in this line of business." She pushed her arms out of in front of herself to stretch and looked at the two men at the other side of the desk. She had already decided that she liked them, but that wasn't a good gauge of trustworthiness. "Tell me, how are you involved with the Beezlebubs?"

Brendan replied, "In a nutshell, we are earning some territory from them and we supposed to be doing this for homage."

"Ah, you men and your egos, they get you into no end of bother."

Both Brendan and Malika smiled at that.

Brendan said, "With the greatest of respect to yourself, we don't want to be involved with drugs at all and the soonest we deliver them, the better. How you deal with the Beezles is up to you. We don't know anything about the financial arrangements and we hope to be rid of everything within three hours."

The woman looked at Malika, waiting for further comment, but she received a shrug.

She made a clucking noise with her tongue as she thought to herself, then stood up. "You're going to have to wait here while I discuss this. How much are we talking about again?"

The question was rhetorical: she was aware how much they needed, but wanted to see their reaction. They looked blankly at her and so she said, as though she had just remembered, "Oh yeah, it was a Kilo, wasn't it?"

The two men nodded, not really any the wiser.

She then asked, "Do you know how much it's worth?" The two men shook their heads, again showing their ignorance. For dramatic effect, she said, "Fifty thousand pounds."

Brendan took an audible sigh, trying to control his stress. The woman gave them a last glance, before walking out of the room.

After ten minutes of waiting, the two Guardians were getting agitated and were also worried about the guys outside. What had surprised them, was the apparent lack of scrutiny from the dealers. But, there again, they hadn't exactly been privy to anything, having been kept in one place. Brendan continued his pacing and Malika leant against the wall with his arms folded. There were some murmurings from upstairs and then the noise stopped and a few seconds later, as before, there was stomping, coming down the wooden stairs. Because of the lack of furnishing, the stomping echoed and seemed a lot louder. The first to walk in, was the black guy that they had met at the front door. He walked over to and stood at the window. In doing so, he blocked out a significant amount of sunlight. Then the racist Pakistani came in and stood just behind the door. All four men stood in silence, looking at each other, waiting for events to unfold. Except for Brendan, the others had their arms folded; he had clasped his hands behind his back. He did this intentionally, to show that he had no need to act defensively – to his own surprise he didn't feel frightened. The thought occurred to him that he was sure it would all catch up, in some physical manifestation.

After what seemed an eternity, the Indian woman entered the room. She acknowledged her men and glanced at the two visitors and even managed a faint smile, however fleeting, for Malika. "Gentlemen," she spoke to Brendan and Malika and made it loud enough so that everyone in the room could hear. "I've considered your request. You are asking to take fifty thousand pounds' worth of merchandise on credit, on the hope that the Beezlebubs will pay. I would have thought that this would be a significant risk for you. It is true that we have dealt with these people before, and yes, they have paid. So, I will give it the go ahead. The responsibility lies with you and your crew. You are an unknown quantity. After all, you could simply disappear and because you are representatives of the Beezlebubs, they too would be pursued with vigour. I'm sure you understand how this type of business works. Our debt collectors are not the same as those that you see on the television."

She let the last statement hang in the air for the two customers to digest. The Pakistani at the door smiled maliciously. She then continued. "There is also the aftermath in the case of your potential poor choices. As I said, we will go after the Beezles and if you abused our trust, we would take it personally and come after you as well. But, I am sure the Beezles wouldn't be happy either and would also want retribution." At this, the Pakistani's grin, became wider.

Brendan didn't like this, he felt that there was fish off, because he was new to this situation, he could only guess what. Unexpectedly, Malika approached the desk and started to speak in Gujarati. "You know, you don't have to do this, you don't suit it."

She looked at him, initially with soft, almost apologetic eyes, but then they hardened. She answered him, in her native tongue, with bitterness. "My husband left me with nothing in this country, I couldn't even speak the language. I had two children and knew no-one, I had no choice."

The contempt in her voice was unmistakeable, no matter the language. She had harboured her hate and used it to shield against the perceived animosity that she thought others had for her. Standing up from the stoop that he had been in when talking, Malika reached into his pocket. The two aides stepped forward expectantly, but the woman held up her hand. They complied and stopped, if not unwillingly. Malika continued his search and produced a business card. He then said to her, "When you decide to give this up." He cocked his head in a gesture that meant their present location and all that it entailed. He handed her the card, which she took gently. She appreciated his intent and smiled wanly. She looked at him and said quietly, "Perhaps."

Brendan said, "OK then, what's next, what do we do now?"

Looking at the smaller black man, the woman said, "We agree to let you have what you ask, but remember, you have been warned." She got up, tucking the card into her sari and walked out. A minute later, Brendan was putting two half-Kilo bags of white powder into a red rucksack, which he then put onto his back. He held out his hand to thank the men present, but none responded. Turning to Malika, he shrugged his shoulders and then cocked his head to gesture that they should leave. Malika and the woman exchanged glances and then the two of them left. It was a big relief to be outside, in the fresh air. Part one of the plan was complete.

Blinking in the sunshine, Brendan and Malika put on their biking gear.

Brendan said, "You go down that way and tell them to go and I'll go the other way and do the same. He nodded in each direction as he said it. Malika nodded that he understood and started up his bike. Brendan quickly followed suit, then they both left in their designated directions. As they approached the bikers at the ends of the street, they started their engines and split up. Each found their own routes through the rabbit warren of streets that was Middlesbrough. By splitting up, they had the idea that it would be difficult for others to follow them.

After about thirty minutes, Brendan pulled into the service station on Longland Road. He noticed Darren's bike was parked up next to the car wash and so he pulled up alongside. As he did so, he saw Darren stood in the queue, in the kiosk area. He tried to catch his attention, but failed to do so. So, he locked up his bike and went to the toilet. As he entered, he took off the red backpack and went into the cubicles. Moments later he heard someone enter the toilets, whistling. He opened the door and saw an averaged sized, dark haired man in a tracksuit. The man had a rucksack, the same as Brendan's. The man nodded and held out his pack, Brendan did likewise and they swapped. The man put the pack on and went to the urinals. Brendan went back into the cubicle and completed his toileting. He chuckled to himself, he was, literally, shitting it!

When Brendan came out of the toilet, the other man had long gone. Brendan washed his hands and as he held his hands under the dryer, Mike walked in. Mike looked around and saw that the place was empty, other than the two of them.

"For Christ's sake, I'm glad that's over with. It should be a case of dump and go now." His anxiety was palpable and Brendan felt for him, but showed no empathy – now wasn't the time. Brendan finished with the dryer and let the noise of the fan die down.

"Yeah, somehow, it seems a little too easy," he replied.

"What do you mean?" Mike asked, more anxious.

"I'm not sure, I'm sure we'll find out soon." As he said it, Brendan walked out of the restroom. He walked back towards where he had parked up, across the forecourt. There was only one bike missing, Muhammad's. As he approached their parking spot, Darren handed Brendan a coffee. Thanking him, he took it and had a sip. The coffee tasted gorgeous. Perhaps the adrenalin that had been pumping through him had enhanced his senses and made everything seem sharper and more real. He noticed that the others all had drinks too and all seemed to be contemplating. There wasn't much talking.

After five minutes, there was a roar as Muhammad's Hayabusa pulled onto the forecourt. Parking up alongside the rest of the gang, he turned off his engine. As the engine went silent a police patrol car pulled into the garage. The officer in the passenger seat looked in their direction. The car stopped next to the pumps and both officers got out. The driver concentrated on filling the car and the passenger walked over to the group of bikers. Our heroes all glanced at each other nervously.

"Hi guys." The officer walked over in a friendly manner and with a broad grin. "Nice bikes," he enthused. He looked admiringly at Darren's Triple and gave more than a cursory glance to Muhammad's Hayabusa. "I know it sounds silly, but are you having a trip out?"

Brendan, returning the smile, said, "Yeah, going to Whitby, you know, the usual, fish and chips and a bit of sea air." Brendan then asked in return, "You got a bike?"

The officer looked wistful. "Yeah, an R1, but it's a nightmare trying to get out, you know, shifts, family and what have yer."

After five minutes of motorcycle-orientated conversation, the driving officer shouted him over.

"Anyway, you guys have a good time." He waved as he left them and the Guardians raised their paper cups in response. The two officers got back into the car and headed off into the traffic. As the car disappeared, there was a collective sigh of relief from the whole crew.

Forming a loose huddle, the group of bikers talked amongst themselves for another ten minutes or so, as they finished their coffees.

"Yeah, I was coming down the road when I noticed them behind me. I assumed, that they thought, there was something up and I considered riding off, but I thought it would be better to stick to the plan or it might confuse everyone."

Brendan nodded and said, "You did the right thing, if you sped off or something, it would have drawn the wrong type of attention and could have made things difficult. Besides, because we were here, it showed that you had a reason for being here." Malika smiled and said, "This is great, really exciting, isn't it!" Everyone rolled their eyes or shook their heads.

Having now finished their drinks, Brendan said, "So far, so good. Remember what's next. We go across to the A174 and then towards Redcar, through Saltburn, Brotton and up to Grinkle Park. Then

Malika and I go up to Ugthorpe and you lot, back to the Angel. There was a feeling of reluctance amongst the group, but they knew they had to accept it.

As Sophie went to put on her helmet, she said loudly, "Malika." He turned to face her. She had a large grin on her face and said, "It is, isn't it!" He smiled back. He put his goggles on, as he did so, Muhammad slapped him on the back. Malika grinned; it was good to be with friends.

One at a time, the bikes started up and as they were back together again, they continued in their traditional order. What was also becoming a tradition, Brendan gave the thumbs up and the rest nodded. One by one, they left the forecourt and entered Longlands Road and headed toward the A174.

As they travelled along, they noticed a patrol car tucked on a side street. The car had two officers in it. As before, Darren kept an eye out, but as in the past, no-one followed. On the final approach to the A174, Mike suddenly pulled up. He quickly put the bike on the stand and struggled to get his helmet off. He took a few steps onto the grass verge and then threw up. The others behind had stopped. Sophie dismounted and went over to him.

"Are you OK?" she asked.

Mike nodded, letting the rest of the puke out and then spat out what was in his mouth. "Just stress, I've never done anything like this before."

She smiled her understanding and sympathy. "It's OK, remember, we're all in this together." She patted his back and nodded that everything was alright to the others. Sophie rubbed his back as the two of them went back to the bikes. Darren handed him a small bottle of water to rinse out his mouth, saying "Keep the bottle" with an unhelpful look of disgust, which got him an angry glance from Sophie. In the middle distance, about two hundred yards in front, Brendan gave a questioning gesture. Sophie gave a 'thumbs up' and two fingers, to indicate a two-minute wait. After collecting himself together, Mike remounted his bike and gave the thumbs up and they all set off again.

No-one had or would criticize Mike for his apparent weakness. They understood how he felt, but if they stuck together, they knew they would be OK. That should be the worst over with. All they had to do now, was to make it back to Loftus in one piece, preferably uneventfully.

CHAPTER 17

27/08/17

The day turned out to be surprisingly warm. The romantic idea of an open bike ride, was just that, an idea. Because right now, they were sat in traffic on the A174. The idea of going down the faster road seemed like a good idea at the time, but because of the excitement and anxiety of their little diversion, it had completely slipped their minds, that it was the Bank Holiday weekend. So now they found themselves sat in the sunlight, watching waves of heat dissipate off the roofs of the surrounding cars. The traffic was packed in such a way that weaving through it would have been a bad move. Brendan had a kilo of white powder on his back, which didn't lend itself to the idea of unwanted attention. So, they sat in very slow-moving traffic, sweating. Craning his neck, Brendan tried to look ahead and see what the situation was. He thought he saw the traffic thinning. It had been fifteen minutes of stop, start, to move about a mile. Sighing, bored, he looked at the stickers on the car in front. It was a typical Chav or Redneck car. It had badges and stickers all over it, along with gonk's on the back-window ledge. Apparently, you had to honk your horn if you thought the driver was sexy. There wasn't much horn honking going on, thought Brendan, smiling to himself. Another badge declared that the car was rubbish, but it was in front of him. The little fat man on the back ledge wobbled, showing the upper crack of his backside. It was stood next to a teddy that said it loved its mammy. Brendan thought that perhaps the parents were giving out mixed messages and a visit from the social services might be appropriate.

After a few minutes of paddling along with his feet, he was getting itchy as the sweat in his leathers began to dry. He lifted his visor and pulled the zip down a little, to let in some air. It made little difference in this heat. Suddenly, a face popped up from the back seat of the car in front. It was boy of about six or seven years old with a big grin. The kid waved. Brendan half-heartedly returned it. Delighted that he had got a response, the boy waved harder. Brendan realised that he was caught in a spiral of silliness, but felt obliged for some unknown reason to play along. Now began the gun fight. The kid jumped up on his knees and with his hands clasped together and two index fingers pointing, he made the form of a pistol. Each time he jumped up, Brendan could see him mouthing 'Peow' as an imagined bullet was fired. Continuing down the spiral of immaturity, Brendan dodged bullets and returned fire. This went on for about two minutes, Brendan unashamedly began to enjoy himself. It was a distraction from the lack of activity elsewhere. It was roughly thirty seconds later when he sensed the presence of one of the other guys beside him. It was Malika. His friend gave him a quizzical look.

"What are you doing?"

"Dodging bullets, what does it look like?" said Brendan, pointing out the obvious. He then added, "You want to watch out."

Blinking slowly and sighing, Malika enquired, "Why would that be?"

Brendan glanced at the Indian and nodded at the back of the car. "Because it appears his sister has a gun too!"

Looking back at the car, Malika saw two wide-eyed smiles, both now taking aim. Brendan looked at Malika expectantly.

"What?" Malika retorted.

"I think the two kids will remember this for a long time; besides, I thought you had my back," said Brendan, semi-seriously. It seemed that Malika was a remarkably good shot – he had four kills to his name already.

With the distraction of the gunfight, they had hardly noticed that the traffic had begun to move. They had almost reached the point at where they could leave the queue behind. The hold-up had been the slip road onto the A172 Stokesley Road, that led to Whitby on a more direct route. At this point, the two kids on the back seat had decided that the alliance they had to kill the evil bikers had come to an end and they began to fight each other. The movement in the car revealed that the adults had had enough and were trying to settle the kids down, probably violently. The distraction of doing this meant the driver lost their footing on the clutch and the car lurched forward, bumping into the car in front. Seconds later, there was a loud bang as the car in front's door opened and slammed shut. A middle-aged man of about fifty years old marched back to the offending driver and began shouting and waving his hands in the air. Seeing this, there was a flurry of clicking and zipping as the Guardians prepared to leave. Within a few seconds they had weaved their way through the remaining traffic. Each of them thought and hoped that their registrations hadn't been picked up by a dash cam. There was a feeling of relief as the air rushed through their clothing and ventilated the sweat and moisture in the heavy clothing.

They neared the end of the dual carriageway, which dipped and met with a roundabout. In the near distance, they saw some more slow-moving traffic. The queue was most likely making its way into Redcar. Families wanting sunshine, seaside and fish and chips. The cars moved at a slightly better pace than the previous jam, which meant a five-minute setback as opposed to the last hitch of twenty minutes. Finally breaking free, they headed toward Saltburn. Yet again, they caught up with some more traffic as they descended Saltburn Bank. It seemed the entire UK was in search of a patch of sand for the weekend.

It was unusually warm; the rise in heat seemed to give a rise in traffic. Following the road up to Brotton, they reached the highest point in their journey.

Looking down, they saw the dark blue of the North Sea on the left and the fields of rape crops, which matched the yellow of the sun. Everything was bright and crystal clear. The Skinningrove Steel Works were still dirty and untidy, but the brightness of the day lessened the effect. Descending the bank, they aimed for Carlin How. Getting past the roundabout that led to Skelton, they ascended a small crest on the road. As they reached the top they were greeted with another blockage of traffic. It was impossible to get past because of the narrow road and oncoming cars. The intrepid bikers sat behind a coach that spat out thick diesel fumes. The Guardians gestured to each other, expressing their frustration. This time, with being closer to the sea, a breeze, thankfully, kept them somewhat cooler. But still, they found themselves paddling along with their dangling legs, inching the bikes along the crowded road. Sod's law, thought Brendan, so near, and yet so damned far.

The coach in front was old. It was 'Y' registered, which Brendan calculated as two-thousand and one. The big yellow sign with the silhouette of two children, showed it was a scholar's bus. Each time it moved forward, in its low gears, big plumes of acrid diesel smoke spewed out the back. The light sea breeze dissipated most of it, but not before the Angels got a mouthful each time. The exhaust roared and rattled each time the vehicle moved, which suggested it was on its way out. Extrapolating this, the bus was probably in the same state throughout. The crew focussed on their breathing to reduce the intake of pollution, without much success. Every now and again, one of them would cough, from a lack of concentration.

Slowly, they got to the brow of Carlin How Bank. This road led to Loftus, on the other side of the valley, or Skinningrove, which sat in the valley itself. To get to either destination, a hairpin bend had to be negotiated, near the bottom of the valley. Moving just past the brow of the hill, the bus began its descent. Lifting his head upward and to the right-hand side, Brendan tried to gauge whether he could overtake. Although the oncoming traffic was thinner, it moved faster, accelerating up the bank. Overtaking at this moment was not an option. Still inching forward, they began to descend. Suddenly, there was a loud bang. At first, everyone looked around. It was hard to tell the direction of where the noise had come from, because of the acoustics of the valley. Brendan and Malika looked behind and as they did so, Darren pointed forward. Looking to see what he was pointing at, they both turned around and saw the bus in front of them beginning to accelerate, only this time, there were no plumes of smoke or grinding of gears.

When it is said, that in times of crisis, time slows down, it does, it really does. The bikers sat transfixed and watched in silent awe as the bus quickly gained momentum. The driver was trying to slow the bus. The red brake lights flashed on, but with no effect. There was faint screaming as the coach occupants realised what was going on. The metal behemoth moved into the oncoming lane, just missing a car. It hit the opposite embankment, but by this time gravity had taken full command of the vehicle and so it bounced off the bank and rocked violently as it did so. Another car, on its way up the incline, swerved to its left, which caused it to mount the kerb. The coach scraped it, as it careened downward and glanced off a couple more cars in the downward queue. Again, the floundering vehicle mounted the opposite kerb. This time, however, the driver managed to force the bus to stay against the grass embankment, slowing it substantially, but it kept going. Another car came around the hairpin, oblivious to the out-of-control metalwork coming towards it. Suddenly seeing the bus, the driver stopped and tried to reverse. Although the impact was lessened because of the manoeuvre, it was still struck, shoving the car backward. The bus reached the hairpin. Because of the now increasing speed, the driver couldn't turn the bus and so hit a metal gate that crossed a track leading to a wood. The gate was ripped off its hinges and it shot into the air, fortunately into the wood, in the same direction of travel as the coach.

The vehicle bulleted down a wood track, but now rocking even more violently, side to side on the uneven surface. It once again hit the embankment on the right of itself as the driver continued to fight for control. It must have been a large protruding root or maybe a deep pothole, but whatever caused it, the front end of the bus left the ground and then came crashing down. Like an injured animal, dying from its injuries, it fell onto its side, its mechanical guts falling around it. The momentum slid the man-made beast across gravel track and just onto the edge of a small ravine. The bus had come to a halt. It was on its side, windows smashed, dented, scratched and most of the underbelly had been scraped off, leaving a trail of metalwork from half way down the bank to where it now lay. The engine was screaming and rear wheels were still spinning. The only thing that kept the bus from falling down the valley were two young trees, one of which was half snapped. It didn't look as though this was going to be the final resting place of the bus.

The acoustics of the landscape made the noise of the engine deafening. By now people were getting out of their cars and the traffic, as would be expected, had come to a grinding halt. The onlookers were dazed and looked down the valley at the carnage below. It was then that time returned to normal. The noises became louder and people moved quicker. A bike drew up alongside Brendan. He turned his head, finding it difficult to process his surroundings, but equally relieved to have his attention diverted. It was Muhammad.

Above the cacophony of the surroundings, Muhammad shouted, "Let's go, let's get them out."

Brendan, considering the situation, said, "What about the bag?" referring to the drugs. Muhammad looked at him, like he was an idiot – 'School kids or drugs?' It was momentary, but Brendan felt ashamed for even questioning the situation. "You're right." He turned and waved for the others to follow. There was a roar of engines as the Guardian

Angels weaved their way through the thickening crowd. They passed the embankment that now had large gouges in it and the resultant debris was all over the road. A pedestrian stumbled on some rubble and Mike, Sophie and Darren were forced to swerve. None complained, it was understandable and they were too intensely focussed on the task at hand. Muhammad was the first to reach the wood track. His bike, not designed for the rough terrain, jarred and squeaked. Although slightly more capable, none of the other bikes managed too well either. After what was only about thirty seconds, but seemed much longer, they arrived at the bus. The engine was still screaming, but the wheels had stopped. They dismounted the bikes about twenty yards past the bus itself, so they would have room to operate.

As they got off the bikes, there was a large creaking noise. It must have been particularly loud, to be heard over the noise of the engine. Running quickly back to the bus, the crew looked around to see what the situation was, so they could decide on the best course of action. As they got closer they could hear the screaming of the children inside. Darren picked up a large stick and walked up to the bus. He struck it hard. Initially there was more screaming, but then he beat a patterned rhythm on the side. The screaming lessened somewhat as the people understood that someone was outside.

Brendan began to formulate a plan. Firstly, he looked around for Sophie and saw her looking down the hill while she was on the phone. He shouted over, "Is that the emergency services?" She stuck her thumb up. He then found Muhammad. "I need you to get on top of the bus with me. We need to see what the sit-rep is and see if we can get anyone out."

Muhammad nodded and looked for a way to mount the vehicle. Before he climbed onto the bus, Brendan grabbed Mike and Darren. "I need you two to figure out a way to keep this thing up for as long as possible." They both nodded and set about working out what to do. Malika was stood by waiting expectantly for a task. Brendan shouted over the noise, "When Muhammad and me get people out, we will lower them down, you grab them and send them to safety." Malika nodded and patted Brendan on the shoulder for encouragement.

Having given his orders and tasks, Brendan followed Muhammad onto the top of the bus. The going was hard because of the broken glass and the sharp edges of the buckled metalwork. Once on top, they carefully moved along the window frames, which no longer had windows to hold. Because of the noise of the engine, which had since been disengaged from the clutch, the two would-be rescuers couldn't make out the voices of the people inside. They did, however, hear the odd scream. Who they assumed to be a teacher, waved at them. Brendan cupped his hand over his ear and shook his head in a gesture that said he couldn't hear them. He then pointed downward, to the other side of the bus. Across the opposite windows, what was now the new floor, there was a scattering of paper. The teacher looked down and then back up and shrugged. Brendan gave a writing sign, then he could see the woman having an 'aha' moment. She bent down and grabbed a couple of pieces of paper. Brendan then gestured the question of how many there were on-board. The woman seemed to have the wherewithal to realise what he meant and began to write. When complete, she waved for a little girl to come to her. The girl crawled over and the teacher explained to her what she was going to do. The girl nodded, obviously very frightened. The woman then put the piece of paper she had just written on, into the child's sleeve. She proceeded to struggle to get the child into Brendan's waiting arms. It wasn't as difficult as expected as she took advantage of the seats that were now sideways and now served as a ladder. As she reached the opening, both Brendan and Muhammad, grabbed an arm each and pulled her clear. The three of them now stood atop the bus. Brendan asked for the paper. She reached into the clothing and gave it to him. The bike leader read it and then looked at Muhammad with trepidation. He handed it to his friend. It read: twenty-eight children, four teachers and a driver. The driver appeared unconscious, but seemingly had no injuries. Muhammad read it and looked back at Brendan. He smiled and shrugged, then gave a flippant expression on his face, as if to say 'well, we're here anyway'. Brendan couldn't help but smile back, feeling a deep respect for the man in front of him. Muhammad then leant forward, back towards the gap below and gestured for the next person to be sent up. Brendan held the paperwork up to the girl's face and pointed to Malika. She nodded and then Brendan helped her slide down what was the roof of the bus. Muhammad was already pulling the next person out of the opening. Brendan sought the attention of the first teacher and gestured for her to turn off the engine. She, in turn, beckoned another adult to take over her position and then she went to the front of the wreckage. A couple of minutes later, the noise of the engine was suddenly cut. The sudden vacuum of sound made everything seem surreal. Slowly, normality returned and the rasping of heavy breathing became prominent.

Meanwhile, Sophie had finished calling the emergency services and had joined Malika in getting people down from the height of the bus. Also, Darren and Mike had found a large log and tried to get it to the undercarriage. This was proving difficult as the bottom of the wreck faced across the valley below. Scrambling on the loose mud and leaves, the two men managed to wedge the log between what was left of the snapped tree and the bus itself. They knew it wouldn't hold forever, but hopefully long enough to get everybody off. Having increased the safety of the bus somewhat, the two guys climbed back onto the track and began to help get the people down off the bus.

Already, ten kids were out and Malika said, "Sophie, you and Mike lead the kids up the track, back to the road." She nodded and so the two of them took two children each by the hand and walked up the track. At the halfway point Mike stopped and told Sophie he would stop there and guide the kids to her. She simply smiled and gestured for the kids to come with her. Bending down to talk to the kids whose hands he held, he told them to go with Sophie. They nodded reluctantly, but complied. By this time, another two kids caught up and so the process continued. Fifteen minutes later, all the kids were off and the extraction of the adults began. The problem of exhaustion was beginning to take its toll.

Both Brendan and Muhammad were breathing heavily.

Darren shouted up, "Hey, do you guys want to swap?"

Muhammad said with wry humour, "And how pray tell, are you, my portly friend, going to get up here?"

Smiling, Darren replied, "I think, my friend, these people are not the only ones who will need to be rescued. I think it might be a good idea if you do stay up there!"

Muhammad chuckled and Brendan couldn't help but smile; Malika smirked.

Brendan shouted down, inside the bus, "OK, so far, so good, how many are left now?"

The teacher who had been their first contact said, "Four teachers and the driver."

Muhammad looked at Brendan. "I'm going in, call Malika up, they're going to need help getting up, especially the driver."

Not happy with the situation, but realising there was little choice, Brendan gave a nod for him to go ahead. As Muhammad descended, Brendan shouted for Malika to come up. The Indian went along the bus and climbed up where the others had earlier. As he was about to set foot on the bus, it lurched. Dropping onto his hands and knees, he crawled as quickly as he could to where Brendan stood, unsteadily.

Darren shouted up, "It won't hold for much longer, it's the shifting weight that's the problem, hurry up." As luck would have it, Muhammad had reached, what was now the floor of the bus before it had moved, thus preventing a fall.

Muhammad nodded to the teacher next to him and said with a sense of urgency, "Let's go!" She grabbed the sides of seats and used them to climb up in the same way as the kids had done. This was repeated twice more. The second to last teacher was a large woman. She stood stock still, terrified.

Muhammad looked at her and said, "You know I'm from ISIS?" She stepped back. He then feigned malice. "I have a bomb that's going to go off in two minutes and if you're not off, you can come with me to visit a few virgins, you're not a virgin by the way, are you?"

Her eyes wide, she scrambled up the same way the others had gone. She slipped a couple of times, but made it. As she got out of the hole at the top of her climb, she fearfully glanced back at Muhammad and then began her clamber off the bus. Brendan, sticking his head into the bus, said with an involuntary half smile, "Muhammad, sometimes you're a right asshole." Muhammad gave him a broad grin; he was enjoying this. Exasperated, Brendan prompted him to go and look at the driver.

As he reached the front of the coach, he saw the driver had a gash on his head. It didn't look too serious, but with a head wound you could never be too careful. Looking around the driver, he thought, how the hell am I gonna do this? He shouted to Brendan, "I'll never lift him out of here, he's too big and not conscious enough to help."

Brendan shouted back, "Give me a minute." Muhammad heard loud voices and then Brendan shouted, "Put your jacket over the driver's head and the two of you get cover, Darren's coming down."

Muhammad scuttled back to the driver and hurriedly took his jacket off and draped it over the driver. As he did so, the bus lurched again.

Darren's shadow fell across the front windscreen. Both Muhammad and Darren acknowledged each other and the Pakistani crouched with the teacher, behind the seating. A second later, there was a loud crash and the bus rocked from Darren's single blow. Popping up from behind the seat, Muhammad saw that the windscreen had all but disappeared. He then shuffled back along to the driver and removed his jacket from his body and put it on. Darren shook his head because of the time wasted. Muhammad looked chastened but justified it with, "I paid a bloody fortune for this!" Unclipping the seat belt, the driver moaned as he fell sideways. Again, the bus lurched, this time with a long, menacing, creaking sound. Darren reached in and grabbed the driver by his shirt and jacket as Muhammad lifted his legs out from under the seat. There was a squeal of protesting metal, they didn't feel any movement, but the sound increased the impetus nonetheless. Muhammad said "Clear" as he lifted the legs above the obstructions and as he said it, Darren pulled. The strength of Darren was impressive. The driver was lifted clean through the windscreen and onto the embankment. Muhammad then helped the remaining teacher climb out the same way. Because of the steepness, Darren couldn't carry the driver and so resorted to dragging him up to the summit.

Muhammad scrambled behind the driver and was about to ascend the final part to the top when he realised that the teacher was struggling behind. He slid back down about ten-foot and reached her. He grabbed her hand and they both made a concerted effort to reach the top. Just as they moved beyond the stricken vehicle, the retaining trees finally snapped. Looking back, like before, everything went into slow motion. The mass of steel hung in the air. For what seemed an eternity, there was no sound. The bus fell, its death throes were a mid-air pirouette and a somersault, until it hit the bottom. There was an almightily loud crash, there were no explosions, no ceremonial farewells and no regrets, simply, what seemed a final sigh, its service had come to an end, with no loss of life.

Darren reached the top of the bank with the driver in tow. Muhammad and the teacher weren't far behind. The three of them sat on the edge of the ravine, on the muddy trail. A moment later, Brendan joined them. After a couple of minutes, the rest of the crew had sat down too. Brendan put his hand on Muhammad's shoulder and said "Thanks", referring to the prompting at the top of Carlin How Bank. Muhammad looked at him and said, "We all did our bit, we were all there; of course, I was the most heroic."

Darren turned his head to his friend when he said this, then said, much to everyone's surprise, "Yeah, you were, you did good."

Muhammad had said it as a joke, but was now embarrassed. But then, everyone agreed. Muhammad was quiet after that. After about a minute of talking and taking stock, between them, the seven carried the driver up to the track entrance then carefully placed him back down, on some coats. The whole rescue had taken twenty minutes from start to finish. Brendan looked up at Sophie and asked if everyone was present; she said that they were. While these events had been going on, a crowd had gathered on the hairpin and when they heard that everyone was off the bus a round of applause broke out, along with a big cheer.

Malika leaned over and said to Brendan, "I thought we were trying to be inconspicuous?"

Brendan looked at him, smiled and shrugged his shoulders, expressing the futility of trying to recover the situation. One by one, each of the Guardian Angels sat on the kerb, next to each other. There were, of course, lots of photos being taken by the crowd. Sophie had phoned the emergency services again, to let them know that there was no immediate danger to anyone any longer, but the driver had a head injury, which would need to be checked out.

It was another twenty minutes before the ambulance and police arrived. This was no fault of theirs. The Bank Holiday traffic, combined with the Rubberneckers looking at the incident, made it difficult to get on the scene. A single ambulance finally approached their location, along with two police cars. The medics made a bee-line for the driver and the police set about directing traffic. Seeing that the situation was now in-hand, the Guardians got up and walked back down the track to retrieve their bikes. They walked in pairs and talked about the events of the day. Each then retrieved their bikes. Surprisingly, none of them had toppled over. Brendan suddenly remembered the red rucksack. He had thrown it off his back when he climbed onto the bus. Taking a moment to think on it, he decided he had a fair idea where it was and so put his bike back on its stand. He walked back to the scene of the accident and rummaged around the undergrowth, for about thirty seconds when he spotted it. With relief he picked it up, only to notice white powder in the foliage. "Oh Christ" he muttered to himself. He checked the bags inside. One had been punctured. Although not much, some powder had been scattered. Kicking the vegetation, he managed to disperse the evidence. Thinking, 'that'll have to do', he put the pack onto his back and resumed pushing the bike up the undulating wood track.

He was a minute or so behind the others, who were stood waiting for him at the junction. He nodded as he approached, expressing his thanks for their patience. Catching his breath, he said, "Well, we have a schedule to keep –are we ready?" They all nodded, suddenly serious again. "We're at least half an hour behind," said Brendan.

They were all sweaty and dirty, but concerns for comfort were long gone; they just wanted today over with. With everyone helmeted, they started the engines. As they were about to set off, a large car suddenly blocked their way. Looking at each other, they couldn't help but be surprised. The men in the car extracted themselves from the high-powered vehicle and walked towards the group of bikers. Turning his engine off and removing his helmet, with a sigh Brendan acknowledged the first man who approached him. The man was balding and had what was left of his hair as a crew cut, thus making no effort to hide the receding hairline. Brendan thought police detective, probably ex-military. The man put his hand out to Brendan, who cautiously took it.

The man said, in a way that showed he enjoyed his position, "I'm Detective McNulty, Cleveland CID. I want to say, thanks for what you guys did." He beamed as he said it.

The other man, presumably another detective, walked down the track where the Guardians had just pushed their bikes up. Brendan, half-heartedly returned McNulty's smile, whilst thinking about the time factor.

McNulty continued, "It's all over social media, you and your heroic bikers." At this, Brendan and Malika looked at each other in dismay.

The detective behind them was walking back up the track, when he shouted his associate over. McNulty excused himself and went to his partner. They stood talking for about a minute and then McNulty returned to the gang. The other officer was on his mobile. Detective McNulty, with a more business-like expression, said, "Anyway, we're here to investigate why the bus fell into the ravine. So, I would appreciate it, if you guys could get off your bikes and give us a statement about what you saw?"

Brendan enquired, "You know, we want to help, but we're on a bit of a deadline – can't we come in to the station by appointment?"

McNulty replied snappily, "I'm afraid not, I need to get the info down, while it's still fresh in your minds. You know, with other distractions, memory recall becomes less accurate. Of course, with the scale of the events that just occurred, that's the last thing we want. There could have been a lot of deaths today. It's only by pure chance that there wasn't."

Seeing that they had no choice, the bikers dismounted, put the bikes on the stands, then took off their helmets and gloves. The group sat back down on the kerb, where they were before. It was then that they heard and saw a police van coming up the bank from the direction of Loftus. They all instinctively knew what it was for. Things were going from bad to worse.

CHAPTER 18

27/08/17

The police van pulled up next to the bikes. It had a riot cage on the front and the windows, at the back, were blacked out. It was a serious bit of kit for some serious kind of police work. The traffic, in the background, was now flowing freely and other than the odd glance, no-one really took any notice of what was going on, on the side of the road. Two burly officers, in stab vests, got out and stood waiting. A few moments later, descending the Carlin How Bank, came two more cop cars, both with flashing lights. Brendan glared at McNulty, who returned the look with a shrug. Once the cars had come to a halt, the sirens were silenced. McNulty walked over to the Guardian Angels, where he was sure they could all hear him.

"I'm saying this to all of you. All six, so-called Guardian Angels. I am hereby arresting you for possession of illegally banned substances, with intent to supply. You do not have to say anything, but it may harm your defence if you do not mention, when questioned, something which you later rely on in court. Anything you do say, may be given in evidence. Do you understand?"

They all nodded, but otherwise remained silent. By the time the statement had been read.out, the other two, late-arriving police cars, had spilled out another four officers, each armoured with a stab vest. The six riot prepared officers made a bee-line for the Guardian Angels. The first one reached for his cuffs, but McNulty stepped forward and put his hand on his arm. The officer looked at him with a confused expression. "They won't resist, stick 'em in the wagon, it'll be OK."

The officer asked, "Procedure?"

The detective reassured him, "Don't worry, I'll take the rap."

The officer cocked his head, but conceded. "On your head be it." He then said to the Guardians, "Follow me, folks." They all filed behind him and walked to the wagon. Brendan was last and asked, "What about the bikes?"

McNulty said, "Don't worry, they'll be taken care of."

Brendan took a few steps when McNulty stopped him by saying loudly, "The bag?"

Brendan smirked, but then wiggled the pack off his back. As he did so, he realised how they had been caught. There was white powder on the outside. When he put it back on his back, the contents must have puffed out.

The officer that led the Guardians to the wagon, opened the door and then the inner cage. Reluctantly, they all got in. Just as Muhammad mounted the step, he turned to the officer and asked, "Do you think you could put the siren on?" He got a semi-smile and a raised eyebrow, but otherwise no answer. Shrugging, Muhammad found a seat next to Darren. He shouted back to the officer, "Why do I have to sit next to the big sweaty one?"

Darren responded with equal humour. "Can I kill him?"

The officer said, "How long do you need?"

Darren looked at Muhammad, who returned the look with a large fake grin. The door of the wagon slammed shut. There was a momentary darkness, until their eyes adjusted to the dimness of the internal lighting. It was ten minutes before the wagon set off. The vehicle juddered and then idled for another minute or so, then they could feel the wagon making its way up Carlin How Bank.

Sophie broke the sombre silence and said, "That went well – at least we're not cuffed."

Mike retorted sarcastically, "Small blessings."

They sat silently again and then Muhammad began to sing, "The wheels on the bus go, round and round, round and round, round and round."

Everyone shouted in unison, "Shut up." He sullenly stopped. Silence fell, across the group. Muhammad then began to hum and tap his feet and then burst out with "Three wheels on my wagon and I'm just riding along."

Mike said, "Pack it in, you're irritating everyone." Muhammad smirked and carried on, purposely winding him up.

Brendan looked at the annoying Muslim. "Listen, Muhammad, we're all in this together. I know you're nervous, as we all are. Please stop it."

Muhammad considered what he had said and stopped. Reinforcing his statement, Brendan said reassuringly, "It will all work out, don't worry."

The back of the wagon was getting very warm and the gang were beginning to sweat profusely. It seemed that there was no air conditioning in the vehicle. The anxiety of the arrest, the stress of the possible negative outcomes, coupled with the excessive heat, was making for very poor conditions. What made matters worse, was the fact that each of them wore body armour and leathers. To get some relief, one at a time, they tried to remove their clothing. Unfortunately, the cramped conditions and the constant rocking of the wagon made it very difficult. The cherry on the cake came, when five of the passengers realised that the remainder got sea sick, especially in enclosed environments. Darren threw up. Spew went all over the crew. Of course, everyone moaned and tried to manoeuvre away from the vomit. As Darren roiled from his sickness, in ashen grey state, the rest of the crew were cursing. In the melee that ensued, jackets were dropped into the ejection, thus increasing the tension and anxiety in the enclosed environment. Darren looked around at the crew, clearly not well and mumbled "I'm sorry" rather pathetically. The other five just sat, having now given up the fight to stay clean. They were all disgusted with him. Although there were a few close calls, Darren didn't throw up anymore. But, needless to say, no one spoke again. They could tell that they were nearing Middlesbrough as the wagon didn't go up and down hills quite as much and they seemed to be going at a slower pace, which suggested that the traffic was getting thicker.

The wagon came to a halt for a longer time than it would for a junction, which could only mean that they had arrived at some sort of police station. They heard some talking and then a squeal, which was assumed to be a large gate. The engine roared again as it set off once more, then they were jarred by a couple of speed bumps. The vehicle finally came to a halt and the engine was switched off. After another minute or so of talking, the back door was opened. The officer who had led them in, in the first place, stepped back. "Oh my god, what the hell?" he coughed and gagged, whilst stepping back to let the air circulate. Taking a deep breath, he unlocked the inner cage and then retreated so the crew could get out. There were no smiles or wisecracks. Still looking sick, Darren stepped out, but not before slipping a little on his own vomit. All six looked sorry for themselves.

Looking them over, with a smirk, the officer said, "Follow me." He led them into the bright, but sparse corridor of a processing area. Stood behind a raised desk, that had computers and various bits of stationery, was a large desk sergeant. The man was a long-serving officer, who had seen it all, but even he smiled when he saw the sorry crew.

"Good afternoon, ladies and gentlemen. Welcome to Cleveland Police HQ. Hopefully we can make your stay here as short and as pleasant as possible." His voice dripped with sarcasm. "Can I ask you all, have you had your arresting statement read to you and did you understand it? Would you like me to repeat or explain it?" They acknowledged that they had understood.

A strange thing happens to people when they realise that they have nothing to lose. Some people get depressed and start looking inward and try to work out where they went wrong, then try not to repeat it. Whereas others, like the Guardian Angels, decided that they couldn't care less anymore. If they were going down, they were going to have some fun on the way. The row of bikers stood in front of the Sergeant's desk. Two were on their mobiles, two were talking and two were having a mooch about. To everyone's amazement, it was Mike who spoke first.

"You're tall, I bet you have a hell of a time getting such long-legged trousers." It was such a corny joke he got a couple of laughs, one from behind the desk, which made the Sergeant turn and glare at the offender. He also glanced at Mike, but said nothing. This was a man who had seen it all, and then some. Having now completed the preliminary paperwork, he looked at the motley crew in front of him and pointed at Mike.

"You, approach the desk." It was said in a no-nonsense manner. Mike went to the desk. "Name?" prompted the Sergeant.

"Mickey Mouse," Mike replied.

The sergeant looked up from his work and down at Mike; he sighed and then said, "What is your name?" emphasizing the 'your'.

"Mike," said Mike.

"Mike what?" said the Sergeant.

"No," said Mike.

Realising quite quickly what was going on, the Sergeant took a deep breath and in a careful monotone asked, "What is your surname?"

Mike too understood that the game had come to a quick conclusion and reluctantly answered, "Jones."

By this time, the rest of the crew were smiling at Mike. Their mobile phones had been put away and they were watching with interest. The common thought was, what a place to come out of your shell! The banter between the Sergeant and Mike was getting funnier.

The Sergeant, now looking at Mike with open contempt said, "I suppose you think you're funny?"

Mike replied, "No, Mike Jones, do you think I'm funny? You can call me funny if you want, I don't mind."

The Sergeant, by this time, was looking bewildered. In exasperation, he said, "Go away."

Mike walked to the door and was about to leave, when the Sergeant shouted, "Oi, where the hell are you going?"

Mike shouted back, "Leaving, like you said."

The Guardians were finding it hard to supress their smiles.

The Sergeant then shouted, "Go and stand next to your friends." To which Muhammad interjected, "That'll be hard!" Even the Desk Sergeant smirked at that. Mike walked back to where had been before the mini-escapade had started. The Sergeant then pointed to Brendan and said, "You're next, no messing about."

The rest of the crew were soon processed and the Sergeant shouted over a female constable. "Take these." He paused before he let himself swear, then said "People" instead, "and get their fingerprints and photos please."

The woman, smartly dressed in her police uniform, said, "Yes Sergeant." Then she turned to the puke-covered bikers and said, "Follow me please."

The bikers trooped behind her, in single file, along another corridor. It wasn't long before she directed them into a side room and told them to sit. There were already two people sat on hard plastic seats. The guardians sat on the row behind the two occupants. After a moment or two, the man and woman got up and moved to the front row of seats, away from the smell of sick. When they did this, Darren leaned over and looked along the row to Muhammad. "Oi, Muhammad, they moved cos of your breath." Muhammad gave him the one-fingered salute in return. Darren's colour had returned to his face; apparently, so had his sense of humour.

When the people in front had been processed, Muhammad was called up first. He approached the fingerprint booth and stood waiting politely, while the officer prepared the card and ink for his prints. Smiling at him, she beckoned him forward. "If I could have your right index finger first please." He complied. She was firm with each finger, making sure that each print was clear. He smirked. She looked at him. "Yes, what's so funny?"

He smirked as he said, "So this is what they mean by a having a good fingering." She looked at him with an expression of disappointment. For some reason, for which he wasn't sure, he suddenly felt ashamed and disappointed in himself. He said nothing more as she carried on with his left hand. As he was about to leave the cubicle he said, "You know, I'm sorry, I shouldn't have said that." At this, she gave him another glance, she could tell in his voice that he meant it. Following on, he said, "Sometimes, I disappoint myself."

She handed him a wet wipe to remove the ink from his hands. She looked at him as he walked away, almost feeling sorry for him. The rest of the crew followed suit and when they were all done, the officer said, "We need to get your photos done and we'll see where we go from there." Once again, they followed the woman out of the room and down the corridor, to the photo room.

As before, the gang were asked to sit on hard plastic chairs, while they waited their turn. Muhammad went first and did as he was told without comment. He was sulking because of his earlier faux pas. He fancied the woman and for the first time in his life, he was bothered about what somebody else thought of him. He wanted to impress her, but he had blown his chance, because of his not-so-smart mouth. When he had finished, he slumped back into his chair. Sophie was next. Her first comment was: "Do you want my best side?" The police officer gave her a blank expression. This wasn't something she hadn't heard a thousand times before, she thought wordlessly. Whereas Darren shouted, "You'll be there a while then?" At this, she turned to him and stuck her tongue out, then giggled. She faced the camera and gave a big smile.

The officer said in a bland monotone, "Look straight at the camera;

do not smile." Sophie dropped the smile, but still had that twinkle of defiance in her eyes. As before, the rest of the gang went through the process, but unlike Sophie, didn't make comment.

After the final DNA swab, the gang were led to the cells, where they would be held for the night. Brendan stopped short of the cell and turned to the woman officer who was ushering them along.

"I'd like to ask a couple of questions please."

She replied, if a little tiredly, "What is it?" It was coming to the end of the shift and she simply couldn't be bothered with the chew.

Brendan asked, "Are we getting charged?"

She said, "To be honest, I'm not sure, but given the allegations of possessing such a large quantity of drugs and the circumstances surrounding your case, I would have thought that the right to hold you for twenty-four hours is being exercised."

"OK." He knew he sounded weak and accepting, but what else could he say?

The woman continued to look at him. "Anything else?"

Grateful for the prompt, he asked, "Any chance of a shower, so we can get this puke off us, you know, health and safety and all that?"

She looked at the faces around her. They didn't seem violent or anything, so she said, "I'll see what I can do, I'll have word with the Sarge."

Malika said, "That would be most appreciated," with a winning smile.

Giving a quick smile in return, the woman said, "For now, I'll have to put you in the cells, two per cell please." Brendan and Malika went in to the first, Muhammad and Mike the second and finally Darren and Sophie went into the third.

Brendan sat on the wooden bed, opposite Malika. He looked at his friend, who he could see, was extremely tired. "Are you Ok" he asked.

Malika looked back. "Yeah, I'm used to the late nights, but not this amount of activity and stress."

Brendan suggested, "Have a lie down and get some rest."

Malika, grateful for the thought said, "I will, once I've had a shower and a clean-up. If I lay down now, I'll not get back up."

Brendan smiled; he felt the same way. It had been a long day, but he was going to have a nap. He nodded to Malika and said, "Excuse me."

He took his jacket off to make a pillow. He had been lucky, Darren hadn't hit his jacket, but he had got one of his legs. Muhammad and Mike were a sorry state – they had got the brunt of the ejection. Brendan and Malika rested in silence within the cell. The noise from the rest of the busy custody reception echoed, but Brendan was too tired to notice and Malika was beyond caring. Mike and Muhammad were having an intense conversation. Mike, with his anxiety, was speculating and trying to work out the worst possible scenario, which in turn fed Muhammad's perpetual need for drama. So far, they were going to be gang raped in Durham Jail and/or they were going to be put in with the paedophiles and nonce's, which ended with the same result as the first. Every now and again the conversation would be exhausted, but then start again, with the same conclusion. In Darren and Sophie's cell, it was quiet. Sophie had cuddled into Darren and had been crying. He tried to comfort her by stroking her hair slowly and rhythmically.

After half an hour or so – no-one could be sure – the cell doors were opened. The new residents of all three cells came to their doors. They peered into the corridor and saw the Sergeant, stood with the woman officer they had seen earlier.

"Ladies and gentlemen, I've come to explain a few things, so please pay attention."

Brendan stood rubbing his eyes, next to Malika, who by now, was particularly exhausted. Both Mike and Muhammad looked tense and wound up. Sophie, still close to Darren was red-eyed and her hair was in a matted mess from leaning against Darren's puke-covered clothes. Darren just looked serious. They all looked at the Desk Sergeant.

"Now I have your attention, please listen carefully. I have had an e-mail from the investigating detectives on your case." He sought a reaction, but got none. "They have submitted the substances and bag that contained it for analysis. However, the lab unit isn't open until tomorrow, at eight AM. The test itself will only take approximately ten minutes, but as you can imagine, there will be a bit of a backlog, so it may take a while for it to get done." Again, he paused for a comment or question, but they continued their silence. "Because of the potential gravity of the alleged offence, as PC Wood said earlier, the right to hold you for twenty-four hours is being exercised." There were couple of sighs and slumped shoulders this time, but other than that, nothing. Continuing, he said, "You will be questioned in the morning at approximately ten AM." To finish, he asked, "Any questions, does everyone understand what I have just said?" Nods all round. Satisfied that he had got his point across, he then said, "I've been told about your activities this afternoon. For that you have my respect. Also, when I said for you to come back–" He nodded towards Mike– "You did. Because of that, I don't believe that you are a flight risk. If I thought you were, you wouldn't be outside of your cells right now."

He let the statement sink in. In not so many words, he was asking if they could be trusted. No one said anything, but he decided that they could be anyway, so he continued. "Down the corridor, on the left, is a washroom with a shower and basin etc. PC Wood has put towels and toiletries out for your use. I'm afraid that there are no hair facilities, such as a brush or dryer, but at least you won't smell." There were a few smiles and looks of appreciation at this news. He continued, "Please leave everything as you found it, this isn't normal practice, but I believe I can trust you, don't let me down."

He looked at them hopefully. They nodded their thanks. "I would suggest being as quick as possible. I'm going to get PC Wood to lock your cells as soon as you're clean; this is for your safety. You have no idea of the sort of individual we get in over the weekend." He left them with that rather ominous thought as he went back to his duties.

PC Wood then said with earnest, "C'mon then, don't stand around, let's get this done, who's first?" All the men agreed that Sophie should go first, then Darren, the middle cell and then the two older men last.

Escorting Sophie down the corridor, PC Wood directed her to the room. When the men saw where she had gone, they returned to their cells and sat down. Each one took their turn, feeling fresher and cleaner.

The night in the cells was a very long one. Other than a few startles, the two older men in the Guardians slept all the way through. The two in the middle cell, Muhammad and Mike, were wide awake. They heard all the goings on. There were fights, scuffles, shouting and the occasional scream. In a cell further down the corridor, a new guest banged against the door and threatened to kill everyone. These threats went on for about two hours, until they tired. The banging became weaker and less frequent. At five AM, all was silent. Every half hour there were footsteps, up and down the corridor, accompanied with a regular clunk. An officer pulled open a hatch on each door and firmly clicked it shut, having checked that the individuals inside the cells were still alive. This was the infamous 'suicide watch'. Mike mentioned this to Muhammad, creating further anxiety and speculation. Every now and again, there was an unexpected noise, whether it be a bang, scream or shout. One of them would whisper to the other, "Did you hear that?" Invariably, the other would say "Yeah, sounds bad." The climax of the night for the two paranoid Angels, was a loud bang on their own door. They assumed, because of the accompanying noise and swearing, that there was a struggle to get an individual into a cell. Finally, a cell door was slammed shut. Moments later, two officers walked past, muttering about the bother that they had just dealt with. Unusually, there were no other sounds of protest. It seemed the person concerned had realised they were defeated.

In Darren and Sophie's cell, Darren was sat wide awake. He had Sophie cuddled into him, asleep. When the loud bangs occurred, she would murmur, but otherwise, she slept through it all. Darren was sat thinking about his mother. She would be past herself by now. He imagined the course of events that would most likely have taken place. She would have rung the police, who would have said that he was being held. So now, she would be beside herself, stewing at home. Christ, what had he got himself into? He looked down at Sophie, he stroked her hair, more for his own comfort than hers. He knew that he had fallen for her and would do this all over again, as long as she was with him. He really had found his purpose in life and would see this out, to the end. Hopefully, that would be soon. He was starting to feel sleepy himself. As his eyes closed, he heard the clicking of their cell door. Somehow or another, it had gotten to seven AM. That had been a long night.

It was apparently Monday morning now. Brendan and Malika woke up as the cell door rattled. Both were bleary eyed and slowly sat on the edge of the wooden beds. Brendan immediately started to put on his boots, while Malika tried to rally himself around. The Indian adjusted his turban, which had moved while he had slept and then he picked up his glasses and rubbed them clean with the edge of his T-shirt. He double checked that they were smear free; satisfied, he put them on. Brendan finished putting his boots on, then stood up, tucking himself in. He asked Malika, "Are you OK?" Nodding slightly, Malika reached down and began to put his own boots on too. After a minute or two, Brendan then prompted, "Ready?"

Malika stood wordlessly and followed his friend to the door. Muhammad and Mike looked terrible. Their clothes were bedraggled and unkempt. The two of them had red eyes from a lack of sleep. Brendan smiled. "Are you guys OK?" They both nodded. Muhammad said, "Knackered, but OK." Mike nodded, agreeing with his friend. Further down the corridor, the two love birds stood looking dazed. Darren had red eyes, like Muhammad and Mike. Sophie had frizzy hair and the side of her face was red and creased from lying on Darren's jacket. Brendan enquired, "What about you two?" Both Darren and Sophie gave a bleak smile.

A minute later, the new shift's Desk Sergeant walked up the corridor. He smiled at them as he approached. He didn't shake their hands, but he did say hello in a friendly manner. "OK you lot. Have a wash-up. Breakfast will be served in few minutes and I believe the duty solicitor will be in to see you, for about ten AM. Any questions anyone?"

Muhammad asked, "Where would breakfast be served please?"

This is when the Sergeant smiled broadly. "Normally, you would eat in the cells, off a plastic tray, but because of what went on yesterday, we're letting you eat in our canteen." The crew looked at each other. The Sergeant said, quite smugly, "You won't have to eat this crap." He then gave a parting smile and walked away. It wasn't long before the gang were washed up and ready to go for breakfast.

They presented themselves to the Desk Sergeant, who directed them to the canteen. They had to ascend a couple of flights of stairs, until they arrived at some battleship grey, double swing doors. As they walked in, the place fell into silence, reminiscent of a Wild West bar. All the people stopped walking and looked at them. People who were facing away, turned and looked too. After a moment or two, people at the tables stood up, others put their trays down. Then the applause began, accompanied with whistles and shouting. Two people at a large table moved their trays to an adjacent table and invited the Guardians to sit in their place. Still dazed from the rough night, they all sat down. The applause eventually faded and a lady from behind the counter came over. She stood next to them with a big smile.

"How can I help you folks?"

Brendan smiled back and said, "If it's OK with you, we'd like breakfast please."

"My dear," replied the lady, "I have been told to let you know, breakfast is on the house, for all six of you. We know you're in a spot of bother, but before it starts, everyone here, as you have probably already guessed, would like to thank you for your efforts yesterday."

The gang looked at each other, becoming embarrassed.

"We only did what anyone else would have done," said Brendan. The others nodded in agreement.

The lady bent over and said conspiratorially, "But they didn't, did they?" Straightening up, she then asked, "OK, orders please."

For a good hour, the Guardians ate a hearty breakfast. Feeling better for the praise of those around them and the good food, they were ready for the rest of the day.

The clock eventually reached nine-thirty and they stood up and made their way back to the Desk Sergeant.

"Feeling better?" he asked.

Brendan replied, "Much, thanks, where do you want us now?"

The Sergeant said, "If you go down the corridor, you'll see a door with a sign 'Interview room 2', that's where you need to be. The solicitor is in there and the interviewing detective will be along in about an hour. He told me eleven, but he's known to be always late."

"OK, thanks," replied Brendan.

They all walked to the room that he had described and filed in. A short man, with receding hair stood up as they entered. He was accompanied by a younger man, with dark hair. Both wore a black suit, white shirt and a red tie. The solicitor and his assistant shook hands with each of the Guardians. After the formality of the greeting, they all took a seat.

"Well, hello to all of you. My name is Rupert McCormick of McCormick & Jones Solicitors and this is my paralegal, Andrew, who is here to takes notes for me." He gave a practised fake smile and then continued. "Normally, what would happen, is that a paralegal would sit through a police interview and then an appointment with the solicitor is made, to make a case for the defence. In this case, being potentially so large and with so many of you, I thought it may be prudent to be in at the beginning, so to speak." Again, that false smile. "If it's OK, for now I'll speak." He looked at the Guardians for assent.

They nodded; after all, none of them had ever been in this position before, so they had no choice but to take his lead. McCormick gave a run-down of the most likely chain of events that would happen in the next twenty-four hours, on the assumption that the police were wanting to go ahead.

After this he said, "It would be a good idea for me to have your side of the story, before the questioning begins, so that we know how to handle the interviews and so on."

The Guardians all looked at Brendan expectantly. It was obviously up to him to relate the events of the last couple of weeks.

Brendan ran through the story of the last fortnight, but withheld the part about the bag swap until the end. "When we stopped at the garage on Longlands Road, I made a pre-arranged swap of the bag, for the exact same bag containing caster sugar, with an undercover police officer."

The others simply stared at him in silence, until Muhammad exclaimed, "Do what?" He couldn't disguise the incredulity in his voice.

Holding his hand up, Brendan cut off any further comment with "Let me explain".

Sophie sarcastically said, "I think you better."

Brendan levelled his eyes at the others, asserting his will. "Because I started this club, I became the de facto leader. So, it is my responsibility to make sure you're all OK and don't come to harm. In the week after our meeting with the Beezlebubs, I phoned the police to let them know we would be moving a Kilo of drugs. Not only do I feel guilty about getting us in that position in the first place, the idea of causing so much misery on the streets is something that I wouldn't be able to live with."

The animosity the others had toward him began to fade. Malika asked, "Why didn't you tell us what you were doing? Poor Mike was sick with stress."

Brendan replied, "Exactly, that's the point, it was real for you, it had to be. We've been watched by the Beezles and the police all along, so everything had to be real, or we would have been scuppered. The police in here don't know about it, just some anti-corruption unit."

At this, they all seemed a bit more relieved. It meant that the tests for the drugs would come back negative, which also meant they would have no choice but to drop the charges.

Brendan looked around at the gang. "This has to remain a secret, not even your mothers can know or the Beezles will come after us." He then faced the solicitor, who was sat, absolutely fascinated by the turn of events. "Mr McCormick." Brendan tried again with a slightly raised voice, "Mr McCormick."

The solicitor shook himself from his reverie "Oh yes, I'm terribly sorry, I haven't come across anything like this before."

Andrew was rapidly taking notes in shorthand, occasionally looking up to see who was speaking. Brendan, with a worried tone said, "Mr McCormick, we have to make sure that we keep this secret, even from the Detective that will be doing the interviews."

McCormick nodded. Brendan continued, "When they come in, we will be told that the bag contained caster sugar and he'll probably tell us that we've been wasting police time or words to that effect, but I suppose we can deal with that, when it arises."

The mood of the Guardians had lightened and the tension had been significantly reduced.

Turning back to his friends, Brendan said apologetically, "I'm really sorry for not letting you in on what I had done, but the only way to make sure you were OK, was to let you act naturally."

The team still seemed a little reticent, but one by one, they relented to his logic and promised to maintain the façade.

McCormick asked, "What are your instructions, or do I forget that any of this just happened?"

Brendan said, "Right now, we'll go back to our cells and have a lie down. I think the Detective will be turning up in half an hour. I also think it might be a good idea if you stay and be a witness, at the very least."

McCormick agreed and told Andrew to pack up. They would go for a coffee and return when they were called. The Guardians got up and left the room. They walked back to their cells that they had spent the night in and tried to have a nap, before the next hurdle.

Malika sat on his bed, whilst Brendan lay back, his head on his jacket.

Malika said, "You could have told us, you know."

Brendan sighed. "It wasn't because I don't trust any of you. Like I said, there had to be a genuine reaction to each situation – if there wasn't, suspicions would have arisen, which would have put the police operation in jeopardy and endangered you all. Even if we all fell out, at least we would be alive to feel annoyed."

Malika lay down onto his own jacket. "I suppose." He sounded unhappy, but Brendan knew he understood.

Muhammad and Mike both lay on their hard beds in their cell. Muhammad looked over at Mike and said, "You know, it was a bit underhand, what he did."

Mike nodded, but said, "On the face of it you're right, but logically, he was correct. If he hadn't done that and we had the actual drugs, we would be looking at least seven years apiece. Human nature would have kicked in: when a trial came up and we would have all blamed each other. That's the one advantage of being autistic, I can't relate that well emotionally, but I can see the logic."

Muhammad went quiet at this and reluctantly agreed, "Yeah, well."

Mike said, "You should be thanking him, I will be."

Muhammad gave a muted response.

Darren and Sophie sat opposite each other in their cell. They didn't speak. Eventually, she looked up at his face and said, "You know he did the right thing. We might be under stress now, but all we shall have to put up with now, is a bit of paperwork and we'll be done. We could have gone down for it."

Darren nodded and held her hand. They waited in silence until they were called to see the detective.

CHAPTER 19

28/08/17

It was eleven fifteen when Detective McNulty rolled in. The Desk Sergeant shouted for the Guardian Angels, who were in their cells. It took a couple of minutes before the bikers had gathered in the corridor. The Sergeant directed them to the same office, where they had been previously. McCormick and Andrew were waiting outside the door, giving their practised smiles.

As they approached, the solicitor said, "Lady and gentlemen, would you like a chat before we start or shall we just get straight on with it?"

Brendan looked at him sternly and said, "Let's get this over and done with."

McCormick knocked on the door; hearing a 'come in', he entered and said, "The Guardian Angels are here for the interview with yourself as requested."

Nodding his acknowledgement, the solicitor then opened the door wide and the gang walked in, in single file. Malika, Brendan, Sophie and McCormick sat at the desk, opposite the detectives and the rest stood behind, against the wall.

Once settled, McNulty said, "Under normal circumstances we

would interview you, one at a time, under caution, but as it is, the test came back from the lab as negative. Of course, having no evidence, we cannot press charges." He looked and sounded disappointed. Continuing, he said, "So, as you will notice, there are no recording devices and we're not taking notes. You are of course able to walk out when you want, but we would appreciate it if you would answer some questions."

The poor man was trying to salvage something from the situation; after all he had arrested probably the most famous biker club in the country. These individuals had just saved more than thirty people's lives and he had thrown them in jail for the night. Brendan looked around at his crew. He felt relief for them that it was essentially all over.

He asked, "Shall we help the man?"

Malika said, "Well, he's only doing his job."

Brendan turned back to McNulty. "OK, ask away."

McNulty couldn't hide his annoyance that things hadn't gone his way, but persevered at being professional. "The first question, what were you doing in the location of the accident?"

Brendan answered, "Going home, or at least to what we call the clubhouse, which is the Angel pub, in Loftus marketplace. We do live there, you know, well, four of us do; Malika lives in Saltburn and Sophie lives in Easington."

Not yet seeing an avenue or opening, McNulty continued, "Why would anyone ride around on a bike, with a bag of caster sugar on their backs?"

Brendan paused, not quite sure what to say, when Darren interjected: "It was mine, I am a baker, as you know."

Thinking that the excuse was more of a ruse, McNulty asked, "Why have it with you on a ride?"

Darren replied, "Because we collected it from Middlesbrough, while we were on a trip out, so I didn't have to make another trip in the car."

McNulty, still believing that something was amiss, pointed out: "If you're the baker, why was it on his back?" He nodded toward Brendan.

Darren's response was fluid, which made it especially convincing. "Have you seen the size of the bag? I couldn't wear it, so Brendan kindly volunteered to carry it."

That road had been closed off, so McNulty changed tack. "Surely, as a baker, you would already have caster sugar, tons of it, I would have thought."

Darren smiled knowingly. "That sugar wasn't going to the factory, it was coming home with me. I live with my mother, who is the main shareholder and originator of the business. She makes experimental cakes with the best gear, like that caster sugar. When she's happy for whatever to be mass produced, we find cheaper ingredients to do the same job, in bulk."

Looking deflated, McNulty conceded defeat. "Just one last thing, why didn't you just tell me this at the start?"

Mike spoke up this time; he had an edge of anger in his voice, probably caused by the poor night's sleep and the frustration of the recent events. "Would you have believed us? Like everyone else, you make assumptions and when you realise you're wrong, you justify it by blaming circumstance or others. That's what's wrong with the world these days. No-one's big enough to accept personal responsibility for their actions, which creates bigotry and malice."

Everyone was stunned into silence, no-one had expected the quietest to speak in that way. Darren put his arm around him and gave him a squeeze of support and Muhammad patted his shoulder. The others smiled at him. He feebly returned the smile; it seemed he was on the verge of tears, but he held back.

After a moment's silence, McNulty looked up at Mike and said, "You know what, you're right."

He stood up, quickly followed by his assistant. "When I say this, I mean it." The Detective looked at the leather clad party in the room. "I apologise for having put you through a night in the cells, but most of all, I want to congratulate you for what you did yesterday. You have completely turned the ideas and assumptions that people have about motorcycle clubs on their head."

He got a couple of nods of thanks as they went out of the door. He quietly closed it behind him, and so ended the interview of the prosecuting detective.

McCormick, who had sat silently throughout the conversation, said with a little trepidation, "Why did you tell him that, why didn't you just tell him about the bag swap and what have you?"

Brendan looked at him and explained, "I was told not to, by the Detective I had made the arrangements with. He said that there may be police corruption involved and he wasn't sure where the problem was. The anti-corruption detective must have gone to the lab or something, because I was told there was a tracking device in the bag, which McNulty never mentioned."

McCormick, concerned, said, "Things seem to be bigger than they appear."

Brendan said to his friends, "That was my worry, I thought we would need back up." When he said this, there was some uncomfortable shuffling in the room, as it had now dawned on the others, what sort of problems they could have been facing. Brendan looked down, not sure what else to say.

Muhammad gave some words of comfort. "We were all shocked initially and perhaps a little hurt, but we know you meant well and with the ways things have turned out, it seems you have been proven right. We're all on your side."

Muhammad smiled and the others gave their agreement, with a nod or a pat on Brendan's shoulder. Feeling relieved, the tension of the last week began to ease.

McCormick rose, along with Andrew, and said, "As the cliché goes, it seems my work here is done. I'll leave you here and let the Desk Sergeant discharge you. Also, Andrew and I would like to add to the congratulations of the Detective and good luck for the future." He shook each of their hands and left them in the room.

With the criminal issues finally put to bed, the gang filed out of the interview room and into the corridor. The place had begun to get busy and the noise level was rising in proportion. The gang walked down the corridor toward the Desk Sergeant's station. As they approached, a moustachioed, short man stepped in their path. The man looked as though he could lose a few pounds. His shirt was stretched across his belly and his tie rested on it too. He wore a dark blue suit, that looked as though it had been worn for too long. His balding head shone in the fluorescent strip lights. He raised his hands for a handshake and said amiably, "Hello, I presume you're Brendan Sykes." A little suspicious, Brendan shook the offered appendage. Giving a quick smile, the man introduced himself: "I'm Detective Sergeant Knowles. I spoke with you on the phone."

Brendan clicked straight away. It was the anti-corruption guy, who had arranged the bag transfer. The rest of the gang looked at each other, wondering what was going to happen next. The Detective turned to the Desk Sergeant and gave him the thumbs up. He then faced the Guardians and asked, "Can I have a few minutes of your time please. You're not in trouble or anything, just need to straighten a few things out."

As before, the beleaguered bikers filed back into the interview room.

Muhammad commented sarcastically, "If we stay here any longer, we might just as well take a mortgage out on the place!"

Knowles heard him and said apologetically, "I won't keep you long, I promise, I know you've spent a night here and can't wait to go."

Having once again settled down, Brendan asked, "So, how can we help you?" Unlike Muhammad, he managed to restrain his tone, despite feeling otherwise. After all, helping the man in front of them had gotten them a night in the cells.

"Firstly, I want to applaud you for the rescue, I mean, well, wow!" Smiling thinly, they waited patiently for him to continue. Taking a breath, Knowles broke the news. "The problem is, the bag swap. It wasn't cocaine, it was caster sugar."

Brendan, being defensive, exclaimed, "Well, it can't have been us, we've had our stuff confiscated and as you know, we never went home or anywhere else, but here."

Knowles, looking concerned, said in a hushed voice, "That would mean, we have a police insider – the bag we gave you had a tracker in it, so did the sugar, in case they were separated. There were two half-Kilo bags, one of which has disappeared. Where it gets hazy with you lot, is when the rescue took place, the signal was intermittent and we couldn't track for about half an hour."

Mike pointed out, "We were in a valley and East Cleveland is in the sticks, with poor reception at the best of times."

Brendan frowned as he tried to retrace their steps during the time of the rescue. "When we started on the bus, I threw the bag into the undergrowth, but once we finished, I picked it up. It was taken from me when the detectives turned up."

Knowles said, "We know it was the bag we gave you, because we went to the lab and extracted the trackers, just in case an insider spotted them. Unfortunately, because there were no drugs and the Beezlebubs didn't take possession, it means we can't go ahead with a prosecution." He looked as disappointed as McNulty had. "Anyway, congratulations again for the rescue and thanks for your efforts. It's just unfortunate that it never worked out." Like many others had done before, he shook each of their hands, before leaving them in silence.

Sophie said rhetorically, "You know, this really is getting deep."

The others nodded, but as there was little that they could do, they rose and tried to get to the Desk Sergeant station without being stopped. Filing out of the room, they made their way to the processing area. Two officers stood two-foot above everyone else, on the platform behind the desk. One of them was the original Desk Sergeant and the other was PC Wood. Both officers smiled at the gang.

"Well, hello again," said the Sergeant pleasantly.

PC Wood smiled and gave a quick glance in the direction of

Muhammad. He still felt an acute embarrassment from the previous night. Brendan was processed first. He was given his chattel, such as his mobile phone, which was now flat and useless, his wallet and change. As he signed for the items, he picked up his keys for the bike and asked the Sergeant, "Can you tell me where the bike is – has it been impounded?"

The officer said, "You'll have to see the officer on reception."

Not happy, Brendan stepped aside, so that Malika could be processed next. The rest of the crew were finished by the end of the hour.

The rest of the Guardians waited at the vending machines, near the exit, when Mike finally caught up with them. Brendan gestured to ask if Mike wanted a drink, but he declined. The five finished theirs and Brendan told them what the Desk Sergeant had said about the bikes. At last, the crew made their way out of the custody area.

Just as they opened the swing door to the reception, PC Wood ran breathlessly toward them, shouting, "Mr Singh, you forgot something."

The crew paused, waiting for yet more drama. Muhammad patted his jacket and felt for his belongings. After a double-check he said, "I'm sorry, you must be mistaken, I've got everything."

Catching her breath, she smiled and held out a piece of paper, "My number."

He looked at her incredulously. Behind him, he heard mutters of 'for crying out loud', then the swish of the doors as the gang entered the reception, leaving him with the police officer. Being serious for once, he stared into her eyes and she blushed. "You know, about last night and my comments. I was nervous and trying to make light of the situation."

She gave him a look of understanding and said, "I know, you wouldn't believe some of the sights that come in here, believe me when I say that you and your gang are very mild in comparison." For a moment, there was silence between them and then she looked at him once more and said, "I must get back to work. You will call, won't you?"

He blurted out "Hell yeah", but then considered it better to try and act cool, so said, "err, I mean, of course, when I get around to it."

Laughing, she turned back to the door and waved to him, before disappearing. He looked down at the piece of paper in his hand and smiled to himself. Perhaps things were looking up after all. He then followed his friends into the reception.

He caught up to the others, who were patiently waiting in a queue, at the reception desk. They were chatting amongst themselves. When he approached, they jostled him and called him a sly dog. Darren said that it was the leathers that attracted her. Sophie said that he was a nice man and she could understand why she would be attracted, which got her a ribbing off Darren. Malika said that the woman was desperate and needed a bit of rough, which got a feigned shock reaction off everyone else. When they finally approached the desk, Brendan asked about the bikes. The receptionist just smiled and cryptically said, "Outside." Perplexed, they went out of the front doors.

The light of the morning sun shone through the glass of the double doors at the front reception. Looking outside they could see crowds of people, pushing and shoving at the bottom of the entrance steps. They looked at each other and Sophie exclaimed, "What the hell's going on here. How are we meant to get to the bikes?"

They noticed two officers trying, somewhat unsuccessfully, to control the throng.

Brendan, with bated breath said, "I don't think we have much of a choice, the bikes are out there, we'll have to make our way through." Remembering the stress that Mike has in crowds, he turned and asked him how he was.

"I'll be fine, as long as I can focus on the task at hand; given the circumstances, like you said, I have no choice." Looking at each other one last time, they set foot out of the building.

The shouting and screaming was almost instantaneous; they were met with a barrage of sound. Reporters rushed up the steps and a surge of people followed. The two police officers were obviously ineffective and so gave up any illusions of controlling the crowd. The best they could do was to make a tight path for the Guardians. The gang noticed a handful of flags being waved with their colours on. Muhammad realised and then explained that when they were doing the rescue, the watchers must have taken photos and copied the design. Malika suggested that they should get a copyright. Smiling and waving, Brendan said from the corner of his mouth, "Let's try to get to the bikes, they're over there." He pointed to a spot about twenty feet away from the steps. They made progress, but it was very slow because of the mass of people, who were constantly surging towards them. The police officers were valiant in their efforts and were being shoved quite violently, but still succeeding in holding them back.

They were within six-foot of the bikes, when a man stepped in front of them, blocking their way. He had a note pad, so it wasn't too wild a guess to realise that he was a reporter. He had a waterproof jacket and jeans on – not the usual image of a correspondent.

"Mr Sykes, isn't it true, that you were arrested for drug running?"

Brendan was about to answer when Darren shouted, "Technically yes, but it was sugar, I run a bakery."

Pursuing this to its next logical step, the reporter then asked, "So you're saying that the police wrongly arrested you?"

Brendan paused for moment and said, "No, not at all, it was simply a misunderstanding."

Seeing that the line of questioning was going to get nowhere, he changed tack. "So, how do you feel about being heroes?"

Brendan looked back at the Guardians, then turned back and said, "We're not heroes, we're a team that works well together and in that particular circumstance, we worked very well."

Brendan and the gang were feeling frustrated and so forced their way through the last few feet to the bikes. At first, they struggled, but were helped by the two battered officers. After lots of pushing and shoving, each of the bikers managed to get to their metal steeds. As they put on the helmets and gloves, a voice came from the crowd and shouted, "Sophie, you're my angel." Lowering her helmet, she looked around, but with such a mass of faces and with so many people shouting, it was impossible to tell the direction of the compliment, let alone locate the individual in the crowd. Smiling, she looked at Darren, who returned the smile and shrugged his shoulders. They put on their helmets and one at a time, started the bikes. As the engines roared into life, a chant began from the crowd: "Guardians, Guardians, Guardians." The chant followed them as they slowly made their way through the parting crowd, towards the exit and the road home.

At the top of the HQ steps, in the background, unnoticed by the crowd, stood Detectives McNulty and Knowles.

Knowles spoke to McNulty, without moving his head. "Well, that could have been a damned sight worse." Knowles meant how Brendan had reacted to being in custody – he could have criticized the police and caused a scene, but had chosen not to, giving McNulty a bit of breathing space.

McNulty was silent for a moment, before he said, "There's more to come, isn't there?" He asked the question because he knew who Knowles was and what he did; he couldn't disguise the worry in his voice.

Again, without looking at the other, Knowles said "Maybe," and he couldn't hide the intent in his. Before going back inside, Knowles said, "It's a bit strange, because there was only one bag in the sack. Whoever took the other believed that it contained coke. Fortunately, it was tracked."

McNulty didn't look at Knowles, but his comment wasn't lost on him. McNulty made for the door and held it open for the other. Knowles nodded his thanks as he passed by and entered the building. McNulty looked at Knowles' back as he mounted the stairs to the offices on the upper floors. When Knowles had reached the top of the first flight of stairs, McNulty reached into the inner pocket of his jacket and pulled out his mobile phone. A few seconds later, with his head bowed, he walked into the corridor that led to the custody suite and aimed for the vending machines. He waited until the phone at the other end was picked up and simply said, "We have a problem, we'll talk later." He then ended the call and got himself a coffee.

When Knowles had turned the corner of the stairs, he had stopped, just out of sight and watched McNulty by means of the reflection in the large window that lit up the stairwell. He looked at his watch and noted the time when McNulty had got on the phone. Internal affairs had been monitoring the Detective for months and had suspicions regarding how he had been able to have such a consistently high arrest rate. He was suspected of having contact with drug dealers, taking a cut of confiscated drugs and receiving bribes. Unfortunately, this time, his greed had meant that he or his accomplices had taken a bag of sugar, with a tracker. If it hadn't been for the Guardian Angels, it would never have happened. It is strange how things work out. He smiled to himself and muttered under his breath 'Good Luck' in the direction of the Guardian Angels.

Outside, the crowd was beginning to clear, now that the Angels had left the car park. The two beleaguered constables stood around, until the crowd had dispersed, then had a quick skirt around to look for possible damage. They saw that everything was OK and went back inside for a break. It wasn't long before the headquarters was clear and everything returned to normal.

CHAPTER 20

28/08/17

The Guardian Angels set off from the car park. They turned left, onto Leadgate Lane and headed toward the A174. The road was quiet – it was a bank holiday after all. As they neared the turn off for the slip road, ahead were two bikers, astride their machines. They were both on the right-hand side of the road, watching the Guardians approach. Brendan wasn't sure if they should stop, but decided against it. Glancing nervously in his rear-view mirror, he checked to see if they were being followed. He thought that perhaps the Beezles were not amused about the lack of drugs and were going to have 'words'. Brendan thought wryly, whatever happened to 'Don't shoot the messenger'? As they made their final approach before the turn off, the ominous-looking bikers nodded as they passed. Was that a gesture of respect or a nod to say they were going in the right direction?

One by one, the Guardians pulled onto the slip road and rode the final stretch to the dual carriageway. As they went onto the road, as they should, they made a life saver head turn, to check for oncoming traffic. As they did, they saw a wall of bikers. The road was blocked by a line of Road Warriors. As they saw the sight, the shock made them unsteady on their bikes. Quickly regaining their composure, they tried to act normally. But as they redirected their attention back down the road, a further group of motorcyclists stood waiting. The Guardians came to a halt: they had nowhere to go. Then, quite unexpectedly, the mass of bikers all revved their engines in salute. The Angels looked at each other in amazement, feeling emotional.

Setting off slowly, the lead bikers rode on down the carriageway. The whole throng of bikers kept the same distance throughout the ride. There were approximately one hundred bikes, which made their way to the end of the A174, until it reached the joining roundabout. To the Angels' surprise, there were police outriders, who had blocked the junctions to let the bike clubs pass. They were waved through the red lights. Making their way to Redcar, the Angels became nervous; they had expected to be going home. They entered the suburbs, pedestrians stopped and stared and a few cars stopped and rubbernecked as the bikes passed. As they approached the coast, the wind picked up, but it was a refreshing breeze, which added to the ambience of the moment. The crew came to a crossroads. Facing them was a narrow road, which went over a bridge. On the left was a Vauxhall garage. The police had, again, stopped the traffic to let the bikers through. The bikes went over the bridge in twos and threes and snaked their way past the roundabout on the other side. They then entered the road that took them to the coast. A small rise on the road hid the sea from sight, but when they rose to the top of the mount, they were greeted by a sea of black and chrome, which glinted in the afternoon sun. The large carpark in front of them was completely dominated by bikers.

As they entered the parking area, a round of applause greeted them. The bikes directly in front of them were pulled apart, to create a pathway to the centre. In the middle of the gathering was a set of plastic garden furniture, around which stood a small group of leather-clad men, one of whom was John of the Beezlebubs. The Guardians assumed that the men were the presidents of the bike clubs that were present. They too were clapping as the Guardians dismounted their bikes. The gap that had been created to let them through had since been closed. Not to prevent escape, but to prevent intrusion. This was going to be a high-end meeting between the upper echelons of the North-East Bike Clubs.

As the Guardian Angels walked to the centre of the circle of bikers, the presidents approached and shook their hands and congratulated them on the rescue, on the previous day. Having gone through the greetings, John invited the Angels to sit. There were thirteen presidents of various biker clubs.

After a minute or so, to allow everyone to settle down, John said, "In the first instance, I would like to thank Barry, for allowing us all to meet here on his club's patch." He nodded toward one of the other presidents, who nodded in return. "I think the first order of business is to officially congratulate the Guardian Angels on their performance over the last couple of days." The Guardians were uncomfortable with all the attention, especially from these people. Continuing, John said, "When you came to us, at our clubhouse, I saw nothing more than a bunch of weird misfits. I was quite impressed by the fact that you turned up at all, then you had the audacity to issue a threat!" At this, the Guardians, especially Brendan, looked embarrassed. Smiling at their reaction, John spoke further, "So, I had a problem. It was true that it was drugs, but not in the way that you thought. Each time we made a request for an assignment, both the coke and cash were disappearing. We know why; the question was how? The reason was because a certain Detective McNulty, somehow, always managed to be there. We had suspected a mole on our side for quite a while, but couldn't prove anything. The question then became, how was he doing it? What we did, was have an arrangement with the Singh's in Middlesbrough. They caught one of their guys, calling McNulty about a delivery – unbeknownst to him, this time, it was caster sugar. The idea was that you would be given sugar, because you were an unknown quantity – after all, you could have gone running to the police."

At that, Brendan and Malika gave each other a sideways glance;

fortunately, no-one else noticed.

"Anyway, when they caught him, they, shall we say, interviewed him and found that he was working with one of our guys, who was also informing McNulty when deliveries and payments were to be made. We, of course, interviewed our guy too." John sounded as though he had enjoyed the 'interviewing', which made the Angels feel a little on edge. "When McNulty turned up at Carlin How, he thought you had drugs, hence your arrest. It has just been put on social media that McNulty has been arrested. It seems that if you hadn't come along with your determination to be an MC, then we would still be losing money and for that we thank you."

The Guardians weren't too sure if that was such a good thing – after all, they had inadvertently removed a log jam for drug sales.

"Another thing, it has been noted that despite all the pressure you have been under, not once did you inform the police. Keeping your mouth shut, in our world, is of vital importance; for that, you have our respect." None of the Angels reacted to these thanks, like Brendan said, keeping quiet was the best course of action. "On a personal level, I want to thank you again for the bus rescue. On that bus, one of those little girls, was my granddaughter."

At this, the harsh exterior broke for a fleeting moment, the light of the sun reflected off some tears in the tattooed man's eyes. Blinking and taking a moment to gather himself, he looked at the Angels. "We will now move onto business." John smiled with what he was about to say. "The gentlemen around this table and I have had a long discussion about your situation. We have come to the following conclusion. The first thing is that we agreed to let you have your colours without argument; neither your name nor the design conflict with anyone else's. Secondly, we have decided to concede some of our territory, so that you can conduct your own activities, without interference or the need for permission. Before you leave, you will be given a map. What we ask is that you follow the same general rules and codes of conduct."

The Guardians looked at each other and shared a smile. They had made it. They had become bona fide members of the biker fraternity, a part of the brotherhood.

Brendan looked at John and asked, "If I may?" John nodded his assent and then the black man spoke. "I, on behalf of all the Guardians, would like to thank you all for your praise and the concessions that you have given us. I haven't had the opportunity to discuss your offer with the others, but I'm sure they would happily agree. I believe that none of us would have a problem following your rules and codes; however, a little guidance on these matters would be appreciated, so we don't step on other people's toes, so to speak." All the presidents nodded their agreement, with accompanying smiles. Brendan continued, looking pensive. "But, and it is a big but, I know the others will also agree with what I am about to say. We don't want drugs on our patch. The idea of you all conducting business under our noses, while you state it is our patch, would be bit rich – even you must agree. We are pragmatic and understand that you are running a business, so would allow for three months, before complete cessation."

This, as expected, got a reaction from the presidents.

John, expressing concern, said, "You'll have to give us a while to discuss this, say half an hour. I would suggest you get a coffee from the caravan, over there." He pointed towards a burger van parked next to the beach.

The Guardians rose from their chairs and made their way through the throng of bikers. As they went, they shook hands with quite a few attendees and were patted on the back a lot as they went. When they got to the stand, the coffees had already been bought for them, along with an open menu.

The gang sat on the low sea wall, feeling like bobbing dogs. As the bikers from the milling crowd walked by, they nodded their respects in the direction of the Guardians. Feeling obliged they returned each kindness, which meant coming close to having repetitive strain injuries.

Sophie pointed out what they were all thinking: "You know what, these are the nicest hog dogs I've had for years."

Mike, who was eating a burger, replied with a serious voice, "You do know what they're made of, don't you?"

With her final mouthful, she half spat her food as she said, "Yeah, that's the reason why I love them."

Looking disgusted, Mike carried on eating his meat sandwich. Darren sat quietly and Sophie looked up and nudged him. "What's wrong with you, titch?"

He looked at her with soulful eyes. He said simply, "I love you."

She stared at him for a moment and replied, "I know."

She puckered her lips for a kiss. The lips were covered in crumbs and her nose had sauce on it. Muhammad walked past and as he did so, he handed Sophie a napkin. "Wipe your face, you're killing the mood."

She snatched it off him and duly obliged. Once her face was cleared, she faced upward for a second attempt at a kiss. Darren craned his neck and their lips met. There were a few wolf whistles in the background and a voice shouted out, "Get a room, will yer!" Looking embarrassed, they both reddened and continued with their meal.

Muhammad was working his way through the crowd to get another coffee, when he saw Mike having an in-depth discussion with Greg and every now and again, the air was punctuated with their laughter. Muhammad smirked, shook his head and made his way to the burger van. "Two coffees please."

He was given the coffees and went to hand the money over when a large biker to his left said, "No mate, the Guardian Angels pay for nothing today."

Muhammad, taken aback, stared at the speaker for a second and then raised a cup and said, "Thanks, mate, much appreciated."

The biker nodded his response and gave a thin smile, then got his own order. Making his way back to where he had been sat, he handed Malika his coffee. "What are you thinking about, my friend, you're awfully quiet?"

Malika glanced at him, sipped his drink and said, "A woman."

Muhammad asked, "Your wife?"

Malika gave him another quick glance, this time with a twinge of guilt on his face. "Actually, no."

Muhammad, sensing his awkwardness, diverted the conversation and said, "Me too." Having fished into his pocket, he retrieved the piece of paper that PC Wood had given him. "Do you think I should call?"

Malika looked at him and said with a gravity that came from many years of experience, "You will only regret the things you didn't do."

Muhammad considered his friend's words. "Thanks, I'll do it when I get home."

Malika smiled and contemplated his own next move. It was just over half an hour before the Guardians were called back to the inner circle. They filed in and sat back down where they were before and waited patiently for the answer.

John spoke for the gathered presidents and said, "We have agreed to what you say. This is because you have brought great honour to the biker fraternity. We have decided that we are willing to take a hit in the business, but we also believe that the three people that were causing us problems, now that they are out of the way, we'll be able to make up the shortfall."

Muhammad spoke timidly, but made his point nonetheless. "I'm almost in a relationship with a police officer; also, the fact that we are now the centre of attention, won't help the cause of your business interests. Of course, all drug related charges were dropped, but as you know, people always say, 'where there's smoke, there must be fire', which means we'll be watched for the foreseeable future. So, it might be best for all those present to keep their distance for a while."

Everyone understood Muhammad's logic, which put the nail in the coffin for any counter arguments. So, John declared loudly, "That's agreed. No biker will be found with drugs, in the patch belonging to the Guardian Angels."

John then stood up and said loudly, "Well, my friends, if we are all agreed, that concludes this extraordinary meeting." He gave a big genuine smile and all the other presidents stood up. After a lot of handshaking and exchange of thanks, the Guardian Angels made their way to the bikes. Putting on their gear once more, the newly inducted MC then mounted their steeds. The engines started and the bikers who had blocked the entry to the inner circle, pulled their machines back to recreate the path back out.

It was just about midday when the Guardian Angels set off from the biker meeting. They were all tired – it had been a long couple of days, both physically and mentally. Once again, they adopted the order of riding that they had done from day one. Brendan turned left onto the road that led to the promenade. As he turned, he saw the blueness of the sea and in the corner of his eye, he noticed the large offshore wind farm. He thought that he must have been really focussed at the meeting, because he hadn't seen them before, despite their imposing size. The road curved to the right and they headed south. As they went on, a few pedestrians were clapping as they passed; the Guardians waved back. Moving onto the main promenade, passing the old cinema on the left, they rode on. As they approached the run-down beach front, a throng of people came into view. It was a bank holiday, so having such a large amount of people at the beach wasn't unusual. What made it surreal was the building of a chant: "Guardians, Guardians, Guardians". With such large crowds, the bikers slowed, in case of any errant pedestrians. Spontaneously, a round of applause broke out and chanting became louder. The gang looked around in amazement, giving polite waves and high fives. Miraculously, they didn't knock anyone over. The crowd began to thin; that's when a handful of kids began to egg the Guardians into a race on their bicycles. The promenade came to an end and so did the kids' stamina, who gave up trying to stay with the motorcycles. They waved as the Angels headed toward Marske.

At the roundabout, they turned onto the coast road. On the left, at the Stray Café, was a smaller crowd, who were cheering. This time there was no chant, but the noise of the cheering did raise a decibel or two as the intrepid bikers filed past. The crowds completely dissipated and so they picked up their speed. The road was a couple of miles long, but was straight and empty. Negotiating the final sharp bend to the right, they entered Marske. Marske is a suburb of Redcar, with a small high street – passing through was uneventful. Turning towards Saltburn, they headed to the coast. Passing the planted coble and down through the town, they came across another throng of people, waving and cheering. Brendan thought, social media has an awful lot to answer for. Malika gave a longing look, as he passed the point where he would have turned to go to his house, but he instinctively knew that he had to be with his friends, until the end.

Descending Saltburn Bank, they passed more people, who waved and cheered. This time, they couldn't acknowledge the crowd – the bank's notoriety would have the best of them, if they didn't concentrate. The line of people continued from the bottom of the incline, all along the short promenade and up to the car park of the Ship public house. The crowd thinned out again as they made their way up the hill to Brotton. As they made their way down the bank toward Carlin How, all was quiet. Strangely, for a bank holiday, there was no traffic. As they crested the final undulation, before the descent into Carlin How village, they were greeted by a sea of people. At this, they came to a stop. They pulled over, just before the first line of houses, keeping their engines running. Brendan took his helmet off, then the others followed suit. Brendan turned and looked at his friends. At first, all was quiet between them, not knowing what to say. They all smiled and at that moment, they became acutely aware of the bond that now held them altogether. They had each found what they had sought at the beginning of this adventure. To be part of something that was bigger than themselves. Brendan nodded sagely, then they all put their helmets back on, ready for the final leg of this epic journey.

As they were about to set off, they heard a rumbling sound; they all looked back. A mass of bikers, were now behind them, taking up the whole road. The bikes had stopped fifty yards behind. The front biker, whom they assumed was John from the Beezles, gave a salute. Brendan returned it and with a smile slowly set off. The noise of the bikes reverberated off the buildings, making a deep throb, like a pulse, as they entered the heart of the town. Both sides of the road from the town signage onward, were three-deep in people. At the sight of the Guardians, a huge cheer went up and the clapping began. It was then that Sophie, Mike and Muhammad, began to cry. Overcome with emotion, it took all their efforts just to keep their bikes upright. Just like in Redcar, kids held out their hands for high fives. Some children ran alongside the slow-moving cavalcade and when that was too much, they waved frantically. The bikes made their way around the bend to the right, just before the now infamous Carlin How Bank. A huge mob stood in their way, making it impossible to go further forward. At the front of the crowd, which had now gone eerily silent, stood two children with white T-shirts, emblazoned with the Guardians colours. The adults who stood behind the children were in tears. They walked over to the Angels. There were two men and two women, presumably the parents of the children in T-shirts. They spread themselves amongst the Guardians and shook their hands and gave them hugs. They constantly repeated their thanks, which, to be honest, was becoming uncomfortable for the bikers. It was difficult to hear anything, because of the mass of noise behind them, from the accompanying engines.

Stepping back from the bikes, after a couple of extra handshakes, the parents allowed the bikes to move off. As there were so many people on the banks, between Carlin How and Loftus, it was very slow going. As they approached the first hairpin, where the accident had occurred, the bikes behind gave a massive roar of engine noise, which echoed down the valley. It was surreal moment; all those who were there, would talk about it for many years to come. As they passed, the Guardians glanced down the wooded track, where they had been yesterday. They could see the broken trees and branches that had given way, when the metal behemoth had made its final descent. The carnage of the bus passed out of sight and they prepared for the last ascent into Loftus.

Draped over the sign that normally greeted careful drivers was a sheet that read 'Welcome to the Guardian Angels'. Smiling at the hastily made sign, the heroes rode on. At the crest of the bank, crowds of people had gathered. The clapping began, slowly at first; as the word of their arrival went through the masses, it became more intense. Muhammad's parents' shop came into view and on the front window a big sign declared 'A Guardian Angel lives here!'. Muhammad waved at his mam and dad; he could see the pride in their faces as he rode on. By now, because of the sheer number of people, the bikers continued at a crawl. There were that many kids gesturing for a high five that they no longer bothered. For Mike, his emotions had become extremely intense and he felt a desperate need to escape the melee. He was getting worried that he was going to have a meltdown. It was because of the good nature of the crowd that he had managed to last this long. Sophie had gone beyond tears and she now found herself with an aching jaw from smiling so much. She thought she would look like an inane idiot when she removed her helmet. Darren, well, Darren was just Darren. Yes, he was smiling, but he took it in his stride and even made the effort to make a high five with the occasional child. This, of course, encouraged more. Malika too, was smiling, but because he now felt welcomed and had a connection with the town that he had previously resented. Brendan was worried about the amount of people in front of them. He dreaded to think of what was happening behind, with the large mass of bikers. He realised that they had brought the whole of Loftus to a grinding halt. Well, maybe it's a good thing, it'll put the town and the Guardians on the map!

They passed Mike's garage, which was on the right and approached the main crossroads. It was now that the police made their presence felt. They were woefully outnumbered, but somehow, they had a semblance of control. Every now and again, a voice would sound over a megaphone, "Can you please stay on the pavement, there is a lot of traffic coming through, this is for your safety." Climbing up the final bank before the marketplace and their clubhouse, unbelievably, the throng of people became even more dense. The crowd had to part, as the six heroes made the final leg. The MCs behind came to a halt. Hundreds of bikers dismounted and followed on foot.

By now, the Guardians were in sight of the Angel pub. On the steps was a mass of white-T-shirted people. It was the staff and children from St Joseph's, the people they had rescued. The kids waved excitedly and the teachers waved and smiled. The bus driver was sat to the side in a wheelchair; he struggled to stand, but was pushed back down by one of the teachers. The Guardians had given up trying to ride the bikes and dismounted. They removed their helmets and gloves and walked towards the Angel. They were patted on their backs and applauded as they made their way through the crowd. Reaching the top of the steps, the Guardians shook the teachers' hands and fussed over the kids. Darren picked up a child and sat the boy on his shoulders, then everyone on the steps held hands. At this, the crowd went wild.

After two minutes of this, Brendan held up his hand, asking for quiet. When the crowd hushed sufficiently, he spoke. "Ladies and gentlemen," then after a pause "and kids." There was ripple of laughter, but the crowd soon became quiet again. "You have come here to congratulate us for the rescue and to demonstrate your love for your children and for each other." Sounding humble, "We cannot accept the honour for the rescue because any of you would have done the same. It is, however, our great honour to be allowed to share this moment with all of you." There was a polite applause. Continuing: "My friends and I formed this bike club because we all wanted to be part of something bigger, something special. It seems to me, when I look at the people in this town stood with us today, we have succeeded and we have made the right choice. Because all I see before me, is a town full of Guardian Angels." The crowd applauded and cheered. Brendan held his hand up again and the noise quelled again. "I would like to make one more statement please. We have had a hard couple of days, I fancy a drink, how about you?" At this he got a big cheer and the crowd, almost immediately, began to disperse into the local pubs and shops to get their partying supplies.

It was about eight o'clock and the six guardians were sat at the back office of the Angel.

"Well, that went well," said Malika. He added, "The restaurant's heaving. I've left the manager in charge and I'm taking the night off."

Sophie said, "I'm lucky, I don't work on Mondays," sounding smug.

Brendan looked around at his friends, feeling pride and an unexpected contentment; he had found his place. "Excuse me." They all stopped and looked at him. He stood and raised his glass. "To my friends, the Guardian Angels."

They all stood and said in unison, "To Brendan." He looked grateful, but embarrassed; they all drank.

There was a quiet knock on the door. Paul popped his head round and said, "There's some people here to see you – shall I show them in?"

Seconds later, Valerie walked in and declared, "I thought we had a date?"

Brendan gave a broad grin and answered, "Yes, we do." Rising, he turned to the others and winked.

As he followed the woman out, Greg, from the Beezles blocked his path. "Can I have a word, with you all?"

Valerie looked disheartened, but Brendan gestured to her that he would only be a minute and re-entered the meeting room.

Nervously, Greg asked, "Can I join the Guardian Angels? I know I'll have to prospect, but I think I'd like it a damned sight more than the Beezles."

Mike blurted out, "Yeah, OK."

The rest of the Guardians looked in his direction. Some smiled and a couple shook their heads. Greg locked eyes with Mike and smiled.

Darren exclaimed, "I know that smile anywhere, Mike, you little tinker."

Both Mike and Greg blushed and dropped the gaze between them. Brendan just smiled and walked back out to meet his date, whilst Mike and Greg made a hasty exit, before any more comments were bandied about. Smiling, Darren shook his head as the two men left. Sophie squeezed Darren's hand to get his attention. He looked down as she looked up. She said, "I think we'd better go to the lounge, our mothers are waiting."

They too went out of the room. As they did so, they passed a strange looking Indian woman in a sari. Sophie stopped and looked at her and said, "Go in, I think he'll be pleased to see you."

The woman frowned at her and asked, "Has he spoke of me?"

Giving the woman a knowing smile, she said, "No, but I know when a man is thinking about a woman."

The woman gave a thin smile of thanks and walked into the room. Malika and Muhammad were in conversation. Her movement caught Malika's attention and he stopped talking. Muhammad turned to see why the conversation had stopped and looked at Malika's face. He put his hand on Malika's shoulder and enquired, "Can Sikhs drink?"

Malika smiled. "I've always been a rebel!"

Muhammad then gently pushed his friend forward and urged him, "Well, go on then, I think you need it."

Malika walked towards the woman and held his elbow out, so that she could hook it with hers and they both went to the lounge. As they disappeared, Malika asked, "You know, I never did get your name?"

She replied, "Bairagi."

Sitting on his own, Muhammad took out the piece of paper that PC Wood had given him. He stared at the number for a moment before fishing his mobile out of his jacket pocket. He tried to turn it on, but there was no power. With not being home, he hadn't had the chance to charge it. Sighing, he cursed his luck under his breath and put the phone away. As he did so, a voice said, "I hate it when that happens." Muhammad looked up. PC Wood stood there, holding two glasses and said, "You know, I love a man in leather."

He returned the comment with "And I love a woman in uniform – then again, leather's pretty good too". She sat beside him and put a glass in front of him.

"I appreciate the thought, but I can't drink alcohol."

She said, "It's shandy, half beer, half lemonade. I wasn't sure, but I don't think it will cause any harm."

He took a sip and smiled; perhaps he was lucky after all. They talked late into the night.

In the lounge, Darren and Sophie found their mothers. The two of them were crying, when their offspring approached and hugged them.

"I'm so proud of you," said Darren's mother.

He squeezed her back and said, "I'm sorry for not calling, it's been chaos for the last couple of days."

"It's OK. Everyone knows what I always knew, you're a hero."

Sophie said, "I think I'm gonna barf." Darren looked embarrassed.

Sophie's mother elbowed her in the ribs and exclaimed, "Pack it in. I suppose you'll be spending all your time here now or in police cells?"

"Mother!" Sophie said in feigned exasperation. "We're Guardian Angels, it's what we do!"

CHAPTER 21

10/08/19

It had been raining the night before. The roads were still wet in patches and the grass still had beads of water, sparkling in the morning sun. It was drying quite rapidly, but the air still had a bit of a chill. The traffic was quite busy for a Saturday. A handful of people stood on the pavement, talking small talk. They were dressed in ill-fitting suits and overly short dresses and skirts. Nearly all of them wore a carnation. Yes, it was a wedding and they were waiting for the happy couple. The chill in the air and the lightness of the clothing, meant that the people who were waiting, were cold and so occasionally walked around to try and warm up.

A car pulled up just along from the registry office, luckily finding a place straight away. Darren's large frame clambered out of the driver's side and as he did so, the other doors opened. From the back, Jean Wood exited and got onto the pavement, where she straightened up her clothes. Darren walked around to the rear passenger side and took the baby from Sophie's tired arms with one arm and helped Sophie out with the other. In the meantime, Muhammad got out of the front passenger side, having put his mobile phone away. Sophie went to the boot and took out the pushchair. With a few practised moves, the baby's transport was ready. Within a minute, the four adults and child were ready for the wedding.

Muhammad said, "Malika will be here soon."

Acknowledging him, they walked on down the path, to meet with those already waiting. As they approached, there were smiles all round and a lot of handshaking. There were, of course, people who didn't know each other, as is always the case at such ceremonies. After a few more minutes of small talk, it was agreed that they had better go in. With a flurry of last second cigarette draws and foot twisting on tab ends, the group made their way inside. Much to everyone's surprise, the reception room was half full already. Near the aisle sat John, of the Beezles. He saw the new arrivals enter the room and stood with a smile to greet them.

Darren said, "I'm surprised to see you here."

John, pretending to be hurt by the comment, said, "I love a good wedding as much as everyone else." He looked uncomfortable in his suit and it stretched in places that showed that he wasn't fit. The two of them firmly shook hands and the four arrivals made their way to the front row. The Guardians were the closest thing to relatives that Mike had, since his parents died.

"You know," said Darren, "I don't know why he's marrying him, he's gay." Sophie ribbed him and there was chuckling from John behind them. There were a few glances in their direction.

Sophie looked around apologetically. She glowered at Darren and said, "You're not funny."

Muhammad leaned toward her and with torment in his voice said, "He is."

Pretending to be annoyed, she said, "You can pack it in too." Jean ribbed Muhammad on his side.

He jumped and exclaimed, "If it's not gay marriage, it's aggressive feminism." Jean gave him a warning sideways smile.

The doors opened, the people in the room expected to see the husbands-to-be, but were greeted with Malika and Bairagi. Malika somehow looked taller and more dignified in his suit and Bairagi looked stunning. The whole front row stood as the two of them walked towards their seats.

Muhammad blurted, "You look amazing."

Jean said, "Stop it, you're making me jealous."

He said, "I'm talking to Malika."

Malika sat next to his Pakistani friend and said quietly, "You better behave yourself."

Muhammad smiled and winked and said suggestively, "You better keep her in sight at all times." Bairagi blushed. Both Jean and Malika ribbed him at the same time.

It was then that the registrar, who had been standing preparing the paperwork, asked everyone to stand. The congregation stood and craned their necks expectantly. The doors opened. It was difficult see to them both initially, because the sun shone directly behind them. Some gentle music started up and the doors closed behind them, revealing two men, locked arm in arm, walking slowly towards the altar. A round of applause broke out, with smiles from the betrothed. When they reached the front, the applause quietened and the registrar began the ceremony. Other than a little fumble by Mike for the ring, which raised a few titters, the wedding went without a hitch. Afterwards, there was, as expected, a huge round of applause and a lot of smiles from the newly-weds.

The main party, unsurprisingly, was held at the Angel, which was a bit of an inconvenient hike from Guisborough. The travel put a dampener on things, perhaps a bit of an anti-climax, but for the sake of expenses and getting home after a few drinks, it was the wise thing to do. When they got back, there were motorcycles parked all over the marketplace. A good crowd had gathered to await the newly-weds' arrival. The entourage pulled into the reserved spots and when they disgorged from the vehicles, a ripple of applause broke out. Mike and Greg waved at the small crowd and ran across the road to the Angel.

The rest of the party followed in little groups. Darren and Sophie were last, carrying the child seat.

As the couple entered the pub, another round of applause filled the air and everyone started to sing 'For he's a jolly good fellow'. When the song died, an anonymous voice shouted, "Which one?", which got a good-humoured laugh. Speeches were made and tears flowed, hugs were given and taken, some wanted, some not. Mike thought, despite the fact that a copious amount of alcohol was consumed, there were no arguments or fights. It seemed, if not just for one day, the stereotype of the one-percenter had been turned on its head. Just for once, they were all friends and came together as a family. Perhaps tomorrow, most probably, things would be back to normal, but for now, well, this was now. He was a man who had never been happier in his life; he decided that he had become the Mike that he had always wanted to be.

The group of strangers, who had become the Guardian Angels, stood in a loose circle, talking amongst themselves. It was Darren who broached the subject.

"So, Malika, when are you and Bairagi leaving?"

Malika took a sip of his drink and replied, "We're going on Monday morning. We're visiting family for a month and then, the idea being, I'm selling up in Saltburn and downsizing to a place in Loftus." He paused for a moment and said to Darren, "You know I've been wanting to sell the restaurant for ages, the staff would like to buy me out and I had a thought about putting in for this place." He referred to the Angel pub. Sophie looked a little disheartened. Her last chance was quickly disappearing. Continuing with his conversation, Malika said, "How about I put in twenty-five percent as a silent partner and get an annual return?"

At first, the information didn't sink in, but then Darren exclaimed "Really?"

Sophie looked up at Darren, trying to understand his reaction, then it dawned on her too. She simply took a stride and hugged Malika. Malika smiled; not only had he defied his father once again, but he had made others happy in doing so. By way of explanation for his actions he said, "I, no we, need to retire. We want to spend time together and I can spend a bit more time being a Guardian Angel, perhaps help Brendan a little."

Brendan smiled and said, "You know, I could probably do with the help. It seems that the romance of being in a bike club has entered the public's imagination and we're getting loads of advertising offers, especially as we're the only known drug-free one-percenters."

Brendan had packed his job in as an accountant and was now running a small advertising firm on behalf of the Angels with Valerie. Valerie handed Brendan a fresh drink. As he did so, she said, "I'm sick of being chatted up by bikers." They all smiled at that.

Then Mike said, "I know what you mean!"

They burst out laughing and Greg playfully punched him on the shoulder.

Brendan looked around at his friends, with the glistening of a tear in his eye and said, "Ladies and Gentlemen, a toast to the happy couple." They all clinked glasses and murmured their congratulations. Then he said, with a tear rolling down one cheek, "A toast to the Guardian Angels." No one commented on his display of emotion. They all raised their glasses silently and drank together.

THE END

Printed in Great Britain
by Amazon